The Halcyon Garden

Or

The 15th Year Revised Edition of Guarding Heaven's Gates

Joshua D. Howell

The Halcyon Garden / Guarding Heaven's Gates is a work of fiction. Names, characters, places, and incidents either are the product of the author's imagination or are used fictitiously. Any resemblance to actual persons, living or dead, events, or locales is entirely coincidental.

Published by Fierce Literature
Fierce Literature is a registered Trade Name.
fiercelit.com
Cover design by Joshua D. Howell
Illustrations by Ilaria Apostoli
Edited by Cindy Roby

AUTHOR'S NOTE

This is me. This is mine. I give it to you, that you may experience the fantastic adventures that lie beyond the windowpane. There, you may find a different moon, a different sun, a different blanket of stars. Still, it is a second home to many, and a place where every mistake can be undone. There is no past, there is no present, and certainly no future to worry about. Just the moment that never existed, but lives on in the back of your mind. This is a place for children, but it should never be outgrown. It is not an easy place to leave, and when you do, it is the hardest place to return to. There is no address, no path to follow, and no certain star to head towards. It simply exists, somewhere between the reality of now and the broken memories we all share inside. Don't shed another tear, and don't waste away another sunny day. When the sun falls, however, this place will be waiting. So flip the switch, pull down the blinds, blow out the candle, and close your eyes. The dream world is waiting....

In the old world, there was once a small kingdom, living out its course along the plains next to a large uncharted mountain range. Like most kingdoms of its time, this one was composed of farmers, merchants, miners, and craftsmen. Most lived in the small village at the center of the kingdom, which was surrounded by farmland. Through the center of the village ran a small river, running down from the mountains and flowing East. To the South of the village were the mountain mines, where miners dug for gold, silver, and metals. To the East of the village lay a small forest that led to the large mountain range said to be too treacherous and vast to be trekked. To the West of the village stretched endless country land that few had ventured off to explore. Finally, to the North of the village stood the castle belonging to King Aldiss and the royal family. The kingdom was called Crestside, but its name mattered not. It simply needed to be a home to its people; a safe place in the ever-changing world. And so it was, for generations, until the sins of its past finally returned to claim retribution.

CHAPTER 1

At the young age of twelve, Eaton Webley had suffered through his share of nightmares. No longer did he run to his mother's bedside, begging for comfort. No longer did hide under his bed, waiting to be found by his parents in the morning. No longer did he pull the sheets over his head and pray for the bad thoughts to go away. Instead, he had learned to simply sit up in his bed and wait for the dreadful dreams to pass. With each breath, each second that passed, the horrible sounds and images that had plagued his sleep would slowly but surely begin to dissipate. At this point, Eaton would usually smile at his internal victory and return to his slumber knowing full well that his nightmares were nothing more than bad dreams that he could conquer.

So, when Eaton found himself sitting up in his bed, on a warm summer's night, unable to silence the distant curdling screams, he knew that this was no nightmare.

After taking a moment to catch his breath and calm down from his initial shock, Eaton recognized the screaming to be that of his family's horses. Had it been once or twice, Eaton would have thought that a fox had perhaps strayed into the barn and caught the horses off guard. This didn't seem to be the case, as Eaton heard continuing screams from the barn as if something horrible was happening to his family's animals.

"Father, wake up. There's something going on in the barn," Eaton said, as he stood in the hallway outside of his parent's room. "Father! Wake up!"

"Go back to sleep, Eaton," his father groaned, as he rolled over and dug his head under the pillow. Eaton's parents tended to be heavy sleepers, and so it was not surprising to Eaton that his father hadn't heard the commotion from the barn. When Eaton failed to convince his father to get up, he sighed and decided to investigate the sounds himself. He quickly put on his garments, grabbed a dagger, and crept out of the house towards the barn.

The Webley's farm sat on the outskirts of Crestside village. In fact, it was the furthest west farm of all the land. The property line stopped only a few miles east of the border with the deadlands. The barn sat off to the side of the house by a few hundred feet, right next to the corn field. When Eaton saw a light coming from the barn, he quickly darted into the first row of cornstalks for cover and made his way closer to the backside of the barn. With a firm grip on the handle of his dagger, Eaton skulked through the cornfield until he could see four figures with torches standing over the mutilated body of Eaton's favorite horse.

"No, no, not Daisy!" Eaton covered his mouth the moment he uttered the words. He quickly crouched down and stared at the figures. His eyes grew wide as they adjusted enough to the darkness to see that the figures were not normal men.

They stood on two legs, as men, with two arms, as men, but their bodies were riddled with holes and lumps, gashes and sores. They were all bald, with no hair on their back, arms, or chest, not even their eyebrows. They wore nothing be tattered fabrics that covered their groin and parts of their legs. Their teeth looked more like fangs, and their fingernails looked more like sharp claws. They hunched over as they stood, with their bones and joints appearing to be disjointed and twisted. Everything about them looked deformed and diseased. Still, as decrepit and disfigured as they appeared, they did not look weak. As one of the hideous creatures tore into the dead horse with his claws, a taller creature slapped him on the back of the head.

"You stupid, insolent swine! Our orders were to steal the horses, not eat them!" The creature on the ground growled and spun around.

"We were stealing them for food. Why can't we have a snack first? We do all the work, but always get the scraps of our labor." One of the other beasts growled in agreement and crouched down to take a bite out of the horse's neck.

"You fool. We steal cattle for food. We steal horses for our soldiers to ride." The taller beast turned and growled at the fourth creature who was inching his way toward the horse corpse. He then turned back to the two that continued to rip the horse to shreds.

"Meat is meat. Let us eat, Captain, and then we can return with the rest." The two creatures continued to feast on the horse as the leader became visibly annoyed. He growled and kicked one of the creatures aside while the grabbed the instigator by the throat and lifted him high.

"In your rash act of disobedience, you injured two of the other horses. Now there are only five left for us to steal." The creature began to squeal and squirm as the lead beast tightened his grip on the creature's throat. Suddenly, the tall beast threw the creature to the ground and ripped his throat open wide with one deep slash of his claws. As the creature drowned in his own blood, the tall beast growled at the remaining two. "Rein the healthy mares and kill the injured ones. We'll stack the bodies under the hay along with this pathetic carcass, and then we'll burn the barn to cover our tracks. Make haste before the family takes notice."

Eaton had fully intended to defend his family's farm but found himself unable to move. He watched as the beasts tore their fallen comrade to pieces, along with the injured horses, and then covered the remains with a bay of hay before tossing one of their torches on top of the heap. At that moment, to his horror, Eaton saw his father and mother walking up to the barn.

"What is this? What the hell is going on here," shouted Mr. Webley as he held a pitchfork in his hand. Mrs. Webley saw the flames and screamed.

"Eaton! Are you in there?" Eaton was about to shout to his parents to run, but it was too late. The large creature walked out from the burning barn to face the parents.

"Who are you?" Mr. Webley held up his pitchfork while the creature walked closer. As his eyes adjusted in the dark, Mr. Webley grabbed his wife and stumbled backward. "Oh God, what are you?"

The beast roared and extended the claws on the tips of his fingers. He ran one set of his claws up the front of Mr. Webley, while the other ripped the man's head clean from his shoulders. Mrs. Webley screamed and tried to run back to the house, but only ended up stumbling in the dark. The creature pounced on top of the fallen woman and shredded her to pieces. The creature stood, drenched in the blood of his victims, and turned back to his group.

"Burn the house as well. Put these two inside." Eaton fell to his knees between the corn stalks, shaking in fear and shame. He had watched his family slaughtered before his eyes and made no attempt to stop it. As the fire grew, the beasts set the house alight and then rode off into the darkness with the horses. Eaton released the dagger from his grip and fell over to the ground, unable to take his eyes off the flames.

CHAPTER 2

Aldiss Castle
The Next Morning

Thomas Clayton, High Knight, briskly walked down the hallway toward the Prince's quarters. The mid-morning sun was peeking in through the stained-glass windows of the castle, illuminating his path in a multi-colored glow. Thomas took a few deep breaths as he tried to calm the fury within him. The morning brief had some grim details regarding some of the local farmers and Thomas had no patience for the Prince's teenage rebellious antics. As he closed in on the Prince's door, he sharply stopped as he witnessed a young barely clothed girl sneaking out the door. She locked eyes with Thomas, and he recognized her to be a daughter of one of the kitchen staff. She nervously scurried past Thomas and down the hallway as she clutched her undergarments and carried her boots. Thomas sighed and rapped upon the Prince's door.

"Prince Aldiss, it's Thomas, are you decent?" Thomas waited for a moment before knocking again. He heard a groan and the ruffling of sheets and blankets.

"Go away. I have not yet drunk enough wine to sooth my aching head, and so I certainly don't have the patience for your lectures, Knight." Thomas gritted his teeth and knocked again.

"Prince Aldiss, please. We must speak." Thomas heard a loud groan and the loud stomping of the Prince's feet coming towards the door.

"How many times, Thomas?" The Prince flung open the door and stood, naked and flustered, in front of Thomas, pointing his finger in the Knight's face. "How many times must I tell you not to call me that?"

"It is your name, young sir." The Prince rolled his eyes and walked back into his suite. He grabbed the nearest open bottle of wine as he waltzed over to his table to pick from the plate of morning fruit.

"You know damned well what I am referring to, Knight. My name is Jerad, and while I do not currently have the power to change my surname, I refuse to be addressed as anything but Prince Jerad." Prince Jerad took a long swig from the wine bottle and toppled down into his seat. He propped his feet up upon the table as he bit down upon a fresh strawberry. "Your insolence does not go unnoticed, Knight. You may be a loyal friend of my father's, but you and I both know he won't live forever. When his time in the sun has passed, and I take up the throne, you will regret these continued acts of disobedience."

"I'm merely trying to…"

"You are merely following the orders of my father in an attempt to raise me in accordance with what you and he deem fit. I am not my father, and I rebuke whatever set of morals he wishes to instill upon me. I've always been my mother's son more than his." Prince Jerad grabbed a knife off the table and flipped it in his hand. He played with it for a moment before violently stabbing it into the wooden tabletop.

"Forgive me, Prince, but you barely knew your mother. Her illness took her when you were barely three years old. I'm sure she wouldn't want you and your father to be at odds like this."

"DO NOT SPEAK OF MY MOTHER, KNIGHT. You did not know her, and I will not hear of your assumptions as to what she would have wanted. If it has not been made abundantly clear to you by this point that I am not inclined to become the man my father wishes me to be, than you are more dense and stupid that I originally took you for. So, now that we've had this same conversation for the millionth time, why don't you get on with telling me why you've intruded upon my morning breakfast."

"As you wish, Prince Jerad." Thomas sighed and attempted to unclench his fists of rage. "You missed this morning's briefing. As Prince, it is your duty to attend and govern over the morning Knight's brief."

"Oh no, not the morning brief," Prince Jerad gasped sarcastically. "However, should I recover from missing such an important meeting? My seat at the table is nothing more than a glorified audience member as you and your armored pissants discuss the uneventful night's watch and whatever petty discord there might be in the town. My presence, or lack thereof, makes no difference."

"You are there to represent the crown and advise my men when events arise."

"Only because my father is too lazy to attend himself."

"Your father, the King, does not have the time to attend every meeting of the castle himself. How are you to become King and take your father's place one day without taking on some of these responsibilities now, while you are young?" Prince Jerad slammed down his drink and stood up, pointing at Thomas with a drunken shaking hand.

"How am I to become King?" Jerad threw the plate of fruits across the room. "The blood within my veins is how I will become King. I don't need your pampering, your training, your uninvited advice to attain my crown. When he dies, the crown is mine. It is as simple as that."

"Be that as it may, Prince, there are urgent things we must discuss from this morning's brief."

"Oh, I could give a shit, Knight. You've ruined

my morning, and I don't wish to entertain your presence any longer." The Prince took another swig of his wine before stumbling into the garderobe.

"But Prince…"

"I am trying to take a bloody piss, Knight! Now unless you wish to get in here and hold it for me, then I suggest you clear out of my quarters and go bend my father's ear." Thomas clenched his jaw, but did as he was told. He was halfway to the door before he changed his mind. Spinning around, he stormed into the privy and grabbed the Prince by the back of the head. "What the.."

"Now listen here, you little shit," Thomas said as he kicked out the Prince's knees and pressed Jerad's face against the chamber pot. "I have put up with your drama for far too long. Your father has been nothing but good to you, and I have been more than bloody patient through these last few trying years. You want to rebel against the crown, against your father? Fine! You want to ignore your duties and tread about the castle like a stubborn, spoiled child? So be it! You can bitch and moan about your daddy issues all day and night, for all I care, but none of that matters right now."

"How dare you touch a member of the royal family! Get the hell off me!" The Prince struggled under Thomas's pressure.

"Two of the village people, your people, died last night! Had you been present at the morning brief, you would have known that the circumstances were suspicious and warranted a visit. You can wallow in your self-pity and drunkenness on your own time, but when the village of Crestside is in need, it is your duty to answer the call." Thomas released the Prince and shoved him over to the floor. He grabbed a towel cloth and threw it down at Jerad. "Now clean yourself up, get dressed, and meet me in the courtyard in twenty minutes. Eight knights and myself will be your escort."

Thomas stormed out of the suite to find his good friend, and fellow Knight, Leif Mayvoy, leaning against a pillar across the hallway.

"He finally broke you, huh?" Leif stood there with a smirk on his face. Thomas rolled his eyes and walked past him.

"I don't know what you're talking about, Mayvoy." Leif chuckled and walked quickly to catch up to Thomas.

"Tisk tisk, Thomas. As High Knight of the Royal Guard, you should know better than to let the twerp get under your skin. What happened to the cool and collected Thomas I know and love?" Leif playfully bumped into Thomas's shoulder, and Thomas shoved him back.

"Again, I have no idea what you are referring to." Thomas stopped at the end of the corridor and looked around to make sure the coast was clear. He then looked back to Mayvoy with a slight grin on his face as he sighed. "This just wasn't the day to test me. That boy better be on a horse in the courtyard in twenty minutes, I'll tell you that."

"Ha ha, and pray tell, High Knight, what will you do if he's not?" Thomas smirked again and continued down the hall.

"The same thing I'm going to do to you if you don't show."

****

Twenty minutes later, Thomas sat upon his horse in the courtyard, along with Leif and seven other Knights. He frowned as Leif chuckled behind him. Prince Jerad was no-where to be found. Perhaps Thomas's tactics had been a bit too rash and had done more bad than good for the situation. Thomas sighed and began to dismount when a figure walked out of the castle and into the courtyard.

"Stay upon your steed, Mr. Clayton," said King Aldiss, the Twelfth, as he signaled for the stable boy to bring him his horse.

"Good morning, your Highness. I was unaware that you would be joining us today." Thomas motioned for his men to get in position.

"Neither was I, until only moments ago, but we can discuss that along the way." The King mounted his horse and proceeded to ride toward the castle gates. Thomas assumed his position next to the King as the rest of Knights took formation with four riding in front and three in the rear. "Have your men give us a wide berth, Mr. Thomas."

"Yes, my lord." Thomas gave a whistle as he put

his fist in the air and spread out his fingers wide. As his men followed their orders, the caravan proceeded out of the castle and down the main road toward Crestside village. “Would you like me to brief you on the details of our visit?”

“No need, Thomas. I read your morning report and will pick up what I need when we arrive at the Webley farm. Instead, I’d like to speak to you about my son. I understand you two had quite the heated discussion this morning.” The King turned to look at Thomas with a grim look upon his face. He stared at Thomas for a moment before breaking into a deep bout of laughter. “You should have seen his flustered face when he came storming into the library. It’s been awhile since I’ve never seen him so distraught! Whatever did you do to him?”

“Admittedly, your highness, I was a bit rough with him this morning. My apologies.” The King laughed again and slapped Thomas on the back.

“Oh come off it, Thomas. Your men are far enough away, you can drop the formalities. Besides the flushed cheeks of an embarrassed twat, I didn’t see any damage on the kid. Perhaps you should have been a bit rougher. Lord knows the boy could use a firm hand, or two." The King chuckled and then coughed a bit. He squinted as he looked up at the sun. "It's such a beautiful day, despite the circumstances. I told him I'd take his place on the ride and give you a scolding. The truth of the matter is, it is the Prince that needs to be knocked down a peg or two. I don't know what's gotten into him."

"He's not a kid anymore. Every boy rebels against his father on his road to becoming a man. The royal family is no different."

"Don't I know it. The funny thing is, I don't judge him for it. I'm sure you remember how much of a pain I was in my father's side when we were young. No child wants to grow up to be the next numbered version of their father." The King sighed and took a bite of jerky. "I was actually quite proud of Jerad when he changed his name. Good on him for becoming his own person. The world doesn't need a thirteenth David Aldiss."

"Are you certain about that? Crestside has always had a David Aldiss on the throne, and we've been better for it." Thomas looked out across the plains and they rode down the path.

"Pish Posh, Thomas. My family has just as much drama as any other. The Aldiss name has always been deserving of the pedestal so many of the villagers put it up upon. You know my family's history and some of the decisions that were made. I wouldn't be surprised if Jerad moved to change his surname when he receives the crown. I'm not sure I'd blame him."

"Bloodline or not, he lacks respect. Respect for you, the crown, and the burden of responsibility. More importantly, he lacks respect for and from the people." The King nodded in agreement.

"As always, you are correct, my friend. Lord knows I've tried to steer him in a direction of empathy and compassion, but the boy bucks me at every turn. When I was ten years old, I remember talking back to my father and getting an ass beating like nothing I'd ever experienced before. Did I learn from that moment? Hell no, I didn't learn. So, the next time I lashed out at my father, he didn't beat me, he didn't scold me, he didn't punish me. He disowned me. I remember he had his head Knight pack a bag of my things and escort me out of the castle. He strapped me to a horse and we rode down this same path into the village until we stopped at the blacksmith's house." The King shook his head and smiled as he looked over at Thomas. "Do you remember that night?"

"There was a thunderstorm, and it was pouring down pretty hard. My father answered the door to see the Knight holding you by your shirt. You were soaking wet and muddy, and fighting against the grip of the Knight. The Knight didn't say anything. My father simply nodded and brought you into the home. My mother cleaned you up and made you a bed next to mine."

"I lived with you for three months. I worked alongside you and your father. He never addressed me as Prince, and was sure to punish me if and when I stepped out of line."

"Which you did, often, at first."

"Oh, yes, I did. Three months felt like an eternity, and after a while, I was dead sure that this would be my new life. That you were my new family. You became my brother, and my best friend. I'm pretty sure you even beat up a couple of kids in my defense."

"I threw a punch or two," Thomas said as he chuckled.

"You were good to me, and so was your family. I learned a lot while in their care. The experience was humbling and enlightening, and it has stuck with me ever since. When my father arrived at your doorstep three months later, I wasn't the same spoiled brat I was before. I did not expect him to take me back and didn't have the mind to realize that it had all been a test, a lesson in humility, but I was grateful for it." The King smiled and took in a deep breath. "My father was a smart man. I tried to copy his tactics and did something similar with Jerad when he was young, and you remember how that turned out."

"The family begged you to take him back after he beat up their boy and demanded they become his servants during his temporary stay."

"Yep. The plan completely backfired. Jerad learned nothing about compassion or empathy for the village family. Instead he took it as a challenge to overcome and conquer the family. To this day, he doesn't understand anything that you or I try to teach him. Lately, I can't help but worry that he's nothing more than a bad seed."

"I'm sure he'll grow out of it someday, in his own way. You just have to give him time."

"He's seventeen, Thomas, nearly grown! Every day it becomes clearer to me that he is more his mother's son than he is mine. If she were here..."

"She's not here, David. You are. Jerad will come around. Don't let it weigh on you."

****

When they reached the farm, Thomas had his Knights form a parameter around the area as he and the King dismounted and walked over to meet with the village doctor. The family home and barn had both been burned to the ground. The air was stale and reeked of burnt meat. Thomas scanned the area until his eyes found the young boy. After speaking with the doctor, Thomas followed the King over to the edge of the cornfield where young Eaton sat. The boy stared, dead eyed, at the barn, as he sat clutching his knees to his chest.

"What happened here, son?" Thomas bent down

and reached out for the boy. Eaton flinched backward, keeping out of Thomas's reach. "It's okay, Eaton. We're not here to harm you."

"What happened to your parents, child? What caused the fire?" The King knelt down beside the boy as well and placed his hand on the child's shoulder. "Did a torch fall on the hay? What caused the accident?"

"It wasn't…" The boy's voice was raspy. His throat must have been parched due to all of the smoke inhalation through the night.

"Speak up, Eaton, so the King can hear you." Eaton looked at Thomas, his eyes widening as he turned and faced the King.

"I didn't… know." The King shook his head and smiled.

"Nothing to worry about, son. Just tell us what happened."

"It wasn't an…accident." The boy wiped a fleeing tear off his cheek. "They… did it on purpose."

"Someone started the fire on purpose?" Thomas

offered the boy a cloth to wipe his face. "Did you recognize the men who did this?"

"They weren't men. They were... monsters. They were hideous, scary looking creatures." As the boy described their appearance, Thomas noticed the slightest change in the King's expression. "I think they originally just came to steal our horses."

"And your parents?" Thomas could see the sweat begin to form on the King's brow. Thomas helped the boy wipe his face clean as he spoke. "What happened to them?"

"They tried to stop it all. They thought I was in the barn, but then the monsters..." the boy suddenly broke down in tears. "The monsters tore them to pieces!"

"That's enough, Thomas. I've heard all I need to hear." The King stood and called over the doctor. "Take the boy into town and set him up somewhere to rest. Thomas, round up your men."

"Yes, my lord." Thomas whistled to his men and signaled for them to mount up and get back in formation. He then mounted his own horse beside the

King. "Could this really be what I think it is?"

"It could be." The King looked back on the boy and then took a deep breath before facing Thomas once again. "Have a few of your men ride ahead. I want your fastest rider to head west. Have him ride until dusk or until he finds something. As soon as he does, he's to hightail it back to the castle and report. Meanwhile, I want you to gather the troops and be ready to ride out tonight should your man find something. I'll address you and the men shortly after we get back to the castle. Those not fit to ride tonight need to be stationed throughout the village. We need to do this quickly and quietly. I don't need the people in a panic, but we need to be ready for the worst."

****

Aldiss Castle
Grand Hall

"Gentlemen, Knights of my Royal Guard, I salute you," Said King Aldiss, as he raised a cup with his men. Fifty of the King's best Knights had been gathered in the great hall and served dinner and drink. The King cheered along with his men before he downed the wine and cleared his throat. "Take another drink and treasure it, but keep your wits about you, for I fear your swords will be needed tonight. I have a story to tell you. Some of you may have been told it as children, if your lineage passed on the tale.

"Several generations ago, when my great, great grandfather, King Aldiss the Eighth, lived in this castle, a group of villagers went out to search the world beyond our western borders. They were gone for years, but when they returned, they brought with them a terrible plague. The plague swept through the kingdom swiftly, infecting most everyone. Some were able to heal, harboring an immunity to it, while others were not so lucky. Leprosy, among other diseases, infected those that couldn't overcome the plague. Close to half of the villagers at the time were diseased with no sign of recovery. Though some of the villagers protested, a camp was set up in the country land to the west, so that the infected could die in peace.

"Not all of the infected died, however, as several survived despite their malformations. Their skin was blistered and had turned colors. Their bones and muscles had decayed, causing deformities in their physical structure. Their minds were the last to go, as they went crazed and turned to fits of rage. Those that could reproduce within the group passed the plague on to their offspring. They became a cannibalistic race, and thus a threat to the kingdom of Crestside. Many of them developed a taste for feasting on the flesh of the uninfected. When they grew tired of stealing livestock, they ventured into the homes of the villagers; stealing babies, children, and the elderly. Their acts of barbarism led to the villagers calling them 'savages.' Finally, the King gathered his knights and ran the savages off, forcing them miles west of the kingdom.

"The King knew that killing them would have been a greater act of mercy, both to them and to the kingdom, but he pitied them and couldn't bring himself to issue the order." King Aldiss took another sip of wine. "So, he had his men continue to drive the horde as far out west as they could, hoping the horde would find some isolated region to live out their final days. If my assumptions are correct, the incident at the Webley farm last night was not that of an accident. I believe it might have been a horse robbery gone wrong, which ended in the death of two farmers by the hands of savages. I believe they might have found their way back to us."

"How is that possible, sir? What makes you so certain," a Knight called out from the crowd.

"The young Webley boy described the attackers to me. His description matches those recorded in my family's archives." A loud murmur erupted in the room as several of the men began to speculate amongst each other. "There's more, I'm afraid. According to the records, the horde of savages were delusional and crazed. They were motivated by hunger alone. They had lost all sense of themselves. No longer could they form rational thought, let alone read or write. According to the young Webley boy, however, these savages were precise with their actions, they were armed with swords and daggers, and they could speak."

"Impossible!"

"The boy is in shock!"

"He's lying!"

"Contain yourselves! Keep your outbursts to yourselves," said Thomas as he slammed his fist down upon the table and stood up, looking over his men. "You will be silent when addressed by the King."

"It's fine, Thomas, it's fine." King Aldiss rested a hand on Thomas's shoulder and nodded for him to sit. "I am well aware of the absurdity of my theories, gentlemen. You are absolutely right. The boy could very well be in shock. The remains of his family were burned to a crisp, but the way that their bodies were mangled, as well the impacts on their bones, suggest that they died of something more than just the flames. I am not ruling out any possibility, but it is my duty, and yours, to prepare for the worst. I sent a rider out west to take a peek over the horizon and see if there's anything there. I'll inform you all when I have more news. For now, I need you here, ready to move if called upon.

"Thomas, with me." The King left the hall, and proceeded down the hall to his study. "Have you located my son yet?"

"Not yet, your highness. He's not in his quarters, and he couldn't be found within the castle. I've sent men to check the local brothel, as well as a few other of his known hiding places." The King stopped and looked back at Thomas.

"Crestside has a brothel?" Thomas raised an eyebrow at the King's shock.

"Yes, sir, be it unofficial."

"I'd say so. I certainly don't remember authorizing such an establishment." The King continued down the hall. "Never mind, all that. I'm sure he's enjoying his normal nightly pleasures. Have him brought to me when he is found. For now, though, I have something I need to show you."

"Yes, sir." Thomas followed the King into his study. The King went behind his desk and pulled a book off the small bookcase built into the wall. Thomas watched as the King reached through the empty slot where the book had been to pull on something behind the books. There was a creek and small burst of air as the bookshelf gave way and swung inward into the wall to give passage to another room. Thomas followed the King through the passageway which opened into a small confined library of old books, scrolls, and artifacts. "How intriguing."

"Yes, well, this is my family's archive room. When a new Aldiss is named King, his father passes onto him the access and knowledge of this room. If the King does not believe he would be able to pass the info along himself, he is to make his High Knight aware, so that the heir can be told eventually. I have no doubt that I will be able to have this conversation one day with Jerad, but I needed to pass on some knowledge to you, nonetheless." The King reached for a scroll high up on a dusty old rack. He brought it to a table near the window. As the evening sun slipped its remaining light through the window, the King spread out the scroll in under the glow for Thomas to read.

"What is this?" Thomas leaned over the scroll.

"For twelve generations, the Aldiss family has protected the kingdom of Crestside. That has always been one of the primary duties of my family."

"One of the primary duties, sir?" The King pulled up a chair for Thomas to sit down on.

"My family has been responsible for one other thing, my good friend. Read this scroll, and you will know the true purpose of Crestside, and why I must ensure that this kingdom never falls."

CHAPTER 3

The sun had set, the castle staff had gone home to be with their families, the kitchen boy had dropped off rations for the night shift guards, and all was silent. The two guards assigned to the West Tower of Aldiss Castle were accustomed to the brisk cold evening wind, the darkness, and the peacefulness that came with that time of night. The village down the road was asleep, the castle was quiet, and only the few fire lanterns along the wall lit the stones upon which they strolled back and forth.

The night shift was a solemn one. Sometimes the guards would play games to keep themselves alert, but it was not uncommon for them to simply go hours without uttering a word to each other. They had each been assigned to this post for years, and for years there had been not one incident for them to engage or report on. Still, after what the King had said earlier that evening, they couldn't help but be on edge as they looked for any sign of the King's rider returning to the castle with news.

About an hour or so after twilight had surrendered to the dark, the two guards heard something in the wind; the cries of a baby. They grabbed their torches and ran back and forth along their stone walkways, scanning the grounds inside and outside the castle walls. Looking out into the night, they searched for the source of the cries until their eyes landed on a figure, standing still, lit only when the clouds gave way for the moon. The pale hunchback stood there, bare of any clothes or coverings, grinning in its deformity, as it gnashed its teeth and smiled up at the tower. In its warped embrace, it held a newborn baby in a tight grip as it licked up and down the side of the child's face. It hissed and growled as it stared up at the speechless guards, who stood frozen in their disbelief and horror.

Almost in unison, the beasts and insects of the

evening grew quiet, and the figure stood in the silence, breathing heavily. The creature turned and picked something up from the ground and threw it closer to the castle walls so the guards could see it. The severed head of the King's rider rolled to a stop and looked up at them with an expression of fear on his face. The creature pointed up toward the guards and grinned.

"Come!" It hissed up at them, snapping its jagged, sharp teeth toward the baby. "Follow me to the West."

****

Within an hour, the group of fifty Knights, armored and armed, rode into the night. The creature had mounted a horse and jetted into the night as soon as it had delivered its message. The Knights tracked the beast across the vast black country, having only the moon to light their way. The freezing breeze iced over the dew on their faces, as they clung to their horses, desperately trying to keep pace. They rode in silence, keeping their eyes peeled on the horizon, looking for any sign of movement. Their commander, King David Aldiss the Twelfth, lead them across the expanse, heading toward the hills and what might lie on the other side. This was the night his father, and his grandfather, and his great-grandfather had warned him about. This was the night that he had prepared for and dreaded all of his life.

"Hold," Aldiss yelled as he signaled for the men to stop near a grove of trees. They had been riding for a few hours now without seeing anything of note. "Two scouts climb those hills and see if anything is visible on the other side, the rest of you take a break. Mr. Clayton, by my side."

As two men rode on toward the hills, Thomas rode up and dismounted beside the King. As the King took a drink from his water pouch, he passed it to Thomas to do the same. Thomas thanked him and took a swig, keeping his eyes on his men and their surroundings.

"The farther we ride, the more I wish I would have forced you to stay behind, Thomas. You have a young child at home. You should be at home tending to their sleep, not riding off on this wild goose chase." The King placed his armored hand on Thomas's shoulder and smiled at him.

"My King was in need, and I am here to serve."

Thomas smiled back before returning his gaze to the dark, staying alert. He thought briefly of his wife, Jennifer, and their three-year-old son, Leland. They would each be long asleep by this hour. "I trust my men on the wall."

"I'm concerned we couldn't locate Jerad before we left, but a part of me is happy he is safe, somewhere back in Crestside." The King sighed and gripped the hilt of his sword. "Do you understand what I showed you back at the castle?"

"Yes, my lord, though I struggle to believe it."

"I'm not asking you to do so. Just know that I believe it. If anything happens to me tonight, I need you to pass on the knowledge to Jerad. I need you to be there for him. I need you to put away that frustration that you showcased with him this morning, and patiently guide him through whatever troubles he will face." The King looked at Thomas in the eyes and smiled. "You've always been a good and loyal friend to me, Thomas. I need you to be the same to him."

"My lord, there is.... a structure on the other side of the hills." The scout looked as if he had seen a ghost.

“A structure? Of what kind?”

“It appears to be an arena of sorts, or one in the making. There are fires and tents surrounding it. We didn’t see anyone, but there must be hundreds of them.” King Aldiss nodded and then got back upon his horse.

“Mount up! Let’s see what we find!” Thomas hopped up on his horse and followed his King.

The group rode over the hill to see the towering rock walls, towering in a circle with one entrance. The walls were encircled by a dark moat, with a single bridge leading to the entrance. Thomas kept his eyes on the tents, double-checking each flap of fabric in the wind. There wasn’t a soul in sight. He looked around for his friend, Leif Mayvoy, and he rode up to his side. They nodded to each other in the night, and then returned their focus on the structure. Fire torches lit the walls all around, but no one could be seen on the catwalks. Thomas didn’t like the look of it, but it was clear that this was an invitation they couldn’t ignore.

“I need fifteen men to accompany the King inside the walls. The rest stay out here and cover our backside!” Thomas rode back up to the King’s side, joined by another 15 volunteers as they rode across the rotting bridge toward the entrance. "Mayvoy, take the rest of the men and cover us. Be ready for anything."

The men trotted through the entrance into the large area. The layered rows of seats circled along the inside of the walls. In the dark, it was hard to make out anything across the empty open space, and so the King and his men rode inward for a bit and stopped. Suddenly the inner walls of the court were lit up as hundreds of torches were set ablaze at once. The rows along the walls were filled with savages, each holding a torch as they hissed and snarled from the stands.

"Protect the King," Thomas commanded, and the King was immediately surrounded on all sides by his Knights on their steeds. Each Knight held a shield that overlapped the shield next to it, while their sword laid on top, pointing outward and ready.

The men were surrounded on all sides as fires were lit through the courtyard. Eyes looked down upon them from every ledge, from every cove, from every walkway of the castle walls. Thomas gripped his sword, unsure of what their next move would be. His men had expected a battle, but there was nothing. Not one savage stepped foot into the courtyard to challenge them.

"What is that, Mr. Clayton?" The King pointed off toward the far side of the arena. Thomas peered in that direction to see a large chair, a throne, sitting alone at the edge of the inner grounds.

"A throne," someone hissed in the distance.

"The Dark One's Throne!"

"A throne for the Dark One!" Several more voices chimed in until the savages were collectively chanting. "The Dark One is coming! The Dark One is coming! The Dark One is coming!"

"Keep formation!" Thomas searched the walls of the court, looking for a door, or a hatch, or something from where this Dark One would enter. He saw nothing.

Suddenly, a booming, deep roar erupted from the clouds above them. The first one was short enough for Thomas and his men to question what they had heard. Perhaps it was a faded crackle of thunder that they had all misheard. When it sounded again, long and more pronounced, they knew for certain that it was no storm. Thomas looked up to see the night sky turn bright red as if a river of fire was flowing just above the first layer of clouds. Through the smoke and flame, he saw the shadow of a massive winged beast flying around, like a vulture circling the dead.

A final roar broke through the silence before a large beast pierced through the clouds and descended upon the arena. It screeched and spewed more fire into the night as it circled the arena for a few laps before flapping its giant wings and landing in front of the King and his men. The horses went wild and began bucking the King and his Knights. Before long, the men found themselves on the ground as the horses scattered to the far edges of the arena.

"Is that… a dragon?"

"Of course, not, you fool. Dragons don't exist."

"Silence," said Thomas as he motioned for his men to be quiet and continue to surround the King. The arena was dead silent, minus the deep breathing of the beast.

"If dragons don't exist, how did you know what

to call this flying monstrosity?" The voice came from across the arena, as a figure stepped out from behind the empty throne.

"I know that voice," said the King.

"Well, I would certainly hope so." The figure walked closer, into the glow of the surrounding torches. "Even a great a powerful man, such as yourself, burdened with all the responsibilities of a King, should be able to recognize the voice of his one and only son."

"Jerad! What is this? What are you doing here?" The King fought to step forward and address his son, but Thomas kept him surrounded by his men.

"I'm here for the same reason as everyone else, of course. To welcome the Dark One!" The arena cheered as Jerad pointed toward the dragon. It was only then that Thomas noticed a figure perched atop the dragon.

"Look at that!"

"What kind of dark magic allows a man to ride a dragon!"

Thomas didn't bother to silence his men, as he

too could not believe what he was seeing. The dragon lowered its head to the ground. The rider, with ease, walked down the dragon's massive wing. The rider was covered, head to toe, in dark golden armor, with a helmet masking all facial features, and long, tattered, black cape flowing behind in the wind. Once again, the King pushed his way closer to the front of the group of Knights. Thomas allowed him to be seen a little, but kept most of his men in front.

"Dragon rider. My name is King David Aldiss, the Twelfth. I demand to know who are you, and what business you have in this land and with my son?"

"My business with your son is no business of yours, old man. Let's just say it involves the fair people of Crestside, the crown that rests upon your head, and above all, the future of this land." The armored rider turned toward King Aldiss, advancing a few paces. "As for who I am, I must admit I'm hurt that you don't remember me. Alas, you were forgettable as well."

"Enough of this." Jerad stepped forward, flustered and impatient. "I brought them here, as you asked. Now give me the crown, as you promised." The armored rider spun and pointed at Jerad.

"Watch your tone, you impudent child. I promised you an army and my support for your reign as King. Nothing else! If you want the crown," the rider turned back to King Aldiss and his men, "you'll have to take it from the head of your father yourself."

"What?" Prince Jerad stood, motionless, as the armored rider spun back around toward him.

"Grow a spine, boy. Did you think I would just hand you the throne, like you've been handed everything else in your life? I will only give my army to a King with bloody hands, but I'm not going to bloody them for you." The rider stomped toward Prince Jerad, reached out and pulled Jerad's sword from its sheath. "Take the blade, boy. Swing it hard and become King, or fall upon it. Either way, make a choice and don't waste my time."

"I cannot simply take on a group of my father's best men. What godly powers do you believe me to possess?" The dragon rider stood there, for a moment, staring at Jerad. Reluctantly, the rider turned toward Aldiss and his men, pulled out two knives and advanced.

"Hold your ground! Protect the King," cried

Thomas. As he stepped forward with his men, he felt the King's hand on his shoulder.

"Hold fast, my friend. I need at least one man at my side," King Aldiss said, as Thomas nodded and watched his men move toward the dragon rider.

As the massive dragon grinned and hissed off to the side, its rider took on the first eight Knights. The rider immediately threw a knife deep into the face of the closest aggressor, then dipped low and underhandedly threw the second knife up into the side of the next man. As the first two fell, the remaining six Knights surrounded the rider. One man hollered and swung his sword. The dragonrider ducked under the blade, spun around, unsheathed a sword and ran it up the length of the Knight's front. Whatever the rider's sword was made of, it cut through the Knight's armor, garbs and ribcage like butter.

The rider kicked the bloodied man aside, spun again, and swung the sword low to slice off the left leg of the next closest victim. Despite their attempts, no man could land a single blow to the rider, let along block an attack. Within moments, the eight men were spread across the ground, drowning in their individual pools of blood. The arena erupted in roars of approval as the rider peered down at the fallen men.

"Were these truly among your best, old man?" The rider stood there; arms open wide. "Surely someone among your ranks can put up a decent fight."

The next wave of Knights advanced on the rider, but each one fell as easily as the ones before. Thomas grimaced as he watched his men die, one by one, by the rider's hand. No matter what tactic they attempted, no matter how many of them attacked the rider at once, none of them could make much of a difference. Some of them landed their attacks, striking the rider's armor here and there, but none seemed to result in any damage. Thomas was proud of his men, but he could sense their overwhelming fear. Despite their years of training, their skills in combat were useless when coupled with their fear. Soon, Thomas found himself standing alone, the King to his back, and 15 of his finest men bleeding to death on the ground before him.

"Don't worry, my King. I will put an end to this." Thomas took out his own throwing knife and hurled it toward the rider. The rider turned quickly enough to deflect the flying dagger with a sword swipe, but not quick enough to avoid the flying shield that followed. The rider stumbled back from the shield hit to the chest, which gave Thomas just enough time to close the distance between them. Thomas swung down his sword, which was blocked by the rider.

The two exchanged swordplay for a few moments, each blocking the other's attack. Thomas side-stepped, crouched down, and retrieved his dagger from the ground. Lunging forward, Thomas rolled under the rider's swinging sword and dug the knife deep into the rider's thigh. Thomas twisted the blade, ran it through the muscle, and then pulled it out as he rolled again, away from the wailing rider. Standing to his feet, Thomas swung around to run his sword up the back of the rider. Before his sword could make contact, however, the dragon roared and swung the tip of its wing to knock Thomas fifty feet to the side.

"Be still, beast," yelled the rider at the dragon. The dragon roared, but was silenced by the rider's hiss. The rider looked across the grounds at Thomas. Seeing no movement, the rider shifted his gaze back to King Aldiss and advanced. Before the King could pull his sword, the rider planted a kick hard to the King's chest, pushing Aldiss backward and to the ground. The rider stripped the King of his weapons and stood over him. Stomping down on the King's leg, the rider crushed Aldiss's knee beneath a boot heel as the King howled in pain. Crouching down, the rider peered into the eyes of the fallen King. "You've grown old and weak, as I knew you would."

"Who are you to do these things to me? Tell me who you are!" The King reached up and yanked the helmet off the rider to reveal a frail old woman with rotted teeth, yellowed eyes, warts and scars across her face, and flakey grayed hair about her head. At first, the King was shocked to see the elderly woman staring down at him. Then, as one remembers the details of a nightmare upon waking, the King's eyes widened as he recognized the face of his attacker. "You! After all this time! Impossible!"

"Inevitable," said the woman, as she grinned and grabbed the King's jaw. Wrenching his mouth open, the woman wrangled the tongue of the fallen King and pulled it tight. Which a quick slice of her knife, the woman cut free the King's tongue and stood up to toss at Jerad's feet. "There you are, Prince. That's all the help

I'm willing to give. Your father's men are down, his weapons have been removed, his ability to beg you has been taken away from him by my hand. You have no more obstacles in your way. Stand here, above your father, and take what is rightfully yours."

Jerad moved forward, stepping over the fallen men that had guarded his home since he was a boy. Some of them stared blankly up at him, motionless and pale in their dying moments. Others reached out for him as they simultaneously clenched their wounds in frail attempts to keep their blood within their bodies. Finally, Jerad stood above his fallen father. The King struggled to stand while globs of blood escaped his lips and ran down his chin and neck. Subsequently, the King resided to sigh and wince in pain as he couldn't manage to do anything more but kneel before his son. He looked up at Jerad, his eyes fresh with tears while burning with rage and disappointment.

"Look at you, groveling in the dirt before my feet. After all the lectures, all the scolding, all the …."

"Get on with it, boy! No one wants to hear your pathetic rants. Are you a whiny little Prince who couldn't amount to his father's approval, or are you a

King who took his reign by force?" As the crowd of savages laughed and hollered, Jerad looked up at the rider with disdain. "Don't give me that look. You've been a coward all your life, Jerad. Do try something different for a change. Rise to the occasion, and earn the glory that I will bestow upon you. "

"I AM NO COWARD, WITCH! I am a King, and no one will dare speak otherwise after this moment!" Jerad yelled out into the night as he lifted his sword, turned and swung it down to the strike the King's head from his shoulders. As his father's head hit the ground and rolled to a stop, the King's body turned limp and sulking over to the side, Jerad reached down and grabbed the crown from the dirt. He smiled as he rubbed his thumb across the golden rim. He then slowly lifted up the crown and placed it firmly on his own head.

"How dare you touch that crown! You're not the King, Jerad. You're not half the man your father was, and you never will be!" Jerad turned to see Thomas climbing to his feet. "He had hoped you'd grow up, that you would become someone worthy of the crown, but we all knew differently you little shit. You want to take the throne? How about you try to strike me down first!"

"You! Your lectures were worse than his! All of your morals and lessons! You were my father's oldest friend, but let's be honest. You were nothing more than a peasant playmate! He grew up to be King, and you grew up to be his head bitch. Why should I waste a breath on accepting your challenge? You're nothing to me!" The crowd roared as they jumped from the stands, some rushing toward Thomas while others ran for the exits to feast on the men outside.

"Wait!" The dragon rider held out a hand as she walked up to Jerad. "This man holds a special place of contempt in your heart, King Jerad. He also landed a strike against me, which means he deserves more than to be torn into slop by your new army."

"Silence, woman! Who are you to question the King? An old hag might have a dragon, but that doesn't give you permission to challenge my decree." The woman quickly turned and backhanded Jerad across the face hard enough to cause Jerad to stumble to one knee.

"What short memory you have, child. You may wear the crown, but I gave it to you. I also gave you this army and this chance to reign." She leaned in close to Jerad. "Likewise, I can take all of those things away. So, once again, I will remind you to watch your tone. Do you understand?"

"Yes," hissed Jerad as he stood and clutched his cheek in his hand.

"Now, then, I certainly wasn't saying we should allow your father's best friend to leave unscathed. Does he have a family? Are there other ways we can make him suffer?" Jerad looked at her and smiled.

"He has a young wife and child. Apparently, he left them at home, alone. Such a loyal servant."

"Hold your tongue, Jerad! Don't you dare speak of them!" Thomas rushed forward to attack, but the dragon roared and lunged forward, blocking Thomas's path.

"Perhaps, instead, a few lucky members of your new army can pay them a visit. A quick death is far less torturous than the knowledge that all you love has been lost." The dragon rider waved her hand, and a small group of savages drew near. "Tell them where they can find Thomas' family, and then lend Thomas an old horse so that he can attempt to return to the village in time to see what remains of his loved ones."

CHAPTER 4

As he rode out of the arena, Thomas witnessed the slaughtering of his men outside. The ground was drenched in blood, and while there were some savage bodies among the dead, the majority were his friends and comrades. He wanted to dismount and help those that were still breathing, but he didn't have the time. The group of savages dispatched to find his family were already at least a mile ahead. Through his own disdain, he forced himself to look away from his dying men and pressed on. Just before he reached the edge of the savage camp, leaving his men behind, he saw two figures fighting ahead. He pulled his last knife from his belt and threw it into the back of the savage's head. As the beast fell, Thomas reached out his arm and pulled Leif up onto the horse.

"Thank you, brother. Where's the King?"

"The King is dead. Jerad killed him. This is his army now."

"That pissant is here? We need to go back, Thomas! We must avenge King Aldiss!"

"We can't! I can't! Jerad sent savages after my family." Thomas stopped the horse near a group of other steads that had run from the carnage. He let Leif down and then dismounted himself, releasing the sickly horse and grabbing the reins of one of the healthier stallions. "Here, take a horse and return to the fight. Kill as many of them as you can. I'd fight beside you, but I have to save my family."

"Wait."

"I can't." Thomas looked over his shoulder and nodded a final time to his friend. "Good luck, brother."

****

Thomas rode as fast as he could, constantly looking around, waiting for something to jump out of the dark and drag him to the ground. He could hear the snickering and screeching of savages in the distance. In the dead of night, their sounds were deafening. He couldn't tell if they were in front of him, or behind him, but he felt surrounded. As he neared the village, he saw several structures on fire. It was clear that Jerad wasn't bent on killing the entire town, but had evidently planned to eliminate any immediate threats to his new reign. With a sizeable portion of his father's army slaughtered, there was little left to challenge his new rule. Thomas assumed Jerad would address the village soon, but tonight was undoubtedly meant to invoke chaos.

Thomas rode down the streets, calling for people to clear the area or get out of the way. He saw mothers clutching their children, boys and girls crying and hiding, old men and women praying. As he approached his home, he saw the front door ajar. Thomas jumped off his horse and bolted inside. The home was a mess; everything torn to shreds and scattered about. He heard a scuffle in the alley and grabbed his spare sword from the wall.

When he reached the streets behind his home, he

saw nothing at first. He called out his wife's name, his son's name, his neighbors' names, but no one answered. His sweaty hands gripped the hilt of his sword as he desperately tried not to lose hope. Then, in the distance, he heard the screams of his wife.

"Jennifer!" Thomas ran down the dark streets toward the screaming, making several lefts and rights until he saw it; a group of savages standing in a circle, tormenting his naked wife as she writhed on the ground beneath one of them. "Get away from her, you bastards!"

Thomas ran up the side of a wagon and launched himself into the air above the group as he brought down his sword to slice in half the savage nearest to him. One of the beasts roared and kicked Thomas into the side of a brick wall. The beast moved toward him while the others continued to pay Thomas no mind.

Thomas ducked under the swinging sword of the savage as it dug into the brick near his head. He sliced at the savage's legs, crippling it, and then dug the sword deep into the beast's back until it fell. Thomas yelled at the group of four or five beasts, which all finally turned to face him. Before he could engage them, however, an empty wagon came barreling down the street and trampled the group of beasts all at once. Thomas turned to see Leif running toward him.

"Well, don't look at me. The wagon was only a slight distraction!" Thomas nodded and followed Leif to the wreck as, one by one, the savages began to climb to their feet. Thomas and Leif attacked the lot before they could completely regain their senses, killing them each swiftly. As Leif stood as lookout, Thomas ran back up the alley and dropped down next to his motionless wife. She was covered in cuts and bruises; bite marks and open wounds of various sizes littered her naked body. He pulled her to him, holding her in his arms, cradling her head as he brought his lips to hers.

"Please, please baby, wake up. I'm so sorry. Please come back to me," he begged as he held her close. Her heartbeat was weak, and she was clearly struggling to breathe, but Thomas could tell she was fighting to stay alive for a moment or two longer. She opened her eyes, just enough to look at him. She tried to speak, but nothing but bubbles of blood escape her lips. Thomas attempted to comfort her, hushing her and rocking back and forth as he fought to hold back the tears.

His eyes scanned the area, not seeing any sign of their son. If the savages had the time to do this to his wife, he winced at the thought of what they could have done to his child. His wife began to convulse, and Thomas broke into tears and held her closer to him. He watched as the light started to leave her eyes. With her final breaths, Jennifer stretched out her arm and pointed across the empty alley toward a group of barrels. Before Thomas could move to check them, however, a second more substantial group of savages entered the alley.

"Looks like we've missed all the fun," said one of the beasts as it licked its lips.

"Leif! I need your help!"

"I'm already a bit busy, brother." Thomas looked to the opposite end of the alley to see another group of savages confront Leif. Thomas gently laid his wife's head down and grabbed large scrap of fabric from the ground to cover her. He stood and drew his sword. The leader of the group snickered and brandished his own two large swords just before turning to his group.

"The wife is dead, now find the child." The group split up to search the area while the leader turned back to face Thomas. "You! Put down your weapon."

"Not a chance, savage. Do you think you can kill me? Let's give it a go."

"Do not call me by that name, Knight. My name is Fellcer. I am a Captain in the ranks for King Jerad's army, and you will show some respect." Thomas spit upon the ground. "I'm not here to kill you. Your wife was sentence to torture and death. Your child has been sentenced to hard labor. You, Thomas Clayton, along with your friend, Leif Mayvoy, will be sentenced tomorrow morning in front of the people."

"You think I would let my son live here under that murderer's regime?"

"Would you rather I have your child killed? Is that really what you truly prefer?" Thomas could hear little Leland cry from one of the wooden barrels. The savage leader turned toward the sound and pulled off the top of the barrel to find Leland hiding inside. He grabbed the young child by the leg and pulled him from the barrel.

"Let him go, you son of a bitch! Don't touch him!" Thomas advanced toward the savage, but the several other beasts raised their swords to stop him. The leader pointed his sword at the child and turned back to Thomas.

"Say the words, Knight, and I'll cut the little runt right here and now." Thomas looked back and forth from the aggressors to his son. Just before he was about to make his move, he felt Leif's hand on his shoulder.

"Thomas."

"Oh, God," said Thomas as he dropped his sword and collapsed to his knees. He saw the savage leader grin as he walked off with Leland in his arms as Thomas and Leif were bound and taken away in the opposite direction.

CHAPTER 5

ALDISS CASTLE

THE NEXT DAY

The large courtyard of Aldiss castle was filled with the citizens of Crestside as they crowded together, trying to keep their distance from the savages that lined the courtyard. As they waited for King Jerad to appear, the crowd sobbed and wailed as they recounted the nightmarish events of the night before. Besides the fifty Knights that had been slaughtered in the West, several people had been rounded up in the night and taken from their homes and families. Certain buildings had been set on fire. Some shops and homes were ransacked. It had been a night of chaos and terror for the Kingdom. When dawn finally arrived, the people were herded together and marched to the castle to hear the first decree from their new King. Captain Fellcer walked out onto a balcony overlooking the courtyard.

"People of Crestside, allow me to introduce your new leader. All hail, King Jerad!" The crowd burst out in cries and moans of sorrow while others chanted and shouted in disgust as King Jerad appeared on the balcony. He raised his hands to silence the crowd, but the discord only grew in volume. Eventually, the savages stationed around the crowd, as well as the ones perched on the catwalks above, began to roar and hiss until the crowd was silent.

"Good people of the land, good morning, and welcome to a new day!" King Jerad looked out over the crowd and smiled as he tipped his crown to them. "If you haven't guessed it yet, my father is dead. Contrary to what you might have theorized, I can assure you that he was not murdered by these people you call 'savages.' He died of his own stupidity and guilt."

The crowd erupted again in fits of rage, defending the honor of their fallen King. Jerad raised his voice and screamed back at them.

"Oh, save your mourning. My father was not the man you knew him to be. He sat on a throne of lies and dirty secrets. Allow me to offer you a history lesson. My father's forefathers abandoned their duty to care for the people of Crestside. When presented with a group of people in need, a group of villagers, like you, who were sick and suffering, my father's forefathers drove these people out West and left them there to die! My great great great grandfather hoped and prayed that he could just wipe his hands of these people, but his wish was not granted.

"The sick citizens of Crestside that had been abandoned and left for dead refused to lay down and die. They continued to travel West until they came across other villages. They increased in population until, even in their weak state, they became a force to be reckoned with in sheer numbers alone. After years of wandering, these poor people were discovered by an ancient one, a powerful dark entity, that saw them and took pity on them.

"The Dark One knew that they had suffered for generations, knowing nothing but violence and hatred. Like Cain, they had been banished from everyone and everywhere, including Crestside. She called them the children of Cain; Cainates. She looked over these crazed people and gave them back their sanity. She could not heal them of their appearance, but she cleaned them of all contagious diseases as well as calm their minds and returned to them some sense of dignity.

"No longer did they need to live apart from civilization. But now, having regained their civility, the Cainates wished for nothing more than to return to Crestside; home. And so, like the long-forgotten prodigal children of this Kingdom, they arrived only to be denied by my stubborn father.

"I tried to reason with him. I tried to tell him that we could have peace with these people, but he would not listen. Now that he is out of the way, I am here to do what he could not. As of now, we are no longer enemies with the Cainates. Our people and their people will be united as one. They will no longer be known as 'savages,' but as equals to us; as friends.

"Still, I believe it only fair to offer reparations to the Cainates for all they had to suffer at the hands of my ancestors. So, to welcome the Cainates into our loving society, all citizens not working directly for the King will hand over their possessions and lands to our new friends. You will continue to work and carry out your jobs within the Kingdom, but you will be overseen by the Cainates. Your homes will become theirs, and peasant lodging will be erected. The families that faithfully do these things will receive Peasant's Pay from me, as the people once did in the old days."

"But my lord, your father did away with that. The Peasant's Pay cannot support anyone with a family or people to care for," shouted someone from the crowd.

"How many times must I remind you people that my father is no longer alive and, therefore, he is no longer in rule over you? Do not interrupt me again! Now then, we will continue with my decree. Any and all families wanting children may have two children only. If the wife bears a girl, the child is to be raised within the family until she is of age to be useful.

"Any boy will be sent off to the mining camp until he is old enough to take on an apprenticeship or go to work in the King's service. Anyone who defies this new law, and any other laws to come, will be put before my mercy. I expect my people to accept the future and move on." Jerad signaled to a few of the

Cainates below, and soon after Thomas Clayton and Leif Mayvoy were dragged out onto a stage in front of the courtyard. "And now, for a taste of what my mercy might be should you choose to disobey."

"You selfish, son of a bitch. Do you truly expect these people to believe anything that comes out of your mouth? You are nothing but a greedy, egotistical boy with bloody hands," shouted Thomas until he was punched in the mouth by the Cainate guarding him.

"Thomas Clayton and Leif Mayvoy, loyal Knights of the Royal Guard, you are charged with treason. You have betrayed me and the crown. You have killed and murdered innocent Cainates, and you refuse to accept the new laws of Crestside. What choice do I have but to execute you both?" The crowd screamed out once again, begging for mercy for the two men. King Jerad dismissed the cries of the crowd. "No, no, I'm sorry. Let this be a lesson to you all. I will absolutely not allow resistance and discord to breed in my Kingdom. There is no place in this land that I do not have eyes and ears. Like my father, these two men are stubborn in their defiance. And so, they must die, here and now."

"Bring out Royal Guard," hollered Captain Fellcer. A gate on the far side of the courtyard opened, and about twenty to thirty Knights were escorted through the crowd to appear before King Jerad. "Kneel before your King!"

"Loyal servants," said Jerad as he looked down upon the men, "You are what remains of my father's Royal Guard. You lucky Knights were not part of the raid last night. Instead, you were stationed back here in Crestside for one purpose or another. I have chosen to spare your lives. As with the rest of those in service to this castle and crown, I will offer you the fair chance to keep your jobs and your lives until I find someone better. For now, I need two of you to volunteer to get up on stage and behead these two traitors."

The crowd cried out again. The Knights looked at each other in shock. Their commander, Thomas Clayton, and a fellow comrade in arms, Leif Mayvoy, were bound and on their knees in front of them. Thomas grunted and gritted his teeth as he glared up at Jerad, while Leif looked at the men, sighed and nodded. Two Knights stood and waded through the crowd to get to the stage. They walked up the steps and took hold of the swords offered by the Cainate guards. They assumed positions and looked up at King Jerad.

"Such loyalty on display. Your obedience will not go unnoticed." Jerad took a drink of wine from his chalice. "You could have retained your position, Thomas. You could have been my High Knight, had you not been such an annoyance to me all those years. I didn't need your grooming. I demanded your obedience. Now look at you. Your wife is rotting in some back alley, your boy is beginning his first day of many as slave labor in the mining camp, and you are on your knees before me."

"You'll regret this one day, Jerad. Mark my word, you will get what you deserve," grunted Thomas as he spat in the King's direction. Jerad chuckled and shook his head as he raised his hands and twirled around.

"Look around you, fool! I already have exactly what I deserve; this castle, this crown, and this Kingdom." Jerad took another sip from his cup before turning his gave to Leif. "You there, Leif Mayvoy. Your only true crime is being friends with this man. You could still live a long life in service of the King. Renounce any allegiance you have to Thomas Clayton, and to my dead father, and I will spare your life."

"Go to hell," countered Leif. King Jerad smiled and nodded.

"Very well, then." Jerad nodded and then signaled to the executioners. "Proceed with your duties, Knights. Earn my gratitude by disposing of these traitors."

The Knights nodded, though reluctantly, and turned back to their kneeled comrades. Leif chuckled a bit until his smile faded and he gritted his teeth in preparation. He looked up at the Knight standing over him and nodded. Thomas kept his eyes locked with Jerad's for a while before sighing and shifting his gaze out into the crowd. He found the eyes of his fellow Knights and tried to reassure them. He then looked up at his executioner and nodded.

"For King Aldiss!" Both executioners swung their swords and cut down the Cainate guards beside them. They each quickly ran a blade through the ropes binding Thomas and Lief and then handed the men swords. The courtyard exploded with chaos as the crowds tried to keep the Cainate guards from reaching the stage.

“Go! Save yourselves,” called one of the Knights as he pushed Thomas and Leif off the stage and down a corridor. The Knight was struck down by an arrow before Thomas could thank him.

“How are we getting out of this one, Thomas?”

“Head toward the kitchen. There’s a staff entrance we can escape through.” The two ran as fast as they could through the castle, down the halls and passageways they had walked so many times before. They didn’t have time to stage a revolt. They barely had time to strike down or shove aside any Cainate that got in their way. Now was the time to escape, and nothing else.

As Thomas expected, there were a couple of staff horses roped up on the outside of the castle, through the Kitchen entrance. Both men grabbed a horse and rode off toward the tree line as quickly as they could, ducking and dodging the flying arrows from the tower guards. Thomas looked back one more time at the castle before they disappeared into the forest. He was on the run for now, but he would have his revenge.

CHAPTER 6

Aldiss Castle

King Jerad sat in the study, looking through the drawers of the desk. When he found nothing of interest, he flung the drawer shut and kicked at the desk as he leaned back in his chair. He saw his reflection in the mirror on the wall and rolled his eyes in disgust. He was ashamed at how childish he was acting. He looked like a child rummaging through his father's private things. Despite not knowing much about this room, or what secrets it held, Jerad forced himself to remember that this was no longer his father's study or his father's desk. He needn't sneak around, looking for hidden treasure or secrets. This was all his, and there was no rush for him to discover what mysteries his father had kept from him.

A knock on the door broke the palpable silence of the room.

"Enter, if you dare." The door slid open to reveal the large Cainate, known as Captain Fellcer, standing in the hall. "Ah, Captain Fellcer, the giant among Cainates, do come in."

"Thank you, sire."

"Please tell me you have some news to deliver on this fine morning. Where are they now, Fellcer? It's been nearly three days since the traitors escaped this castle. Where have they gone?"

"The hunt for the two Knights continues. I have several of my men scouring the forest, looking for tracks. Clayton and Mayvoy have likely gone in search for a cave in the mountain in which to spend the rest of their lives."

"What a boring life that would be." Jerad gulped down the glass of beer on his desk before standing up and loudly belching. "Well then, I expect you to deliver some better news by the end of the week. Until then, I'm guessing you're here to remind me of our afternoon's activities in the courtyard."

"The men and Cainates are ready for you, yes, my lord. First, there is something else that requires your attention. A hooded rider has arrived and is waiting for you in the private dining room of the east wing."

"A hooded rider? Are you simply opening the door of my home to any no-name that shows up to the castle?"

"No, sire, of course not. He refused to give a name, but he claimed he was an envoy of the Dark One. He stated that he would speak only to you. I have him guarded for now, as he awaits your arrival." Jerad scoffed at the idea that some stranger could summon the King's presence but then threw his hands in the air, and shook his head.

"Well then, as if I don't have anything better to do today, let's go see what he wants. We mustn't keep our guest waiting."

****

Thomas woke up to the sounds of water splashing against the rocks near his head. He opened his eyes to find that he was lying beside the twisted river. The river flowed down from the mountains and ran through the forest down and through the town. Once, a great stream broke off to connect with the Aldiss Castle Moat, and a lake existed between the village and the castle, but that was a long time ago. Thomas saw his friend, Leif Mayvoy washing his face down the way a bit.

"Well, good morning, Thomas. Good to see you awake, my friend," said Mayvoy as he returned to their makeshift campsite.

"Was I out long?"

"You passed out around mid-day yesterday and slept through the night. By the look of you, I'd say you had a bit of a fever you needed to get through. I tried to keep you cool with a wet cloth, and it looks like it did the trick."

"Ugh. I feel terrible."

"Well, I imagine you would be. I found us a secure place to stay for the night, but the forest floor isn't necessarily the most comfortable of places to rest." Mayvoy chuckled a bit. "I'm sure you're hungry. I cooked up some breakfast for us. How about you get some food in you, and then we'll plan out the day."

"You've been busy. Did you go hunting overnight?"

"Ha, nope. A little old lady traveled into the forest last night with some food for us. Once I knew the area was secure, I met up with her and thanked her." They ate in silence for a while, keeping their eyes on the forest around them, looking and listening for anything that would warn them of an attack. "So, commander, what's the plan?"

"I don't have one at the moment. At least not one that wouldn't likely result in the death of my son." Thomas sighed at the thought. "Since we fled the castle, the Cainates have infested the kingdom. They're everywhere, and the likelihood of us getting close to Leland without running into trouble is slim."

"We've been through worse."

"We've been through worse with a group of comrades to rely on. We are just two men. They have an army of savages, as well as countless hostages to dispose of should we force their hand. They've already built up and fortified a barrier around the mining camps. Those Cainates work fast. Let's be honest here,

Leif, more innocent lives will die if we allow our emotions to dictate our next actions." Mayvoy grunted and tossed a stone into the water.

"So, what then? Do we just hide out here forever, like cowards, evading Jerad's search parties and watching the kingdom deteriorate over time? I'm not a coward, Thomas. I refuse to believe that's the only option left for us." Thomas finished his food and went to the river's edge to splash his face.

"Of course not, my friend. We must preserve the lives of innocent, but that doesn't mean we do nothing. We need help, outside help."

"Outside help? From where?" Thomas pointed to the mountains.

"Before we rode West to find the savages, King Aldiss shared with me a secret. He told me that, long ago, the Aldiss family had sworn to two oaths. The first was to protect the people of Crestside. The second, a secret but just as equal an oath, was to safeguard the entrance to an unknown land."

"An unknown land? What are you talking about?"

"According to the King's archives, there is a secret land on the other side of these mountains. I didn't have time to read all the details, but the Aldiss family has a history with the residents of that land. So, my only hope is that we can find our way there and convince the people of that land to join our cause and save Crestside."

"What children's book were you reading, my friend? Do you know how ridiculous you sound right now? Are you seriously telling me that the people of Crestside have lived just outside of a secret land for 12 generations without ever knowing it?" Mayvoy laughed and shook his head. "I'm trying to be as optimistic as I can here, buddy, but I don't know if I'm ready to go off on a wild goose chase because you read something in an old book."

"It was a scroll, actually, and what other choice do we have? We are outnumbered and, currently, have no chance in saving this kingdom ourselves." Thomas stood up and brushed himself off. He held out his hand toward Mayvoy. "Sure, it's a long shot, but I'd never take the King for a liar. I have to believe he showed me that scroll for a reason. Right now, it's the best chance of saving my son. Will you come with me?"

"Ah, hell," Mayvoy said as he stood up and shook Thomas's hand.

****

Jerad arrived at the dining room, where two of his Cainate guards stood watch outside the door. He waved them out of his way as he pushed open the door and entered the dark room. A figure sat at the far side of the table, shrouded in darkness, his feet propped up on the table. The air was thick with the smoke from the figure's cigar. Jerad rolled his eyes as he plopped down in the chair across the table from the figure.

"I have neither the time or the patience for your theatrics. So, let's skip straight to the point. Who are you, why are you here, and where is the Dark One?" The figure chuckled at Jerad's words and nodded.

"A king is always busy, I guess." The figure stood and grabbed a candle from the bookcase to light the room just enough for Jerad to see him. "I hope you don't mind chatting in the dark. I prefer to limit how many people truly see my face. "

“I don’t care. Get on with it.”

“The Dark One has given you an army, she has given you the crown, and she expects you to hold up your end of the deal.”

“Besides doubling our mining efforts south of the village, the Dark One gave me no direction. I had assumed she would relay to me her wishes in the days after I seized the throne. I’ve heard nothing from her since the night I killed my father.” Jerad leaned back and started filing his fingernails. “I was beginning to wonder if the bitch forgot about me.”

“Watch your tone, boy. No one speaks of the Dark One in that manner and gets away with it.” The figure took another puff of his cigar. “My name is Fitch. I have been employed by the Dark One many times in the past. As she is currently engaged in other matters, the Dark One has sent me to relay a message as well as be of service to you.”

“What services do you provide?”

“It amuses me how cut off from the world Crestside really is. In other kingdoms, the name Fitch is associated with only one man: the faceless assassin. I have hunted down and killed more men than I can count. I can change my form so that I am not recognized, and I can always get my man."

"If you always get your man, why do you need to be faceless?" Jerad stood and walked over to the small bar to pour himself a glass of wine. "How can a man recognize you if he's dead?"

"Never mind the details. I've heard you have two traitors on the run. It's no surprise these beasts can't find them for you. Let's face it; they're more brawn than brain. Perhaps I can help with that." Jerad nodded. He couldn't argue with that.

"Perhaps. First, give me the message from the Dark One. What does she ask of me?"

"The Dark One has a special interest in Crestside. Yours is not the only kingdom that she has a stake in, but she does have plans in store for you. While she handles her other affairs, she wants you to locate your father's family archives. She believes there are secrets to behold in there that would benefit her greatly."

"I've been looking for those already, but I've found nothing so far. What does the Dark One want with a bunch of old family journals?"

"It is not for you to question the wills of the Dark One. You have been given everything you asked for. Be glad that this is currently all that the Dark One has asked in return." Fitch put out his cigar by squishing what was left into the tabletop. "The Dark One has paid me well to assist you in your new duties. Once I track down and kill your traitors, you will grant me a position within the castle, and I will remain here until the Dark One returns."

"I don't need a babysitter. I am the King!" Jerad pounded his fist on the table. "How dare you presume to think I need your help to run my own kingdom."

"As I said before, mind your tone. I don't need much, and I won't get in the way. I have my orders from the Dark One, and I don't intend to disobey her. Do you?" Jerad scoffed and took another drink of his wine. "Now then, we can discuss those details further once I get rid of your traitors. Tell me who they are and I'll be on my way."

****

Aldiss Castle
Courtyard

As the hooded Fitch rode off on his horse, King Jerad entered the courtyard and took off his cape. Setting it aside, he rolled up his sleeves as he crossed the courtyard and picked out his sword of choice from the weapons cart. Around him stood several of his father's former Knights as well as several Cainates. When Jerad found a sword to his liking, one with a weight that he approved of but something dull enough not to cause too much harm, he stuck it in the ground and addressed his audience.

"Now then, here's what's going to happen. You will shed your armor, you will pick whatever weapon you wish, and you will fight. To the men before me, you may have been good enough to serve my father, but I will decide if you are worthy of being one of my Knights. These Cainates before you believe they are better fit for the job. This is not a fight to the death, but the ones standing at the end will be honored with a spot on my royal guard." Jerad picked up his sword and swung it around.

"My lord, if we are sparing with the Cainates,

why do you require a sword," asked one of the Knights. Jerad smiled at the man.

"Oh, was I not clear? You won't be trying to take down the Cainates. You'll be trying to take me down." Jerad watched as the men walked over to the weapons cart. He had a feeling a few of them were a little too excited to attack their King, but none the less, he welcomed them to try.

As the Cainates stood back to watch their human counterparts make the first attempt, the men each bowed and then proceeded to attack. The first man swung low at the King, but Jerad blocked it and kneed the man in the stomach. He turned around and elbowed the man in the face. As the man fell to the ground, Jerad clashed swords with the next Knight. The two exchanged blows back and forth until the Knight swiped at Jerad's midsection.

Jerad sucked in his gut to avoid the tip of the sword and then swiped his sword to block the next attempt. He lunged forward and punched the man in the face before kicking him to the ground. The next Knight took the opportunity to attack Jerad from the side, knocking the King in the jaw. Jerad stumbled to earth, but quickly swung his legs around to kick out the Knight at the knees. Jerad hit the man in the throat and pushed him aside.

"So far, I'm less than impressed. Let's see how the rest of you perform against the Cainates." The Cainates nodded at the King and roared as they raised their weapons and attacked the remaining Knights. Jerad watched as the Knights took long swings at their opponents, while Cainates preferred to move around and counter with quick small cuts from their daggers. The small cuts began to overcome the Knights as they became weaker in their attempts to fight back.

One of the Knights, clearly irritated, hit one of the Cainates across the head with the dull side of his sword. The Knight then tackled the Cainate and proceeded to break the beast's skull with the butt of his sword. Seeing this, several other Cainates attacked the Knight. Before the men could pull the savages away, several large chunks of the Knight's flesh was ripped from his body.

"That's enough! Control yourselves!" The Cainates stepped aside as the man bled out on the ground next to the dead Cainate. "You men just can't follow the rules. I said this was not to be a fight to the death, and yet here we have one dead Cainate and one dead man. Now I want a few of you to pick up your friend and bury him outside the castle. Bury the Cainate with him. They need to be friends, even if only in the afterlife. For now, you will remain Knights, but I will be adding some Cainates to your ranks. You all need to learn to get along." Jerad waved them off as he wiped his forehead with a cloth. He looked over at the Cainates and smiled. "Bring me Captain Fellcer."

The Cainates cheered as their captain emerged from the horse stables. He stood at least a foot taller than the largest of his men. He was just as deformed as the rest of them, but he had some muscle mass about him. Jerad smiled and waved him over.

"The Dark One spoke very highly of you. Your own men call you a giant. You've served me well over the past few days, but I haven't yet to see how you fight. I've indulged your title of captain for long enough. Let's see how you hold up." Jerad lunged forward and dug his fist into the Cainates gut before swinging up to catch the beast in the jaw. Fellcer shook his head a little but didn't appear to show much pain. He punched Jerad hard across the face, dropping the King to the ground. Jerad launched himself off the ground and grabbed the savage by the waste in an attempt to tackle him. Fellcer wrapped his arms around Jerad and tossed him across the courtyard.

Jared coughed a bit as he righted himself. He took a breath and pulled a dagger from his belt. Jared sprinted toward Fellcer, dropping to the ground at the last moment to slide past the giant and run his blade along the side of the beast's knees. Fellcer hollered in pain as he fell to the ground. As the beast climbed to his knees, Jerad quickly landed a hard punch down into the beast's face. He then whipped his blade across to strike the beast's cheek. Fellcer growled as he cupped his bleeding face, but did not move to attack. He sighed and stayed down on his knees before the King.

"You live up to the hype, Captain, and you clearly know when to bend the knee." Fellcer winced and bowed his head. "When that cut heals, let the scar remind you to never underestimate me. Clean yourself up and come find me later. I have a position I'd like to discuss with you."

Jerad turned around to see a servant girl staring at

him. Still young and thriving, the girl gawked at him with burning lustful eyes. He looked down at her ragged clothes and how they flowed over her maturing body. Her mother shunned her away and threw a glare at Jerad. Apparently, she had a problem with the King eyeing her very young, very clearly virgin daughter. Jerad smirked at the mother and then continued his walk back into the castle, knowing full well that he would have whatever he desired.

CHAPTER 7

Crestside
Eastern hills

"I think this is it, my friend." Thomas and Leif stood at the bottom of what appeared to be a path leading up into the mountains.

"Looks like quite the hike."

"I imagine it will be, but the risk is worth it." Thomas took a step forward but then froze when he heard the slightest of movements behind them. He unsheathed his sword and spun around. He stared into the empty forest in front of him, searching for anything out of the ordinary, but he could see nothing but trees.

Leif followed suit and pulled out his blade. “I felt the air shift. I can’t place it, but I feel like we aren’t alone.”

“That’s because you aren’t,” said a voice from the forest as Thomas and Leif struggled to find the source. “Your days of running are over, gentlemen.”

“Show yourself, coward!” Leif’s shouting went unanswered.

Suddenly, a knife flew through the air and dug deep into Leif’s right arm. As his friend crouched low to the ground in agony, Thomas grabbed him by the back of his garments and pulled him to the side to hide behind some rocks. Taking cover, Thomas looked out across the trees, desperately searching for a target. He looked down at Leif, who was pulling the dagger out of his arm. Thomas grabbed the blade and brought it to his nose. When he couldn’t smell anything, Thomas sighed in relief at the likelihood that the knife had not been dipped in poison. He heard a twig break nearby and quickly popped up to throw the blade in the direction of the sound. Thomas watched as a shadow, hiding in the darkness between trees, deflected the blade.

"Gotcha." Thomas jumped over the rocks and sprinted toward the shadow. He could barely make out the figure and noticed that the face was masked in some kind of supernatural blur, but it was enough for him to make a move. Thomas swung his sword at the shadow, but his blade hit nothing but the trunk of a tree.

"Behind you," cried Leif. Thomas flipped his sword behind him just in time to block an attack. Thomas swung his arm out to hit whoever it was that evaded his eyesight. He hit nothing but quickly felt a fist punch him across the face. Thomas swung wide again and was punched in the face again from a different direction. Leif now joined Thomas at his side. "He's out here, somewhere. Keep swinging until you hit something."

The two stood back to back as they swung their swords out into the air. The shadows of the trees seemed to conceal everything from them. Their swords swiped through the air back and forth, coming up with nothing. Suddenly something crashed in between them and forced the two apart. Thomas and Leif turned around to see a shadowy figure standing between them holding a sword in each hand.

"I could have killed you both so many times over by now, but this is a bit more entertaining."

"Aaagh! Leif swung high as Thomas swung low, and the shadowy figure blocked both as the three of them engaged in combat. Swords clash as Thomas and Leif try their best to keep their attacker in sight. Thomas is sliced in the leg, while Leif swiped his sword along the arm of the shadow. As Thomas stumbled to a knee, the shadow turned both swords toward Leif. Blocking each blow as best as he could, Leif stepped backward until he slipped on a fallen branch and lost his footing. Hitting the ground hard, Leif attempted to roll to his slide but was met with a sword digging into the ground on either side of him.

The shadow dropped down on top of him and rained several hand punches to Leif's face. Leif blocked the first few, but then found himself unable to stop the shadow from beating him senseless. Tired, Leif spat a wad of blood up at the shadow and snickered a bloody grim up at him.

"Get it over with, you slimy, shadowy shit!" The shadow brandished a dagger and brought it high above his head before swinging it down for the kill.

"Not today," cried Thomas as he ran towards his fallen friend and tackled the shadow to the ground before the dagger could meet its target. Knocking the blade out of the shadow's hand, Thomas rained down punches until he was kneed in the side and pushed over. Thomas rolled to his knees and thrust his sword forward just as the shadow did the same with his dagger.

"I've hit my mark, Knight," said the shadow as he twisted the dagger into Thomas's side. Thomas groaned in pain but held his ground.

"As well, have I," said Thomas as he tightly gripped the hilt of his sword and pushed it deeper into the belly of the shadow. The shadow dissipated to reveal a man wincing in agony. Both men withdrew their blades at the same time and stumbled backward, clutching their wounds. Leif took Thomas by the arms and dragged him out of the forest, into the sunlight.

"How bad is it, friend? Let me get a look at it?" Leif pulled back Thomas's coat to see that his undershirt was already drenched in blood. "Ah, hell, that doesn't look good."

"You don't look so great yourself, buddy,"

chuckled Thomas. Leif looked down at himself to see his right sleeve covered in blood. He also had a growing red stain on his thigh where he must have been clipped during the exchange.

"Looks like you're right. If you hadn't dived in to save my ass again, you'd be doing better than me right now." Leif tore off a long stretch of this shirt to tie around Thomas's stomach. "How many times you going to save me this week?"

"How many times you gonna need saving?" Thomas chuckled through the pain as Leif tied the bandage tight.

"Let me get you set up here, and then I'll hustle back to the village and get some better medical supplies." Thomas smiled and spat out some blood.

"Forget it. In your condition, I'd be concerned with you making it back through the forest." Thomas groaned again, but grabbed onto the rockface and pulled himself up to a seated position. "We have to press on. Perhaps there's someone on the other side that can stitch us up. It's really our only chance."

"Thomas, come on now. You're in no condition

for hiking."

"I'm in no condition to fail, buddy." Thomas stabbed his sword into the ground and used it to prop himself up against the rock wall of the mountain. Getting to his feet, he put his arm over his friend's shoulders and limped forward. He used his sword as a cane and pressed onward. "Come on, Leif. Let's get going. Time isn't really on our side."

****

Aldiss Castle
Two Days Later

King Jerad walked down the steps toward the castle infirmary, following the Cainate that summoned him. Having grown impatient, waiting for his assassin to return, Jerad had sent scouts into the forests again to find any trace of Fitch or the traitors. As Jerad walked into the infirmary to see a sickly looking Fitch sprawled out on the table, he rolled his eyes and came to his own assumptions.

"You look like shit, Fitch. Did someone finally get the best of you?" Jerad circled the table, as Fitch groaned and coughed.

"He is weak, my lord. We found him propped up next to a tree with a severe wound to the gut. He's been stabbed by a sword," said the healer. "He's lost a lot of blood and is suffering from a fever, but with some care he should make it."

"Forgive me for my condition. I managed to severely wound both traitors. There's probably lying dead somewhere in the…"

"But then we would have found there bodies and not just yours, you worthless little worm. Where's the disrespectful, ultra-confident, self-praising assassin who dared to speak down to me? You were given a job to do, and you failed."

"My scouts found a trail leading up into the mountains. The traitors appeared to be dragging their feet heavily and looked to have lost a lot of blood. If they successfully made the climb, they likely died somewhere upon the rock," said the Cainate beside Jerad. "Do you want me to send a search party?"

"Don't bother. I've wasted enough time on those two bodies already." Jerad couldn't stand the stench any longer and headed for the door.

"We will take care of the assassin and nurse him back to health, my lord," said the healer. Jared waved his hand.

"No, you will not. I have no more use for this fool. Reopen the wound and dump him in the pig trough." As Fitch protested in vain, Jerad proceeded down the hallway towards the stairs leading back to the castle keep.

****

Somewhere in the Mountains
West of Crestside

Thomas limped through the snow, his body brittle and frozen to the core. He followed the frozen river as a guide. His hope was that it would lead him across the frozen wasteland until it split off to head down the other side into the hidden land that King Aldiss had spoken of. Each step was painful. Each breath of air, excruciating. Each time he stumbled, Thomas wondered if he would find the strength to stand back up again. The ground was hard and unforgiving. As a freezing breeze whipped by, Thomas brought his arm up to cover his face. Doing so only made Thomas lose his balance and sent him hurtling back to the ground. For a moment, he sat there, on his knees in the snow, and looked back at the way he had come.

Somewhere back there, in the snowdrift, he had buried his friend the night before. They had both begun the hike in less than favorable conditions. Had they started as they had planned, healthy and full of motivation and vigor, they would have crossed this frozen desert with ease; certainly, with a much quicker pace. Instead, they had braved the elements while still suffering their wounds from the assassin's attack. They had held onto each other for as long as they could, but it was only a matter of time before one of them gave out.

"I'm sorry, brother." Thomas winced as the cold wind licked his flesh. His skin burned with such intensity, he might as well have been standing in the middle of a furnace. Thomas grunted in anguish as he forced himself back to his feet. If he allowed himself to fall now, then it was all for nothing. They could have faced the odds back at the forest and attempted to seek help from a villager, but both men had committed to the mission of finding this hidden land. His friend had died for that mission, and Thomas would only dishonor his comrade's memory if he fell now. "My name is Thomas Clayton, and I will not die today.

"My name is Thomas Clayton, and I will not die today!" He repeated it again, and again, as he got to his feet and pushed onward. Each time he slipped, each time he found himself crashing to his knees again, each time he doubted his ability to preserver, he repeated those words. He chanted them, screamed them out into the cold. His tone of desperation evolved to rage and then to determination as he recited his mantra again and again and again. He found a faint warmth in his fortitude and clung to it with every last ounce of his being. "My name is Thomas Clayton, and I will not die today!"

Finally, he came upon a crossroads. Beneath the ice, he could see a fork in the river. The main stream flowed down from the north and broke off into two smaller streams. One ran back the way he came, Westward to Crestside, while another stream ran East.

Though Thomas knew that this likely meant that he was only halfway in his journey across the frozen wilderness, he at least knew that he was heading in the right direction. He forced himself to embrace the optimistic point of view as he trudged on, following the Eastbound frozen stream.

Eventually, his path dipped downhill, and Thomas's strides took him slightly farther with each easier step he took. His frozen surroundings became less and less until he found himself walking on a softer rock and dirt path through a canyon alongside the flowing river waters. The path took him down into a cave network that followed the raging river deeper and deeper into the mountain. Thomas clung to the walls as he forced himself to stay upright. He walked, and walked, and walked until he came to the end of the path and dropped to his knees beside a high waterfall shooting out into open air.

Thomas gazed out at the beautiful sight. From this height, he could follow the mountain tops encircling a great valley. Clouds filled the majority of the space between his vantage point and the ground hundreds of feet below. He could see what appeared to be a dense, colorful forest beneath sections of the clouds. Otherwise, he couldn't make out much of anything. He had arrived at the hidden land that the Aldiss family had kept secret for generations but now was left without a clue as to how to get down to it. Surely, he couldn't ride the waterfall down through the clouds.

Thomas forced himself to stand as he looked over the edge of the cliff. The sun's rays played off the water to create several mini rainbows that reflected off the walls of the cave. His eyes followed the splendid displays of color until Thomas noticed a large crack in the rock wall. As he limped toward it, he found that it was more significant than it first appeared; large enough, in fact, for him to fit through it to find an ancient stairwell carved into the mountain, leading down.

Thomas felt his heart begin to race as he took the first of many steps down the spiraling rock stairs. Eventually, the sunlight from the waterfall failed to light Thomas's path as he found his way through the dark, continuing to take each step one at a time, down through the dark of the mountain. The stairwell continued on forever until Thomas's momentum gave out and his feet failed him. Missing the next step,

Thomas found himself falling forward, hitting the rock wall of the stairwell and then crashing down the stairs on his back. Each stair dug into him as he reached out into the pitch blackness to try to stop himself. His attempts to halt his fall were unsuccessful, and the pain soon overwhelmed him. In his final moments, he struggled to call out his mantra one last time before he lost consciousness.

"My name is Thomas Clayton..."

CHAPTER 8

Prison Camp / Crestside Mines
Twenty Years Later

Once again, prisoner 452 woke from a restless night. Tortured, as always, by an endless stream of nightmares, prisoner 452 found his nights to be more exhausting than anything else. He still found himself waking up earlier than the rest of the camp. The guards wouldn't be around for another two hours or so, and the sun wouldn't rise for at least another three. As he was never able to calm himself back to sleep, prisoner 452 would simply sit up and wait. The chain around his neck, which was connected to the other ten people who shared his tent, prevented him from moving around much. So, he would sit and wait for the guards to come around and unlock them for the day's work.

Every day was like the previous. Before heading into the tunnels, the prisoners would all line up for breakfast. Breakfast usually entailed standing on the edge of an empty ditch that would eventually be filled with slop. The prisoners would huddle on one side of the trench, while pigs would line the other side. The prisoners would have five minutes or so to battle amongst each other as well as fight off the pigs for a handful or two of slop. Meanwhile, the guards sat at a table nearby, eating their sausages, pancakes, and toast. The aroma of their coffee always filled the air, teasing the prisoners. When the guards were full, the workday began.

Roll call was taken after every meal, and again before bed. Each person was assigned a number. Prisoner 452 used to be prisoner 453, but one man died recently. So, everyone moved down a number. The prisoners would line up in rows according to their specific task. If a person was late or missing, everyone in that row would be whipped until the prisoner was found. There wasn't a single prisoner without a back full of scars from when the skin had been ripped open by the crisp leather whips. Once everyone was accounted for, the prisoners would go to work.

Prisoner 452 was assigned to the mining tunnels. It was a dirty job and a pointless job. From dawn until dusk, with only a break for lunch, the miners would dig deeper into the mountains for no apparent reason. It had been generations since anything of worth had been found in these caverns. Gold may have lived within the walls at one point, but all of that had been found long ago. Now, the miners simply dug deeper, wider tunnels into the mountain. Of course, there didn't need to be a point to the work. Prisoners were there to work, not to find meaning in their work. The same job, every day, every year, with no result or objective, could make a weak man go crazy.

With the small, dull tools that they were given, the work was slow and tedious. Each prisoner was either assigned to hauling the rocks or chipping away at the mountain with what would barely be described as a shovel. Undoubtedly, the guards weren't interested in arming a rebellion. Inadequate tools or not, the guards demanded a steady pace be upheld within the tunnels, and their whips would provide the encouragement. Prisoner 452 learned that the deeper into the mountain he worked, the fewer guards would be present. He cherished that time of minimal supervision and used it to listen and learn from the older prisoners. They would share stories of the old days with him and teach him the history of Crestside.

Every once in a while, there would be an incident where the tunnels would collapse, and miners would get trapped within the mountain. Procedures required miners to exit the tunnels no matter who was left behind. When the guards deemed it safe to return, the miners would go back to work. Sometimes they would unearth their fallen comrades; sometimes people would never be found again. Prisoner 452 had never been victim to the mountain before, but he had certainly been through worse.

Though he had little to no memory of his life before serving as a prisoner, he definitely remembered his first few years at the camp. The guards were under strict orders to give him extra attention. They would continuously torment him, even as a small child. They would scare him, taunt him, starve him, and, worst of all, they would break him. He would be beaten on a regular basis, which generally resulted in a broken bone or two. He'd be allowed to heal, and then the beatings would return. This routine would eventually build up his body to be stronger over time, but that knowledge didn't help the pain. When he was old enough to pull his weight in the mines, the beatings stopped.

At the end of the day, the prisoners would be allowed to eat dinner and then sent to the water pool to bathe. A hole had been dug in the ground and lined with bricks. The water was only changed once or twice a year with water from a nearby well. To wash off the hard day's work, each prisoner would jump in, one by one, and wade across to the other side of the small hole where they'd climb out. After a final roll call, the prisoners would then be escorted back to their tents, chained, and left to rest.

This had been prisoner 452's life for as long as he could remember. Little change occurred, save for the past few years. One evening, awhile back, prisoner 452 had been summoned to the warden's quarters. The warden of the prisoner camp, known as Captain Fellcer, had a proposition. The guards had been growing bored with their evening activities. Either prisoner 452 could once again become their punching bag, or a deal could be arranged. The warden wanted to organize a fight club amongst the prisoners. Prisoners would be assigned to guards, and bets would be made as the fights were arranged in tournaments. The warden wanted Prisoner 452 to fight for him. Nothing would be granted to Prisoner 452 in exchange, other than a guarantee that the guards wouldn't touch him during the workday.

Having eaten his dinner and bathed with the other prisoners for the day, 452 was separated from the group. As the rest of the men and women of the camp were sent to bed, Prisoner 452 was taken to a separate tent to prepare for his fight. He was always given some rags and rope to tie around his hands and forearms. He was given a fresh bowl of water to hydrate as well as splash across his face before the bout.

He never knew who he would be fighting, as the other fighters were always kept in secret. During the workday, guards could take their fighters aside for training. Of course, that training could be anything from lifting rocks to getting beat by other guards to teach fighting styles. Either way, 452 would only know his opponent seconds before the fight would start.

"Good evening, 452. How are you feeling tonight?" 452 stood up immediately and bowed his head in the presence of the warden.

"I am well, sir. Ready to serve." 452 avoided eye contact as he spoke. The warden circled 452, inspecting his body. Besides the hand wraps, fighters were allowed to wear nothing more than a loincloth.

"That's good to hear, 452. You look well. I'm not sure if you have been keeping track, but tonight in your one-hundredth fight. You have served me well over the past five years, and I've made a lot of coin. Face me." The warden stopped in front and waited for 452 to lock eyes with him. "Win this fight tonight, and there will be a reward in store for you. Do not let me down, 452."

"I will not, sir. Thank you, sir."

Prisoner 452 followed the warden out of the tent and down a path leading to a large group of guards. 452 waded through the crowd until he reached the pit; a large wide rectangle dug about ten feet deep and surrounded by tall torches. 452 climbed down the ladder into the pit as the guards cheered and roared about. The torches lit the pit reasonably well for such a dark evening. 452 stretched and danced around his side of the pit as he waited for his opponent.

"Fellow Cainates, welcome! Tonight, we have the long-time champion facing off against the rising star of our slave tournaments. Allow me to introduce to you, Prisoner 667!" As the crowd cheered, a large rugged man climbed down into the pit. 452 recognized him from the mines. He didn't know 667 personally but had definitely noticed the man had increased in muscle over the past months. His guards must have been training him well. 452 had not seen 667 at the slop ditch in some time, either. No doubt his guards had been feeding 667 well. "Retract the ladders! As always, once the fight commences, it will not end until the better mad remains on his feet. Fighters, are you ready?"

452 nodded at 667 and then up at the guard that was speaking. 667 did the same as he smashed his fists together.

"Alright then! Beat the shit out of each other! Fight!"

Prisoner 667 sprang forward in a dead sprint toward 452. At the last moment, 667 ran up the side of the pit and launched himself forward. 452 caught the punch hard in the chin as he stumbled backward. Before he could collect himself, 452 was slammed against the pit wall as 667 hit him repeatedly in the chest and gut. 667 locked his hands and arms around his prey and pummeled 452 in the stomach with his knees. As the guards roared and cheered about, prisoner 452 struggled to get free. Loosening 667's grip, 452 pushed his opponent off of him and struck his elbow hard across the side of 667's head.

Maintaining his momentum, prisoner 452 jabbed at 667, hitting him a few times in the face. 667 grunted in frustration, put his head down, and charged at 452. Dodging to the left, 452 tripped his attacker and sent 667 headfirst into the mud. As 667 climbed to his feet, 452 kicked the man across the jaw, sending a spurt of blood across the pit. 667 cried out in anger and rushed toward 452, swinging wide and hard. 452 ducked or blocked each blow and replicated with a jab or an uppercut.

To the crowd's delight, the fight continued for

quite some time. Eventually, all of the rage and venom behind 667's muscle couldn't contend with 452's calculated hits. Prisoner 667 found himself on the floor of the pit once again, but this time he couldn't seem to stand. Taking a knee, 667 looked up at his guards who were shouting at him to get back in the fight. 452 looked up at the warden, who seemed very content with the night's proceedings. Just before the fight judge announced the end, however, an ax was dropped down into the pit next to 667.

"Kill that bastard, 667!"

"Get 'em!"

"Slice him up, 667!"

The crowd roared with new life as 667 grabbed the handle of the ax and used it to help him stand. 452 looked up to see the warden arguing with the judge. Weapons had never been allowed in the pit, and the fights had never been to the death. 452 looked over at 667, who seemed to be drinking in the newfound attention. Now to his feet, prisoner 667 looked down at the ax and then smiled back at 452.

"Don't do this," said 452, as he backed up to the

far side of the pit. "This isn't what we do."

"What do you care? You beat your fellow man whenever the warden commands. You're nothing but a lapdog for the guards. At least I'll have some time on top for a while," said 667 as he swung the ax forward.

Prisoner 452 ducked out of the way as the ax dug into the wall of the pit. 667 quickly pulled it free and swiped it around as 452 dove out of the way and rolled to the other side of the pit. Glancing up, 452 noticed a sense of worry on the warden's face. 452 knew, however, that this was more due to the money on the line and less about 452's actual wellbeing. He dodged another few swipes of the ax, trying his best to stay out of 667's range. Eventually, 667's adrenaline began to fail him again as he stumbled to the side. 452 took the opportunity to lunge forward and smack 667 in the face with his knee. 667 dropped the ax and fell back into the pit wall before crashing to the ground.

"Finish it! Kill him," the crowd chanted above as 452 back away from his fallen opponent. He looked up at the warden who was no longer protesting but had rejoined his comrades in clapping and cheering. He nodded at 452, approvingly, and chanted the same. 452

turned back to see 667 had risen to a crouching position and was reaching for the ax. Though he had not intended to end the fight this way, Prisoner 452 knew he had no option if he hoped to be allowed to climb back out of that pit. Grabbing the ax, 452 swung it high and brought it down hard, digging the blade deep into 667's head.

CHAPTER 9

Usually, Prisoner 452 was escorted back to the group tent after a fight, but that wasn't the case this time. Instead he was escorted to the warden's quarters. In the past, the warden had addressed 452 on the porch of his cabin. No prisoner had ever been granted permission to step inside. When they arrived at the cabin, the guards shoved 452 up the stairs and inside where they left him and closed the door. The interior of the cabin was just as magnificent as the outside. It was built by slave labor, and it was built well. The warden walked in and motioned for 452 to sit at the table. While most of the guards were hideously deformed creatures, the warden had a massive frame and muscles to compensate for his deformities. The scar along the warden's face appeared to be the only battle damage on his body, and no one spoke of where that came from.

"You did well tonight. My apologies for how it played out, but I had every confidence that you would rise to the occasion."

"Thank you, sir." The warden brought over a plate of meat and fruits and set it in front of 452. He then proceeded to pour a cup of wine and set it next to the plate.

"Eat! Drink! Enjoy your well-deserved feast." Prisoner 452 stared at the majestic offering for a moment, but soon quickly dived in. The warden sat down across from 452 with his own drink in hand. "Slow down, Leland. You can't enjoy the taste if you shovel it down like that."

Leland almost fell out of his chair at the sound. No one had called him by his name since he was cared for as a child. He stared up at the warden in shock before composing himself and returning to his food.

"I have some news for you, Leland. In case you didn't know, today is your twenty-third birthday." This time Leland did fall out of his chair, having never known his age, let alone the day of his birth. He quickly righted himself as the warden laughed. "Although there aren't many young boys who grow up in this prisoner camp, there is a policy in place. At the age of twenty, you should have been released from here and sent into the village to serve as an apprentice in some craft. I'd like to say that your records were misplaced, or that someone forgot, but truthfully, I didn't want to let you go. Your performance in the pit fights have made me quite a bit of coin, and I selfishly didn't wish for that to end.

"All things, of course, do come to an end at some point. Prisoner 667 was the last fighter the guards were willing to bet on to bring you down. They invested time and resources into preparing him, and you still bested the man. Suffice it to say; I wouldn't be able to enter you in another fight without paying the other guards off myself. So, I have decided to set you free from this place." Leland almost choked on the wine and then decided he couldn't eat anymore. He simply stared at the warden and listened intently.

"I have already made the guards at the gate aware,

and there is a horse waiting outside this cabin for you to ride into town tonight. I've secured some clothes for you, a few coins, and some other essentials have been prepared and packed for you in that sack by the door. You will live in one of the housing units set up near the village, and you've been granted a position with the local blacksmith." A human woman in a silky dress walked into the room. "For now, I want you to follow this young woman into the back room. She is going to clean you up and prepare you for your trip. Don't be shy; she'll take good care of you."

Leland nodded in silence, still too shocked to speak, as he stood and followed the woman past the warden into the back room. The woman proceeded to escort Leland down a hall toward a room with a large tub filled with steamy, clear water. After closing the door behind them, the woman ran her hand along Leland's back and brought him over to the tub. She removed the wraps around his hands, as well as his loincloth, and helped him into the tub. The water was hotter than it had appeared, but the woman forced Leland all the way into the tub until she pushed him under.

Having never been in this situation before, wholly submerged in clean, clear water, Leland was content to stay beneath the surface. When he finally ran out of air, he rose back up until his head emerged from the warm depths. The woman had removed her dress and was now climbing into the tub with him. He had never seen a woman, let alone another human, appear so clean and delicate as she did. He had also never been in the presence of a naked woman; certainly not one has fair as she was.

"Hush now. Close your eyes and relax as I take care of you." Leland did as he was told, as the woman sat behind him in the tub, her legs wrapping around him, as her hands caressed his body. She rubbed him down with a smooth, soapy cloth, years of dirt and grime, blood and sweat were wiped free of him. The air was filled with heavenly aromas as the woman scrubbed Leland from head to toe with ointments and oils. The experience was almost enough to put Leland to sleep, but he forced himself to stay awake in fear that this was all a dream. The woman cut his hair and shaved his face while they sat in the water, and then proceeded to massage his shoulders; addressing the knots and sores about him. When she was finished, the woman exited the tub and helped Leland out as well. She stood naked and bare before him as she used a fresh towel to dry him off.

"There you are, all clean." She ran her hand along his face and then motioned to the far end of the room. A stack of fresh clothes sat on a stool next to a bed. "You may now get dressed. Or, you can lay down on the bed and spend some time with me."

The woman stepped forward and kissed Leland, pressing her body against his as her hands ran through his hair and over his body. Leland's hands began to roam as well as he returned the kiss. After a moment or two, Leland broke the kiss and stepped back.

"Thank you for your kindness. You are beyond beautiful, but I believe I have indulged in enough delicacies for one night." The woman grinned and nodded. She kissed him once more and then walked him over to his clothes.

"I'll leave you to it then. I have a long walk back to the village. The warden wishes to speak with you once more when you're dressed and ready." The woman dressed herself and then left the room while

Leland gathered himself and attempted to calm his racing heart. When the woman left, Leland immediately regretted denying her offer, but he could only focus on his freedom at this point. He still did not believe that he would be allowed to leave the camp tonight, and so he couldn't allow any further distractions until that point. Dressing himself in the fresh linens that had been provided, Leland felt like a new man. He donned the nice leather boots that had been supplied and proceeded back to the front of the cabin where the warden was waiting by the fire.

"There he is. I'd say you look and certainly smell much better, wouldn't you Leland?" The warden applauds as Leland walks into the room. "I think it's time for you to be on your way, young sir, but before you go, we must address the issue of your name."

"My name, sir?"

"Your surname, to be exact. I'm not sure how much you are aware of your family past, but the Clayton name is deeply disdained within the Kingdom. Your father disgraced the crown, which resulted in the tragic death of your mother. This is also, of course, why you were sentenced to hard labor." Leland nodded and listened. Out of fear of repercussions, the elders amongst the prisoner camp had never told Leland much about his family. All he knew was that his father had been a Knight in the royal guard, and had done something wrong against the crown. His dishonor had brought shame to the Clayton name, and Leland and his mother had suffered the consequences.

Leland could barely remember his mother and father. He couldn't really remember their faces, their voices, or their touch. Leland had no memory of his home or his life before the camp. He could only remember the feeling of home. No matter how terrible life had been for him in the mines, no matter how many broken bones, bruises, beatings, Leland had clung on to the memory of that feeling of home. He didn't know the details of his father's crimes, but he had eyes enough to see the injustices of the prison camp. The other prisoners may have never been brave enough to divulge his family's history, but they still treated Leland with a level of respect that did not go unnoticed. That was enough for Leland to know better than to hate his father.

"I still remember the first day I met you. You

were hiding in a barrel in the corner of a back alley. You were only three, but you were a spirited little fella." The warden took a sip of his wine. "You shouldn't have to bear the weight of your father's sins any longer. So, in order for you to leave this camp behind, you will need to leave your surname behind. You will no longer be known as Leland, of the house of Clayton. Instead, you will be a Toller; a good and shameless surname."

"Leland Toller," said Leland, trying it out.

"See, there you go. It fits you well. With the skills you'll learn as a blacksmith, you'll grow into a respectable servant of the King. Nothing like that silly savage your father was." Leland's ears perked up at the word. He hadn't heard it in a long time, but he understood it had a history in this kingdom. It once referred to the enemies of this land; the enemies of the King and of the people. It didn't feel right that it would be associated with his father though. Thomas Clayton was a Knight, a member of the royal guard that protected the kingdom from savages; beasts that preyed on the innocent.

The warden, Captain Fellcer, and all his guards were the true savages. After all he had suffered, after all

Leland had endured, he suddenly felt a wave of anger engulf him. He couldn't leave it all behind like this. He couldn't act as if he were grateful to the beasts that broke him so many times over. Leland's eyes quickly scanned the room until they landed upon a rack of weapons mounted on the wall. While the warden took another sip and briefly turned his back, Leland sprung forward and grabbed a large dagger from the wall. He leapt over some furniture and launched himself up onto the warden's back.

"No, Fellcer. You're the savage," whispered Leland as he dug the dagger deep into the warden's neck. The warden quickly grabbed Leland and threw him across the room. As Leland crashed to the floor, he rolled to his feet and sprinted back toward Fellcer.

"You selfish little bastard!" Fellcer clenched his bleeding neck wound as he grabbed a knife and threw it toward Leland. The blade sliced through the side of Leland's stomach. Wincing, Leland scaled a large chair and launched himself into the air. Distracted by the deep gash in his neck, Fellcer was too slow to block Leland's advance.

Leland tackled the mighty Cainate and brought

the blade down swiftly into the warden's left eye. Leland covered the Cainate's mouth and quickly stuffed it full of linens to muffle the warden's cries of pain. Twisting the dagger, Leland dug it deep into the warden's head until the Cainate stopped moving.

Leland stumbled back, distancing himself from the massive beast. He stared at the warden for a moment before quickly righting himself and grabbing his things. Even at this time of night, there was no guarantee that a guard wouldn't show up to the cabin and discover the fallen warden.

Leland stepped outside to find the horse tied to the banister, waiting for him as the warden had mentioned. Leland tied the sack to the saddle and mounted the horse. Every instinct within him wanted to sprint the horse for the gates and get away from the camp as quickly as possible, but Leland knew he would only look suspicious.

Slowly but surely, Leland galloped through the camp, avoiding eye contact with anyone he came across. Finally, he arrived at the gates and nodded to the two guards standing a post. They growled at him briefly, but eventually opened the gates and said nothing. Leland turned back and looked at the camp one more time. He saw the prisoner tents in the distance and, for a moment, he almost missed the false security they had granted him. He turned back around and rode through the gates, nodding once again to the guards before continuing on.

CHAPTER 10

Leland wasn't quite sure what to do now. He couldn't simply follow the warden's instructions and head into town. Sooner or later, Fellcer's body would be found. The guards would put two and two together and come hunting Leland down. He needed to run, but he didn't know where to run to. Leland had never seen a map of the kingdom, let alone know which direction to steer his horse. It was only when Leland was far enough from the camp gates that he noticed a pain in his side.

Pulling up his shirt, Leland saw a sizeable bloody gash where Fellcer's blade had sliced him. In all of his rush to get out of the camp, Leland had forgotten altogether that he had been wounded. Though he was still very much in fear of his life, Leland felt the adrenaline leave him as a sharp pain steadily took over. He groaned and leaned forward on the horse as his vision began to falter. The night was dark, and the road was hard to see. The trees started to sway in the wind, and everything spun in a dizzy haze around Leland. He was about to lose consciousness all together when he heard a voice pierce the pounding in this head.

"Is that you, Leland?" In his slumber, Leland frantically looked around, searching for the source of the voice. He groaned and clung tight to the horse, not wanting to surrender. "Leland! Are you alright?"

Despite his efforts, Leland fell off the side of his horse and hit the ground hard. He grimaced at the pain while he simultaneously struggled to get back the air that had abruptly escaped him on impact. Rolling over, Leland focused on the stars in the sky, trying desperately to stay awake. He couldn't be captured now. He couldn't be sent back to that place; not when he was just on the cusp of freedom. His view of the night sky was momentarily blocked when a shadowy figure rushed to his side and knelt over him. Feeling the smooth touch of a woman's hand, Leland's eyes focused to see the woman who had bathed him taking his head in her hands.

"Please...please...," but Leland couldn't speak much more after that. The woman tore off a strip from the bottom of her clothing and used it to dress Leland's wound.

"Hush now, I've got you. I know just where to go."

****

Leland woke to a man standing over him with a knife. He jerked up and tried to get away but found himself strapped down to the table. Leland tried to shout, but his mouth was gagged. Leland struggled as much as he could trying desperately to get loose, but the restraints were too tight.

"No, no, no, stop that, please," said the man, but his words fell on deaf ears. "Sweetheart, please, I need your help."

"Hush, now Leland. This man is trying to help you." The woman he had seen on the road rushed to Leland's side. She put her hands on his chest and pushed him down as she looked into his eyes. "He's a healer, Leland. He's almost finished stitching you up."

Leland slowly, but surely, stopped struggling as he breathed in deeply and looked down. The healer pulled a string tightly from Leland's side before using the blade to cut it off. He then proceeded to wrap fresh bandages around Leland's torso, nice and tight, before using a pin to secure it.

"There we are. That should do it. If you take it easy over the next week or so, you should heal up easy." The healer smiled down at Leland, and then looked over to the woman. "Why don't you help me remove these restraints, Melony."

"Sure." Melony assisted the healer in removing the straps around Leland's wrists and legs before turning and helping Leland up and off the table. Leland winced at the pain and quickly slowed his movements. "Take it easy, now. Let's sit you down over here."

"Thank you," Leland said as he looked into her eyes. He then turned and nodded toward the healer. "Thank you, as well, sir. My apologies for all the trouble."

"Don't mention it. I'm just glad Melony brought you in when she did." The healer pulled up a blanket that was covering a window and took a glance outside. "There's still a few more hours until sunrise. I'm guessing you need to stay out of sight."

"What happened, Leland? I thought the warden was set to release you." Melony wiped Leland's forehead with a damp cloth as she handed him a cup of water.

"He did, release me, but... well, I couldn't leave without a parting gift." The healer frowned a bit and nodded. "I'm sorry to bring this to your door, sir. I can leave if you just... *cough...* point me to my horse."

"Oh, stop that. No need to rush. You have some time to rest a little before getting on your way. It's the least I could do for Thomas Clayton's son." Leland's eyes widen at the sound of his father's name.

"You knew my father?"

"Of course, I did. I used to serve in the castle as the head healer for the crown. I serviced the King, the royal family, and all of the royal guard, including your father." The healer had the sack that Fellcer had given Leland. After rummaging through it for a moment, he began filling the sack with bandages, bits of food, and some other materials. "It's a shame what happened to him."

"What did happen to him?" Leland unknowingly began to grip Melony's hand as he longed to know what details the healer could tell. Melony smiled and held his hand in return.

"Well, of course, you wouldn't know. I imagine the Clayton name isn't spoken of much in the place where you came." The healer put down the sack and pulled up a stool. "I was there when your father and his friend, Leif Mayvoy, escaped their execution. They caused quite the scene in front of the town folk but were able to make it out of the castle and up into the hills.

"King Jerad sent an assassin after them, but only the assassin's body was recovered. In his dying breaths, he swore that he had wounded your father and Leif. Your father was believed to have found a highland pass and escaped up into the mountains. To my knowledge, he and Leif were never heard from again."

"What did they do…*cough*… to deserve such a sentence? Why is my mother dead, and why was I left to rot in that hellhole?" Leland couldn't get the questions out quick enough. It was the first time, in all his life, that someone was willing to tell him his own history.

"Ah, son, that's a long and depressing story. The short version is, your father was a trusted, loyal High Knight of King David Aldiss the twelfth. The King's son, Jerad, turned on his father and brought the Cainates back to Crestside. His first official act as King was to get rid of anyone who posed a threat or reminded him of his father. Thomas Clayton was the first of many to go. You and your mother, through associated, reaped your own punishments." The healer got up from his stool and went back to filling the sack.

"The kingdom has been at the mercy of King Jerad ever since. Now you need to rest for a moment while I prepare some supplies for your journey. You can stay here for another hour at most. Then you must head for the hills, and Melony and I must return to the housing units before we are missed." Leland wanted to ask more questions, but he felt a deep sense of exhaustion overtake him. Before he could protest and ask more questions, Leland found himself laying back into Melony's embrace.

"I'm glad you found me," Leland said through his pain.

"I'm glad I did as well. I'm surprised you had the energy to take down the big Cainate. When you turned me down, I figured it was because you were too exhausted to participate." Leland chuckled at the thought.

"Not at all. Despite what I certainly wanted at the time, I… didn't feel it was right." Leland looked over at Melony. "Why did Fellcer elect you to take care of me?"

"It's what I do, sweetheart. Under Jerad's rule, women with my looks and my… talents tend to be loaned out for certain… things. I was happy to learn that you were to be my center of attention instead of catering to Fellcer or his guards again." Melony looked away for a moment and cleared her throat before returning back to Leland with a half-hearted smile. "It's not a glorious profession, but I've seen worse."

"I'm sorry…."

"Don't be. Had I not been walking home tonight,

I wouldn't have found you. Now rest for a moment, while you have the time." Melony ran her fingers through his hair and pulled his head back.

Leland did as he was told and closed his eyes. Though his mind was racing, he couldn't fight the weight of his eyes. He knew that, come morning, the Cainates would be on the hunt, looking for him. Like his father, he would be on the run. Had he not killed Fellcer, he could have been waking up to the first day of his new life as a blacksmith's apprentice; as a man named Toller. Perhaps he would regret his decisions one day, but he didn't have the strength to do so now. He lost himself in Melony's arms and dozed off to sleep.

****

When he woke, the healer was tying the sack of supplies to the saddle of the horse. Melony secured a blanket to the horse as well and then turned to give Leland a hug. For a moment, Leland considered asking her to join him, to run off with him, but he knew better. Despite the demons she faced on a daily basis, she was, for the most part, free. Leland, once again, was not. He had lost his freedom when King Jerad declared his father a traitor, and he had lost his freedom again when he took the life of Captain Fellcer. This was his burden to bear, and it seemed, for now, he would carry it alone.

"I've taken the liberty of drawing you a map, as I'm sure you don't quite know your way around these parts," said the healer as he patted Leland on the shoulder. "You can either head West, and hope you find another Kingdom somewhere out there, or you can follow the river up through the forest and into the hills. I've marked the general area where your father was last seen. Perhaps you can trace his steps and… find some closure."

"Thank you, sir, for all you've done." Leland shook the healer's hand and turned to Melony. She smiled and gave him a gentle hug.

"Take care of yourself, Leland. Don't go falling off your horse anytime soon." Leland smiled and hugged her back. The healer helped Leland up on the horse and then turned to close up the shop. Leland folded up the map and put it in his pocket. Nodding one more time at Melony, Leland brought the horse around and headed east, toward the mountains.

CHAPTER 11

Leland rode all through the day, climbing farther up the hills, deeper into the forest, closer to the mountains. Stopping only to allow the horse a drink from the river, Leland didn't allow for a moment's rest for himself. Again, he wondered how much easier this would have been had he simply escaped in the night after a day's work as an apprentice. He didn't regret killing Fellcer, but he was definitely aware of the predicament he put himself in.

Towards the evening, Leland reached the mountains and headed North along the edge of the ridge. While the healer didn't know exactly where Leland's father had escaped to, he knew the general region based on the assassin's report. Leland used the map to guide him but kept his eyes open for any signs.

It wouldn't be long before night took over the kingdom. Leland was tempted to set up camp and wait until morning to resume his course. Considering all the events that happened the previous night, Leland knew that a lot could happen in the time he took to stop and sleep. He pressed forward and desperately looked for a break in the rock wall. Leland watched the last rays of the setting sun slowly crawled down the mountainside, and in the last flicker of light, he saw it.

What looked like a fold in the rock wall was actually a passage that wound up and through the mountain. Finding a new wave of energy within him, Leland turned the horse onto the path and began the journey through the rocky canyon. After an hour or two of climbing, Leland arrived at the top and stared out across a long, frozen plane that stretched to the Eastern horizon. There was nothing in sight, or at least nothing that Leland could see at that hour.

If his father had indeed taken this path, then he would have likely stood in the same spot that Leland now stood; looking out across the nothingness. Having not found a gravesite or a cave along the way, Leland began to lean toward the chance that the healer's wilder prediction could actually be true. Perhaps his father decided to journey across this open space to find whatever lied beyond. A part of Leland was saddened by the thought, knowing that it meant his father would have made the conscious decision to step forward instead of turning back to rescue his own son. It wasn't a pleasant thought, but surely his father had his reasons.

Finding the mountain stream, Leland dropped to his knees to drink alongside his horse. Leland found a spot for them to rest along and spread out his blanket on the ground. Taking some food from the healer's supplies, he replenished himself and then laid down to rest. Once again, Leland found himself staring up into the night sky. Unlike the previous night, Leland wasn't fighting to stay conscious as he looked up and took in the splendor. He let his mind roam to thoughts of what he might find the following day, but soon his fatigue took over and took him down for the night.

****

When he awoke the cold breeze biting at his face, Leland opened his eyes to find that the horse had left him in the night. He still had the sack that the healer had prepared, the blanket from Melony, and the dagger he used to kill Fellcer. Leland wrapped the blanket around him as he sat up and leaned against the mountain rock. This was the first time in the past twenty years that he could remember waking up with the sun already present in the sky. While he was thankful to have achieved such a deep and restful sleep, he did not want to waste the day. Tying the blanket around his shoulders and securing the sack to his belt, Leland began his trek across the frozen frontier.

The first few hours maintained a slight but steady uphill hike. Each step took him deeper into the cold and further from the troubles behind him. The ground turned to snow, Leland's breaths became visible, and all was deathly quiet. There were no birds in the sky, and no tracks on the ground to suggest any mountain wildlife. Leland was alone, but for the most part, he enjoyed it. While he was tempted to speculate what he might find on the other side, Leland forced himself to stay focused on the task at hand.

While most of the ground was covered with snow, Leland could still see the faint outline of the mountain stream still flowing beneath a solid layer of mountain ice. He used the stream to guide him across the frozen plane if only to keep him from accidentally turning himself around.

His pace began to slow as the elements became more and more an obstacle to his journey. Leland wrapped the blanket around him, covering his head and upper chest, as he powered on through the stiff winds and blistering cold. At some point, he found a split in the stream. A larger stream flowed down from the north and split into torrent toward the village, and an eastern torrent toward Leland's assumed destination.

Soon enough, the weather became too much for Leland to bear. If the window wasn't blowing him over, the frozen tundra compromised his footing. Each time he crashed down to the hard, snowy surface, the pain in his side became increasingly evident. While climbing to his feet for the fourth or fifth time, Leland looked down to see several red pellets in the snow. Pulling back the blanket, Leland discovered that his wound had reopened and he had bled through the bandages and his shirt. Leland gripped his side as he forced himself to his feet.

This would not do. Leland did not grow up, having every inch of his body beaten and broken, time and time again, just to give up now. He did not endure the ghastly summer heat of the dark and dirty mines just to fall prey to the chill that currently surrounded him. He did not kill Fellcer, and lay waste to what could have been a simple, uncomplicated life, just to die a couple days later in the snow. Unable to see, unable to feel anything but the numbness that immersed his body, and hardly able to breathe, Leland kept his head down and carried on.

Eventually, Leland resorted to covering his face thoroughly with the blanket and walking blind as far as he could. Every once in a while, he would peek out to find the frozen steam and verify he was still on course. Otherwise, he kept himself wrapped up as much as possible and kept moving forward. Finally, after hours of agony, Leland noticed the ground beneath his feet beginning to thaw. He felt the ground slowly shift into a downward slope.

Longing for warmer weather, or at least a place to get out of the cold, Leland summoned what strength he had left to pick up his feet and tread faster through the snow. The snow beneath his feet soon turned to slush as the cold slowly began to dissipate. Leland quickened his pace, telling himself that the journey was almost at an end. If he could just make it a little bit further, he would be able to rest in a much warmer, more secure environment. Unfortunately, Leland allowed his excitement to get the better of him.

While his reinvigorated momentum definitely powered his legs to move faster and his footsteps to quicken, Leland's enthusiasm ultimately distracted him beyond caution. While the snow melted around him, so did the layer of ice that ran atop the eastward mountain stream. Forgetting to mind his whereabouts, Leland soon felt the ice begin to crack beneath his feet. By the time Leland realized that he was no longer trekking alongside the stream, but was now running along on top of it, it was too late. The ice finally gave way, and Leland fell through to the watery depths beneath.

Leland fought through the pain in his side to suck in as much air as he could before his head went underwater. As agonizing as it was to open his eyes under the freezing water, Leland desperately tried to find the hole in the ice so that he could swim back and pull himself out. The stream's current, however, was too strong and immediately pulled Leland along. Leland finally made his way to the ice as the river dragged him eastward.

No matter how hard he tried, he couldn't break through the ice, let alone find something to grab onto. Knowing that the water was flowing so much faster than he could have ever traveled on foot, Leland tried his best to stay as close to the layer of ice as possible. He knew that he could only hold his breath for a short time longer, but he also knew that eventually, that ice would thin enough for him to break through.

Leland focused on limiting the air bubbles that escaped his lips while simultaneously keeping his eyes on the surface as the water raced toward the east. Sure enough, the ice above him began to thin until he saw chunks start to break off and float along the surface. Seeing this, Leland frantically swam for the surface and forced his head above water.

As the air rushed into his lungs, Leland fought to stay above the surface. His arms were tired, and no amount of desperate adrenaline could overpower the strength of the current. Reaching out, Leland tried to cling to passing blocks of ice but found that he couldn't maintain any type of grip. Out of options, Leland looked ahead in hopes of finding a low hanging tree branch or vine, something, anything, that he could cling to.

The water flowed faster by the minute as it sloped downhill more and more. After burrowing through a canyon, the stream appeared to be heading toward a cavern in the mountain. Leland desperately tried to swim to the water's edge, knowing full well that he'd be doomed once the upcoming cavern swallowed him up. Sadly, his efforts were fruitless, and he soon found himself engulfed by the darkness of the mountain. If it wasn't hard enough already to stay above the surface, it was near impossible to do it the pitch black of the cavern. Leland was swept underwater, again and again, slamming into rocks, bumping into cavern walls, and desperately trying to remember which direction was up.

Finding the surface again, Leland choked on the air and cried out in pain. While he might have thawed from that frozen plane behind him, his body felt like shattered glass; brittle and fragmented. As he struggled to stay afloat, Leland's eyes caught a shimmer of light dancing off the wet cavern wall. There was a light, somewhere ahead in the tunnel.

"Please! Help me! I'm here!" Leland's voice was weak, and his throat was sore, but he shouted as loud as he could. He kept his eyes on the light as the water raced toward it. Perhaps it was a lantern hanging on the wall or a someone holding a torch to light their path. If he could just find the strength to stretch his arms out far enough, someone could grab him and pull him free of the current. His fantasies of being saved were soon demolished as the light at the end of the tunnel became clear. There was no lantern or torch lighting the cavern up ahead.

"Oh.... God...," were the only words that could escape his lips as Leland felt every ounce of hope leave him as he was swept out of the cavern and over the cliff, following the waterfall down through the clouds.

****

"Where am I?" Leland struggled to speak but got the words out as he struggled to focus his eyes through the haze.

“Take it easy, bud. You’ve been through a lot.” Leland turned his head toward the man’s voice, still unable to see anything more than fuzzy shapes in the low light.

“Who’s there?” Leland tried to reach out, but his arms were too heavy to lift.

“It’s your father, Leland. It’s me, son.” Leland could now make out the shape of a man sitting next to the bed. He couldn’t make out the more delicate features, but he could see the man reach out and touch his arm. “You’ve been through a lot, son, but you've found me.”

“Where…where were you… all this time?” Leland groaned as his body ached all over.

“I had to go away, son.” The man stood and leaned over the bed. Leland still couldn’t focus as he stared up at his father through the blur. He felt his father’s hand run through his hair and caress his face. His father's hand then found their way down to Leland’s neck where they gripped his throat tight.

"Ugh! Stop! I can't...breathe!" His father only tightened his grip on Leland's neck and pressed down. Leland winced at the sharp pain in his throat as he struggled to breathe.

"You shouldn't have come here, Leland. YOU SHOULDN'T HAVE COME HERE!"

****

Leland screamed as he opened his eyes to find himself submerged underwater. His lungs were on fire as they begged for air. Leland clawed his way to the surface and gasped for air as the evening rays of sun stung like daggers inserted into his eyes. He coughed up a bunch of water as he gasped for more air. He struggled to stay afloat as every one of his limbs felt like they were tied to sacks of bricks, pulling him back underwater.

Leland looked around to find himself in a wide stream, flowing eastward through a dense, green forest. No one seemed to be in sight, though he doubted he had the strength to call out to them if he saw them. Cranking his head to look downstream, he saw an upcoming fork in the flow. The larger portion of water continued to the right while a smaller, calmer stream flowed off to the left. If Leland had any hope of overcoming the power of the current, he knew he needed to make it to the smaller stream on the left.

Grunting through the pain, Leland tried to swim to the left. Barely having enough strength to keep his head above water, it was a miracle to Leland that he did indeed make it to the smaller stream that flowed off to the left, deeper into the trees. He let out a sigh of relief as he tilted his head back and floated along the top of the water to regain his strength. If he could conserve enough energy for one more struggle, he could probably make it to the shore, or at least close enough to grab hold of something.

The sun was setting, and Leland found himself, for the third time, peering up at the stars. He contemplated whether making it to shore was worth it at this point. His body was in shambles. Even if he managed to pull himself from the water, he knew for sure that he couldn't walk. Lying beneath the trees might provide him some shade, but he'd likely die just as quickly as if he stayed in the water.

Before he could truly make up his mind, he felt

the water dip beneath him. The small, peaceful stream had transformed into fast-flowing rapids as the water's surface turned into waves that crashed up against large rocks randomly placed in the stream. Unable to get out of the way, Leland hit the first boulder hard before the current dragged him under and swept him over a bed of several submerged rocks as well.

Leland tucked his arms and legs into himself as best as he could as he weathered the rapids until the boulders were no more and the stream emptied out into a small lagoon. It seemed clear, by now, that Leland was without a choice in how he would die. The lagoon was much deeper than the streambed had been, and Leland was now content to sink to the bottom instead of scrambling his way back to the surface again. Someone once told him that drowning wasn't such a horrible way to die. If it meant he no longer needed to bear the pain that engulfed him, he was certainly open to it.

He smiled and closed his eyes, letting his body relax as he sunk to a lower depth. In his last moments of consciousness, Leland didn't care to think about the troubles behind him, but only hoped that he'd find some peace ahead. When his body found the bottom of the lagoon, he accepted his fate and waited for his sweet release. His sense of peacefulness was suddenly interrupted when he distinctly felt his body being pulled to the surface.

Leland opened his eyes in confusion only to be equally as dumbfounded when he focused on what was in front of him. Leland shook his head in the water, opening and closing his eyes to readjust, but the outcome remained the same. Pulling him to the surface, with her arms wrapped around his, was a woman with the torso of a human and the tail of a fish.

The mermaid smiled at Leland before calling upon her friends to help her haul Leland to the surface. Several more mermaids, each strikingly beautiful with long flowing hair of different colors, matching the different colored scales of their tails, swam up to grab hold of Leland and expedite his climb to the surface. Their eyes were squinted like that of a cat's eyes, radiating through the water with a green tint. Their fingers were webbed together, and long nails protruded out from their fingertips. As they ascended together, the closest mermaid leaned in, taking Leland's face in her hands, and brought her lips to his. She breathed cool air into his burning lungs while holding him close.

When they finally reached the surface, the mermaids slowly escorted Leland across the water. The lagoon reflected the night sky above, making Leland feel as if he were genuinely floating among the stars. His eyesight began to waver as everything around him jumped in and out of a dark shroud of blurriness. He had taken ten or twenty too many hits in one day, and the repercussions were starting to surface. The moon, in its full state, smiled down upon Leland. It shined it's borrowed light past Leland and the mermaids and landed on a tall rock looking over the far end of the lagoon. The mermaids brought him closer as he struggled to focus his vision.

There, atop a rock which protruded out from the tree line over the waters, sat the most gorgeous of creatures Leland had ever laid his eyes upon. The woman sat in solitude, a sadness surrounding her, so thick Leland could see it. Her head was bent, and the bangs of her hair hung down over her face. She held her knees up to her chest with her arms wrapped around them. She wore a long black dress, which contrasted against her pale skin. The mermaids called out to her as she guided Leland closer.

"Katrianna, look what we found!"

As they drew closer, Leland could see that the woman had been crying. Tears ran down her face, only to hit the rock beneath her and continue on their way to the waters below. The mermaids called out to her again. Slowly, she raised her head into the light of the moon that seemed to hover over her alone. Her eyes found their way to Leland. As she peered down upon him, a set of large, magnificent, grey feathered wings emerged and extended from her back. Her beauty astounded him beyond words. Despite the drastic turn of events Leland had suffered through over the past few days, nothing could have prepared him for such a sight.

Her wings swiftly lifted her up off the rock before gently dropped her down into the shallow edge of the lagoon. The mermaids guided him towards her as she locked eyes with his. Leland stared into the mist of green clashing with a layered blue in such a stunning display of fusion within her irises. She stared at him with an awe about her expression, as if he were somehow just as rare a sight as she was. She caressed his face and then looked back to the mermaids with concern.

"He's fading."

"Wait." Leland tried to speak, to protest her concerns, but alas, he could not. At that moment, the moon almost seemed to brighten, engulfing everything around them into a thick white light. The light covered all, and then dissolved into a darkness Leland was all too familiar with. He felt himself go but hoped he would wake again to see such sights once more.

CHAPTER 12

3 Days Later

As a fresh breeze carried the fragrance of sweet morning dew into the cottage, the heat of the morning sun shined through the window frame and spread over the bed where the man laid. Over the past three days, she had supervised his recovery. He had yet to wake up from his sleep, but that was probably for the best. She had called upon the fairies as well as some other friends to help mend his broken body. The fairies were already aware of his presence in the valley, having seen him fall from the waterfall three days before. Had they not been there to slow his descent, he would have hit the water below like face diving into a solid sheet of rock.

They had cut away his clothes and cleaned him. They used herbs and ointments to address the exterior wounds and a bit of magic and address the internal ones. The man had clearly suffered through a tremendous journey before arriving at the lagoon. According to the mermaids, the man had almost seemed at peace when he sunk to the bottom. While she was sorry to rob him of that peace, she knew that her friends could at least help him heal.

He certainly was a sight to behold. Beyond the prominent features that she found herself attracted to, this man represented the first human to enter this land in a very long time. The elders, of course, we against keeping him there. In the olden times, humans had been barred from this place. Events happened, times changed, and centuries later they found themselves in this predicament. Despite their reasonably valid arguments, she couldn't leave this man to die. The mermaids would not have saved him if they sensed a darkness within him. They are gracious and beautiful creatures, but the intuition is beyond reproach. Things would have ended much differently if they didn't recognize the man to be worth saving.

While waiting for him to recover, she couldn't help but allow herself to speculate as to who he was and where he had come from. She dreamed about him and couldn't get over the look in his eyes when she had dropped down beside him in the lagoon. He had seen her in her full form, something she rarely allowed within this land, and he had smiled. Though she knew absolutely nothing about him, she found herself yearning to see that smile again. She had him set up in the cottage beside the castle where she could easily visit throughout the day and check in on his progress. After three days asleep, the man had shown signs of waking. So, she was summoned to the cottage to greet him.

As she waited by his bedside, having brought a plate of food, she watched his eyes move back and forth beneath their eyelids. She wondered what he was dreaming about. His body was riddled with scars from wounds long before his trek to this valley. He had been beaten, whipped, stabbed, twisted, and mangled time and time again. Perhaps the memories of those times haunted him in his sleep. If so, even more reason for him to wake and find peace in this new place. Finally, the man's eyes began to open as he squinted at the sunlight. He lifted a hand to block the rays as he looked around the room. Eventually his eyes landed on her, and she smiled in silence.

"Hello," he said, as he slowly put down his hand and stared at her.

"Good morning. I'm happy to see you finally awake." He smiled at her words and then took in the room once again.

"Where…am I?"

"I've put you up in the spare cottage by the castle. You've been here for the past three days while you recovered from the injuries you sustained on your journey to our lands." The man listened to her but didn't seem to comprehend.

"I… don't remember how I got here."

"Well you were pretty banged up, and you lost consciousness in the lagoon."

"The lagoon?" The man massaged his head as he sat up in the bed. He looked back at her and smile. "Do

I know you?"

"You don't remember me? From the lagoon?" She sat back in her chair, slightly disappointed, almost hurt that he couldn't remember their first encounter. She tried to sympathize and leaned forward again. "Let's slow down and start with something simple. I'm Katrianna. What's your name?"

"My name? My name is…my name…is…"

Katrianna stood up and walked across the room to grab the sack that had been found tied to the man's belt. They had tossed most of the items which had spoiled due to the water, but there had been a paper in there that they managed to salvage and dry out. She found it and brought it over to the bed.

"This letter says it belongs to Leland Toller, a blacksmith apprentice. Is that you?"

****

"Leland… Toller. Leland, yes... that's my name." Leland recognized the name and clung to that recognition as he struggled to remember anything else. Instead, his mind kept coming up with nothing. He looked back up at the beautiful woman who sat patiently beside the bed. “I’m sorry, it’s so…frustrating. I can’t… my mind is so blank.”

“That’s understandable. When we found you, you were in a pretty bad way. We have worked to heal your injuries over the past few days. You had injuries from head to toe. Some things take longer to heal. I’m sure your head will clear sooner or later.” He clung to her words, hoping they were true. If what she said was true, that this wasn’t their first encounter, then he couldn’t help but feel a bit embarrassed. He struggled to contemplate how he could have forgotten a face like hers. Her eyes pierced through him, her smile resonated to his core, and her fair skin almost seemed to glow in the sunlight. She appeared to be close to his height. Her long brown hair flowed to her shoulders. Her thin frame was wrapped in a blue dress which flowed over her body down to her long, smooth legs. He caught himself staring at her for far too long and quickly averted his eyes.

“Uh…well…thank you, then, for taking care of me. I appreciate your kindness.”

****

Days passed before Leland was able to step out of bed. Up until that point, he had only made contact with Katrianna. In the night, between dreams, he swore he could hear voices in the room, but the room was always empty when he managed to open his eyes. Katrianna was plenty company, but being cooped up in that bedroom was beginning to turn Leland a little stir crazy.

Katrianna clearly played things cautiously. She was very pleasant in his presence. She was quick to provide encouragement, tell him he'd heal soon, assuring him his memory would return. Since he didn't have much to add to the conversation, she would bring him food and stay with him while he ate. She seemed willing enough to care for him but wasn't yet ready to tell him much about her, or the land in which she resided.

In fact, the only thing he had gathered, outside of knowing her name, was that she was a sort of Princess in these parts. There was no royal family, and no one else resided with her in the castle. She wouldn't quite divulge why she was considered a Princess and not a

Queen, but it was undoubtedly something personal. He tried not to prod her with questions she evidently wasn't ready to answer. Instead, he remained grateful and respectful. Needless to say, when he found that he could stand, he begged to be allowed to walk around outside of the cottage.

Finally, after a week or so of trudging around the inside of the cottage, Katrianna permitted Leland to step outside. He would be allowed to roam the area immediately surrounding the cottage but was forbidden to travel any further without supervision. Katrianna promised to take him on long walks in the near future, but he assured her he was content enough to take in the fresh air and stay close to the cottage for the time being.

It was on one lovely afternoon, when the sky was particularly blue, that Leland had a visitor stop by the cottage. He had pulled a chair out into the garden and was resting in it when he felt a presence nearby. He heard no footsteps but definitely was aware of someone watching him. He tried not to be nervous but found himself searching all around him for whoever it could be.

"Hello? Is someone there? I can't… see you… but

I'm fairly certain you can hear me." Leland looked around some more but continued to find nothing. "Please… I won't bite, I promise."

"Oh, I'm sure you won't. Pardon my intrusion, as well as my apparently terrible hiding skills, but I wanted to watch you a bit before introducing myself." To Leland's surprise, the presence he had sensed was not a person at all. Instead, Leland watched as a small elderly fairy dropped down from the trees above him and hovered in front of him. "My name is Mrs. Doodles, and I'm the resident healer in this valley."

"Oh, …uh, hello. I'm…I'm Leland." Leland tried to keep his composure but found that his jaw was hanging so low it was beginning to cramp.

"Pleasure to meet you, Leland, but I already know who you are. I helped nurse you back to health and have been checking in on you regularly at night."

"So, you're one of the voices I hear in the dark. I knew I wasn't crazy."

"Oh, heaven's me, my apologies for disturbing your sleep. I try to keep my assistants from jabbering on, but they can't seem to keep quiet when I tell them to." Mrs. Doodles flew to the left and sat herself on the head of a large sunflower. "I'll remedy that, but for now let's focus on the situation at hand. Katrianna tells me you're still unable to remember anything."

"Yes, that's correct." Leland couldn't keep his eyes off the fairy. She wore a tiny green jumpsuit and boots. A pair of thick-rimmed glasses sat on her face as she looked down at the notepad she was jotting down words upon with her tiny writing tool.

"Have you had any trouble remembering anything about the ten days since you've been awake?"

"Not at all. Everything about the last ten days, though intriguingly questionable, is clear as day." Mrs. Doodles smiled at his response.

"Well, that's good to hear. It means your brain is functioning well enough. My guess is, due to the traumatic nature of the injuries you endured on the journey here, your brain went into a defensive state and locked down. We just need to find a way to unlock it." Still mesmerized by the fact that he was looking at an actual fairy, Leland took a moment to notice that Mrs. Doodles had stopped talking.

"Oh! Sorry. Yes, okay, so what can be done to… unlock my brain?" Mrs. Doodles put away her writing pad and flew up to him.

"Well, you've been getting more exercise lately. I suggest we take longer walks during the day when you're able. I've also requested that some paper and a writing utensil be provided to you so that you can do some journaling."

"Journaling?"

"Why yes, of course. The act of writing down your thoughts is a great exercise for the brain. Working overtime to document your current thoughts might eventually trigger your mind to remember your previous thoughts. Trust me; it's worth the try." At that, Mrs. Doodles began to fly back into the forest.

"Wait, where are you going?" Leland grabbed his cane and stood up.

"Don't worry, Mr. Toller. I'll be back around tomorrow to check in on you."

****

Later that day, Katrianna arrived at the cottage to take Leland on his first walk. They didn't stray too far from the cottage, but she took him around the forest for a bit, through the vineyard, and over to thewater's edge of the main stream that cut through the valley. They walked in silence; for the most part, exchanging smiles every now and then. Leland's head was full of questions, but he didn't want to ruin their time together. At the stream, they both take a break and sit down, dangling their feet in the water.

"You seem to be recovering well. You barely need that cane," Katrianna said as she cupped some water in her hand and took a sip.

"Yes, thank you. Though I'm not sure if I'm ready to discard it just yet, I've become fairly dependent on it." Leland followed suit and drank from the stream before wiping his face and turning back to Katrianna. "I met Mrs. Doodles yesterday."

"What?" Katrianna looked shocked, as if she wasn't aware of the visit.

"Yes. She dropped by to visit and introduce

herself. I... never knew creatures...pardon me... I never knew fairies like her existed. Are there other magical creatures in this valley?"

"Yes, there are, though I wasn't planning on divulging that information to you just yet. We don't typically have strangers visit this land, and so I wasn't quite comfortable with sharing secrets with you." Katrianna sighed and looked out across the water.

"I understand. I mean you no harm, I swear it. I just wish there were a way for me to prove it to you." Leland looked at the gorgeous woman sitting next to him. Every time he was blessed with her presence, he couldn't help but eventually get lost in the moment. She was without flaw. Her small frame appeared both delicate and strong. Her demeanor and the way she carried herself told him many things about the level of responsibility she carried on her shoulders, as well as the genuine emotions she had in regards to this place. He did not blame her for taking caution around him, but he wished he could overcome that somehow. "I don't suppose your friends have any kind of potion to make me tell the truth. I'll gladly drink it if it means clearing up any of your doubt."

"That's funny." Katrianna looked back at him and smiled. "Even if we had such a potion, what truth could you reveal when you can't remember anything past 10 days ago."

"True." Leland looked into her eyes and found them staring back at him. He broke her gaze and looked out at the forest across the river. "Are there more humans around here somewhere, or are you the only one?"

"I'm not…" Katrianna suddenly caught herself and stopped speaking before she gave too much away. "I mean to say that I'm not alone, but I am the only one of my kind. Many of the other magical kind, like the fairies, speak a common tongue. So I am not without friends."

"How did you come to be here, then? If you have no family, and you are the only human here, how does something like that happen?" Leland saw a shift in Katrianna's eyes and realized she was raising her defenses once again.

"That's a story for another day." Katrianna pulled her feet out of the water and stood. "We best get back."

****

The Enchanted Castle
That Evening

"I'm not sure if that was necessarily the best course of action, exposing Leland to some of our secrets." Katrianna ate her dinner as she spoke to Mrs. Doodles.

"Well, what was I supposed to do. I can't properly treat him if I'm only allowed near him when he's asleep. Besides, the mermaids already vetted him. What is the point of keeping this up? You might appear human, and therefore normal to him because you're able to hide your wings from the naked eye, but he's going to eventually notice the rest of us."

"I've already received pushback from the south. They don't want him here." Katrianna opened up a bottle of wine and poured herself a glass.

"Well, that's no surprise. They don't want anyone here." Mrs. Doodles plopped down on a shelf and leaned against a candle. "Don't act like you don't want him around. I've noticed how you've been acting lately. A young man, certainly not ugly, around your age, without an evil bone in his body, happens to drop down into your territory. There's nothing wrong with recognizing the benefits of all of this."

"The mermaids are not enough. Without knowing who he really is, where he's from, and why he's here, I can't put much faith in him. No matter how much I want to." She took a long drink from the glass as she peered out the stained-glass window toward the cottage.

"It's very commendable how careful you're approaching all this, but don't be afraid to live in the moment a bit. The north side of the garden has given you their blessing. Allow yourself to relax with him a little. If he regains his memory, he'll be more of an open book to you if you earn his trust now. If it isn't obvious already to you, take it from me, the man has eyes for you. That, my dear, is certain." Katrianna smiled at the comment and nodded.

"Fine. I'll heed your advice, as always, but I'd rather take things slow. I'd prefer it if there are no more surprise introductions, for now, without my approval."

"You're the Princess. I'll make it known."

CHAPTER 12

Over the following few weeks, Katrianna did her best to let down her defenses a bit. What Mrs. Doodles had observed in her behavior was accurate. She was not without eyes to see the attractive man who had entered her lands. Her heart wasn't so cold as to not flutter when she caught him staring or smiling at her. He had invaded her thoughts, her dreams, and her entire mindset. She found herself wondering what he was doing, what he was thinking, what he was writing in his journal.

She went on longer walks and hikes with him on a more regular basis. She had even granted him permission to walk on his own, so long as he followed specific parameters. He was not allowed to venture south of the stream. He was not allowed inside the castle without an escort. He was not allowed to be outside the cottage past dark. She didn't like limiting him, but it was necessary to protect both Leland and the valley.

The magical creatures of the valley knew they were not to interact with him or expose themselves to him unless given permission by Katrianna. Besides Mrs. Doodles, the fairies had kept their distance. The rest would be introduced to Leland if and when Katrianna thought it was safe. She kept telling herself that it was all for the better good, but she grew tired of keeping secrets from Leland. Despite her caution, she was overwhelmed with pleasure, having someone she could talk to. Before Leland, this land had been a very lonely place of living for her for many years.

Her visits became more frequent. She stuck around longer each time, sometimes joining him for dinner and staying up till well past midnight. Their chats were simple, but being near him was undoubtedly more comforting than walking the empty halls of her castle.

"Happy three months," said Katrianna as she walked into the cottage garden, finding Leland writing in his chair.

"Excuse me?" Leland put down his pen and paper and looked up at her with a smile.

"As of today, you've been here for exactly three months." Katrianna pulled up a chair of her own and sat.

"Huh. It feels like so much longer. Despite having forgotten a lifetime of memories, I feel like I've built up so many new ones here." Leland closed his journal and sat up straight in the chair. "To what do I owe the pleasure of your company, Princess?"

"Well, if you're not busy, I'd like to introduce you to some of my friends." Katrianna loved seeing the spark light up in Leland's eyes. He jumped out of his chair and ran his things into the cottage, only to emerge just as quickly.

"I'm ready when you are." Katrianna laughed at his over the top excitement and nodded.

They walked for a couple of miles, trudging

along the same forest paths she had taken him on before. Eventually, Katrianna took a turn that she hadn't made in the past, and Leland was quick to notice the new territory. She led them through the forest into a large clearing where he hadn't been before.

"When I was young, I used to come out here and sleep at night. The night breeze would rock me, and the sweet sounds of the forest would be my lullaby. The stars would be the blanket over me, and the moon was the light that kept me safe." Leland smiled at the thought.

"It certainly looks peaceful. I'm sure it got lonely at times, though." His hand slid into hers as he stared out into the clearing. She looked down at it and gently clenched it. She turned to him and looked him deep in the eyes.

"You're not wrong. As independent as I was forced to be, growing up here, I did get lonely from time to time. So, I made friends, like the ones I'm about to show you. But before I do, I need you to promise me something. No matter what happens down the road, no matter if you regain your memory, no matter if you decide to leave this place, I need your word that this will remain secret." Katrianna looked deep into Leland's eyes, searching for a reason to back away from this whole ordeal. In the morning, she had felt so certain about it, but now she felt more vulnerable than she had been in a very long time. Leland never broke eye contact with her, but simply held her hand tighter and nodded.

"No matter what, I promise." She let his words sink in for a moment as she gathered the courage to continue. Smiling and nodding back at him, she turned back to the clearing and whistled into the silence.

****

He could see the seriousness in her eyes. He could feel the rapid beating of her heart as it resonated through her all the way to the hand that he now held in his. He was a little shocked that he had actually reached out to hold her hand, but when she held his back, he couldn't imagine letting go. She was shaking when she spoke to him, but she smiled when he responded with his promise. When she turned back to the clearing and whistled, Leland looked out to see who she was signaling too.

It took a moment, but eventually a relatively large herd of horses began making their way into the clearing from the far side. White, black, brown, they appeared wonderfully calm and cordial as they emerged from the tree line into the light of the sun. As they trotted closer and Katrianna pulled him deeper into the clearing, Leland froze for a moment as he processed what he was seeing. The horses were, in fact, not horses at all. Instead, Leland found himself taking in the beauty of a herd of unicorns. The sun illuminated their fair colors and reflected off their spiraled pearl alicorns.

"They're so… majestic." Leland found himself at a loss for words as he stared in awe.

"Come close, my friends. There's someone I'd love for you to meet." Katrianna spoke in the softest of voices, almost to a level that Leland could barely hear, but the entire herd raised their heads in response. The unicorns encircled them in the center of the clearing, allowing the little ones to push through and greet Katrianna first. She pet a few of them and brought Leland's hand to the mane of the closest one to do the same. The largest of the herd stepped forward, white as fresh snow, and nudged Katrianna gently with its head.

She hugged it and ran her hands down its neck. "This is Leland. He's been staying in the cottage for the past few months. I think he's a friend."

The unicorn looked at Leland and neighed a bit. Katrianna laughed and calmed the unicorn down.

"I call him Aubade because of how beautiful his coat shines in the morning sun. Don't worry, Aubade, you're still my favorite." She hugged the unicorn again and then retook Leland's hand.

After spending some time with the herd, playing with the young foals and chasing them around the clearing, Katrianna and Leland said goodbye and watched as the unicorns returned to the forest from where they came. The evening was on its way, and Katrianna suggested they get back before it was dark. She kept her hand in Leland's and pulled him back toward the path. He stopped her for a moment.

"I just wanted to thank you for trusting me with this. I've tried not to push you, to riddle you with questions since I've been here." He sighed and smiled at her. "This was amazing. I'm very grateful."

"I'm glad." She leaned in and kissed him on his

cheek. She then turned back to the forest and pulled him along. "You can ask me anything you want. I can't be certain I'll always give you an answer, but I'll try."

The two walked in silence for a moment while Leland gathered his thoughts. It was everything he could do not to ramble off a list of questions he had been building up since he first woke up in the cottage. Some of them seemed less relevant now, while others felt just as prominent in his mind. Having met a fairy, and now a herd of unicorns, but classes of creatures he never imagined existed, he couldn't help but wonder what this valley really was. So, he figured he'd start with that.

"This is such a magical land, but something tells me there is more to it than just a valley beyond the mountains. What is this place, and why are so many magical things congregated here?" Katrianna nodded and smiled as she looked around at the forest.

"That's a fair assumption. I'll tell you what I was told. While you call it a valley, most of the residents here refer to this land as the Garden. It refers to a place, much like this one, that existed long ago; back then it was called Eden. Things occurred, and mankind was banished from the Garden of Eden. Not too long after,

Eden itself disappeared, leaving the remaining occupants stranded without a place to call home."

"It disappeared? How?"

"Eden had been created as a heaven on earth for man to reside in. Having lost its chief resident, the Garden no longer had a reason to exist. One morning, the remaining residents woke to find themselves living in a barren place that no longer resembled the plentiful, nourishing land it once was. So, the fairies, the unicorns, and the rest of the magical creatures dispersed in search of a new home.

"Generations later, a woman by the name of Asielle began searching for the magical creatures that once lived in Eden. She said she was on a mission from the Creator to find and secure these creatures before an epic event occurred that would surely kill them all. While a man named Noah was said to have harbored two of every creature on a giant boat built to survive a great flood, Asielle gathered all the magical creatures she could find and took them here.

"This would be the Garden of Eden, reborn. A vast mountain range surrounds this entire valley. With a lot of hope, and a little magic, the mountains remained tall enough to weather the storm, and this valley was left untouched by the flood. Asielle brokered a sense of peace between all the magical creatures, as some had become more territorial than others. The new Garden was divided up, and those boundary lines have remained ever since.

"Asielle told one human about this place, a young man named David Aldiss; a distant descendant of Noah. He was to build a Kingdom on the other side of the mountains, west of this place. He called it Crestside. He took an oath to not only take care of the people in his Kingdom, but that his lineage would protect the secret of this place, and essentially guard the Garden from the outside.

"Once Asielle was satisfied with the arrangement and had helped King Aldiss build his Kingdom, she returned to the new Garden where she lived for many generations before passing. To thank her for all she had done, the inhabitants of this place named her Queen and built her a castle; the place where I currently live. When she passed, the people here swore to uphold their pledges to keep the peace. This valley was as close to the

Garden of Eden reincarnate as any place would ever be, but it would never hold that name. Instead it would simply be called the Garden, and it would always be a joyous, safe, halcyon home to those that lived here."

"That's such a beautiful story. I can see why you, or anyone else that lived here, would be so protective of this place." As they finally made it back to the cottage, the darkness of the evening in full swing, Leland couldn't help but think of one more question for the evening. "Okay, one more. This should be a lighter question, I might think. If you live in the castle, who was this cottage for? Did Asielle live here before the castle was built?"

"No," said Katrianna, as she half-smiled and then looked down to the dirt a bit. "My…father lived here. We both did. He raised me here after my mother died while giving birth to me."

"Oh, wow, I'm so sorry. I didn't mean to bring up…," but Katrianna raised a hand to stop him.

"No, of course not. I don't mind. My father was a good man, but he died of illness the fairies couldn't treat. I was about ten then. The fairies took care of me after that and moved me into the castle. It wasn't easy, but at least I had the time with him that I did." Katrianna walked him up to the door and finally let go of his hand. "I had not stepped foot in this cottage a day since I moved out. That is until you arrived. It's been nice to see it again, and your company has helped me get past certain things. I'm very grateful for that."

Once again, she kissed him on the cheek and then backed away to head back to the castle. Leland thought about asking her in for a drink, but he didn't want to push his luck. The day had been fantastic, and Leland felt as if he'd finally had a moment to be close to her. He hoped it would continue.

"Goodnight, Princess." Katrianna turned around at his words and smiled brightly in the night.

"Goodnight, Leland."

****

Later That Evening

Unable to sleep, Leland lit a candle and took some time to write. While journaling sounded like a good idea when Mrs. Doodle's suggested it, he had struggled to think of much to jot down. While there was plenty of things going on around him, he almost didn't want to spoil it all by trying to document it. Without knowing anything about his past, he didn't have a history of feelings and experiences to reflect upon. So, he instead wrote he felt like writing. Almost on a nightly basis, he'd sit and work on a poem about the only thing that was on his mind; Katrianna.

He'd written quite the catalog at this point, though he became increasingly worried that she, or someone else, would happen upon them. He thought maybe he should burn them, or hide them, but those actions would only come off as suspicious. His relationship with Katrianna, amongst the circumstances, was so delicate that he tended to avoid acts that would jeopardize it.

After jotting down some lines, he decided what he needed most was some fresh air. Putting away his papers, Leland stepped outside and leaned against the cottage wall in the dark of the night. He peered up at the castle to see no light in any of the windows on that side. He imagined the Princess was asleep, as with most of the valley. While he would be happy to dream about today's events, he wasn't able to stop his mind from running.

He replayed the moments that Katrianna had kissed his cheek, and they were beyond pleasant. Every time he tried to focus on those moments, however, he would find himself ever more frustrated that he had made no progress on his memory. If there was anything keeping him from expanding on his relationship with the Princess, it was the fact that he remained a stranger to everyone including himself. He alone could put together the remaining pieces, but for the life of him, he could not figure out how.

His frustrated thoughts were interrupted when he heard a couple of small voices nearby. Gently stepping around the cottage, Leland found two little fairies, one male and one female, pressing their faces against the window of the cottage.

"Do you see him, Daphi?"

"Keep it down, Demmy! It's the middle of the night! He'll hear us." The two flew back and forth up and down the window, peering inside.

"Why do you think he's up so late, Daphi?"

"How should I know? Maybe he's a night owl?"

"He's not a night owl, Daphi! He's a human! He's the only human in the whole Garden!"

"You're dumber than I thought, Demmy. But yes, you are correct. He's the only human in this valley."

"Aren't you forgetting about someone?" Leland interrupted them as he crossed his arms while leaning against the cottage. The two fairies jumped and screamed for a moment, but then composed themselves.

"Holy…Daphi, it's him!"

"Shut it, Demmy!" The two fought back and forth for a moment before facing Leland again. Leland smiled at the sight. Daphi cleared her throat and spoke first. "My apologies. My name is Daphi, and this is Demmy. We already know who you are. We didn't mean to spy, but… well we did mean to spy. Anyways, what were you saying? Who did we forget?"

"Well, the person who lives up there, obviously," said Leland as he pointed to the castle. Daphi and Demmy looked up at the castle and then back to Leland. Demmy, especially, looked confused.

"Who? You mean the Angel Princess?" Leland raised an eyebrow at Demmy's words.

"What did you say," asked Leland as he leaned forward.

"Demmy!" Daphi immediately punched Demmy in the shoulder.

"Aagh! Stop it." Demmy rubbed his shoulder and then turned back to Leland. "What? What did I say?"

"That's what I'm asking you. What did you call Katrianna?"

"Who? Oh, her? I called her the… the Princess, of course." Daphi rolled her eyes as Demmy stumbled over his words. "She's the Princess… uh, right? So, that's what I called her."

"Nice recovery," said Daphi, sarcastically.

"She certainly appears human, but clearly you know something I don't." Leland acted as casual as possible, not wanting to scare the two off.

"She's only half human, silly." Again, Daphi punched Demmy in the arm. "Would you stop that!

The cat's already out of the bag, sis."

"Yea, cause you took it out to begin with, doofus!" The two began to quarrel, but Leland put his hands up to stop them.

"Guys, guys, stop it! There's no need to fight. So, what if Demmy spilled the beans. I can keep a secret. I'm really good at that." Daphi peered at Leland with a curious look.

"Hm, I don't know," said Daphi, as Demmy rolled his eyes at her.

"She's only half human. Her father was a man, but her mother was a fairy, like us." Leland pulled up a chair as the fairies flew down and sat on the window seal.

"Now, how does that work?"

"It doesn't." Daphi left it at that, but Demmy clearly couldn't.

"Don't mind my sister. She's never been much for stories. That's where I usually come in." Demmy flew up closer to Leland. "So, the story goes that a man, like you, had made his way to this valley. Unlike you, the man didn't throw himself off the waterfall to get here."

"Wait. What?"

"You really did lose your mind, didn't you?" Daphi leaned back against the window. "Several of us fairies saw you falling down that giant waterfall on the west ridge. Had we not been there to conjure enough magic to slow your fall, you'd have likely dug yourself a hole ten feet beneath the riverbed."

"Wow. Well I guess I should thank you, then. Without you, I wouldn't be here." Daphi took notice of Leland's sincerity and smiled a bit.

"Would you stop interrupting, Daphi! I'm in the middle of a story here!" Demmy flew back in Leland's face. "Like I was saying, the man didn't arrive here by way of the waterfall. He found the secret staircase that takes you down to the forest floor, only he stumbled on his way down and banged himself up pretty good. A fairy by the name of Seira found him."

"She was always a rebel." Demmy frowned back at Daphi but then nodded in agreement.

"Yes, she was. She knew the magical folk of this

land wouldn't be too keen on a stranger showing up unannounced. So, she nursed him back to health and hid him away in the forest. Over time, the two became great friends, but Seira wanted to be more than that."

"As I said, always a rebel," said Daphi.

"Shush, Daphi! On the castle grounds, near the lagoon, there's a fountain dedicated to the late Queen Asielle. Well, the whole castle was dedicated to her, but the fountain was built after she passed. Atop the fountain is a small statue of Asielle. Seira flew to the fountain and sat on the edge, crying and begging Asielle for an answer to her troubles. She had grown to love the man, but she couldn't entirely do so in her current state.

"Somewhere, out there in the cosmos, Seira's pleas were heard. As it began to rain down upon this valley, Seira felt her body begin to change. She grew and grew until she found herself human size. She still had her wings, and nothing else about her had changed, but she was now only about a foot shorter than the man she loved, instead of the size of his palm."

"Wow, that's incredible." Leland was entranced

by the story, and Daphi was too.

"Indeed, it was. So, Seira and the human became more than friends, and soon enough, Seira was with child. The entire fairy community was split. Some were intrigued and curious, while others were concerned and thought it blasphemy to mix the two races. Fairy pregnancies are quick affairs, only lasting a few weeks. Many healers in the fairy world, Mrs. Doodles included, assisted with the birth. Sadly, Seira was lost in the process.

"She had given birth to a beautiful girl, a hybrid of human and fairy. She was the most beautiful creature this land had ever seen. While she mostly took the traits of her father, she wasn't without features that clearly were influenced by her mother. Due to the drastic differences between our species, Katrianna wasn't necessarily part fairy, but she certainly had aspects about her that were similar."

"And that's as much as you're going to say about that, Demmy," cautioned Daphi from the window seal.

"I'm not dumb, Daphi." Demmy turned back to Leland and shrugged his shoulders. "Sorry, pal. You'll have to figure the rest out yourself."

"Who gave you two permission to come around here?" Mrs. Doodles flew into view and scolded the two fairies. "Not to mention, it's in the middle of the night! Get on out of here. I'll deal with you two in the morning for sure!"

"Yikes! Bye, Leland," shouted Demmy as he met up with Daphi and flew off into the forest. Leland sat up straight, almost expecting to be scolded by Mrs. Doodles as well.

"My apologies, Ma'am. I had encouraged them to stick around." Mrs. Doodles sighed and shook her head.

"You should get your rest, sir. From what I hear, you had a big day." Mrs. Doodles flew off into woods and left Leland to think about the story. Katrianna was definitely a mystery to him, but now there was even more about her that he found intriguing. He hoped he could one day discover this magic side of her. That is if he could convince her to let him in.

CHAPTER 14

The next morning, Leland took a walk around the castle grounds in search of the Asielle fountain. Though he had taken many walks during his time in the valley, the area was so dense with trees and plant life, that he wasn't surprised he hadn't come across the fountain yet. Eventually, he came upon a small garden on the eastern side of the castle walls, and the fountain stood prominently in the center of it. It was a large, stunningly carved. From the center of the round basin, a spear rose up to showcase a small statue of Asielle. Leland smiled at the sight.

He dipped his hand in the water and sat on the edge of the basin. Perhaps this was the spot where Seira had sat, begging for relief from her troubles. As silly as it sounded, Leland wondered if he could find his own relief by doing the same. He chuckled at the thought, and felt the likelihood was slimmer than he cared to bother with.

Walking around the garden a bit more, he found a path that led down a small hill. Following the path through some incredibly thick foliage, Leland ultimately arrived at the edge of a hidden lagoon. Save for the more middle areas of the water, the bulk of the lagoon was covered in the shade of long, luscious tree limbs that stretched out overhead. The area seemed quite peaceful and private. With the heat of the sun already in full swing, Leland could think of nothing better to do than go for a swim.

Abandoning most of his garments on the shore, Leland waded into the cold water and swam out farther into the lagoon. He dove deep into the dark waters and rose again to float on the surface. Having only slept a few hours in the night, Leland was more than happy to lie back in the waters, close his eyes and relax. The waters were calm around him, the area around was silent and undisturbed, and Leland found himself at immense peace.

"Mind if I join you?" Leland had dozed off for a while but was brought back by the lovely sounds of Katrianna's voice. He looked up to see her standing at the shore. He smiled and nodded. As Katrianna began to remove her dress, Leland quickly turned around in the water and faced the other side of the lagoon. "What are you doing, silly?"

"Looking away, of course. Out of respect for the Princess."

"Out of respect, huh?" Katrianna grinned and waded into the water. Swimming over to meet him in the middle of the lagoon, Katrianna was reminded of all the scars across his body. She had seen them before, when he had first arrived, but had forgotten their severity. She rubbed her hands over them, tracing their lengths across his back, over his shoulders and, as he turned around in the water to face her, across his chest. "Perhaps the memories of a life where these originated from aren't worth remembering."

"Bad memories only make the good ones sweeter," said Leland. Katrianna blushed as she ducked her head back in the water to wet her hair.

"I see you've found one of my hiding places."

"Oh. Did I intrude? It was not my intention." Leland treaded water as Katrianna did the same only a foot or two away from him.

"Not at all." As rays of light peeked through the trees above and lit the water around Katrianna, she looked around and took in the splendor. "I usually come to this place in the nighttime, when I'm sad and wish to be alone. I've almost forgotten how beautiful it can be in the daytime."

"It only compliments your beauty, my Princess." Katrianna simpered at his words and swam closer to him. As their legs touch, every so often, while they stay afloat, she looks at him fondly.

"I'm your Princess?" Her eyes locked with his, Katrianna held her breath as she longed for an answer. She inched closer to his and repeated her words. "Your Princess?"

"I'll swear my allegiance, just tell me what to say and I'll say it." Katrianna breathed in quickly and draped her arms around Leland as she pressed herself against him for a long, fevered kiss. Overtaken by waves of sensation, Leland abandoned treading water and wrapped his arms around her to return her affection. The two slowly sank as they held their embrace and locked lips to share each other's air.

The lagoon engulfed them, but Leland was without care to notice. Instead, he tried only to process every bit of feeling that overwhelmed him. Katrianna's fingertips roamed over Leland's back and neck, while her arms and legs held him tight in her embrace. She kissed him with a passion that he had only dreamt to one day experience. After a while, the two opened their eyes to stare and smile at each other underwater.

Katrianna caressed Leland's face and then kissed him briefly once again before releasing him to swim back up to the surface. Leland remained in her wake for a moment, still in a mix of shock and utter harmony, before he too began to ascend to the surface. When he reached the top of the lagoon and took in a deep breath of air, he noticed Katrianna was swimming away.

"Wait! Where are you going?"

"Stay there. I want to show you something." Katrianna didn't swim back to the shore but towards a large rock that jutted out from the trees and over the edge of the lagoon. She climbed the stone and sat on top, looking over the water and down to him. There was something about the sight of her up there, looking down at him, that Leland felt was familiar. Before he could figure it out, however, he felt something swim by him.

"Whoa!" Leland spun around in the water, trying to see what it was. "There's something in the water."

"Don't be alarmed, Leland. I'm surprised it took them this long to show themselves," called Katrianna from the rock. "Swim closer to me. They won't bother you, I promise."

Leland was still a bit nervous but soon complied. As he made his way over toward the rock, he noticed another large object swim by him, then another, and another. They swam past so quickly, so fluidly underwater that Leland couldn't get a true glimpse of what was encircling him. Before he reached the shallow waters just beneath the rock, the movement around Leland ceased. He turned around in the water again, looking in all directions until he saw a long haired woman rise up from the water. Another woman swam up beside her, followed by several more until Leland was surrounded. As they drew in closer, he could see their scales and realized what they indeed were. Again, Leland was overwhelmed with a sense of deja vu, as if he had lived this moment before. He looked up at Katrianna, who was smiling down at him.

"Right there, about where you are now, is where I first laid eyes on you." As Katrianna's words rang out, Leland was suddenly flooded with clarity as his memories of his first night in the valley came rushing back to him.

"I…I remember." Katrianna's expression quickly changed to excitement as she jumped down into the water with him.

"Wait, you do?" Leland looked around at the mermaids, at the lagoon, at the rock and then at Katrianna. It was all still a bit foggy, but the more he looked around, the more the pieces were coming together.

"I was …dying, I think. Drowning! I was drowning in this lagoon." Leland looked at the mermaids as they smiled and murmured around him.

"You. You all saved me and brought me back to the surface."

"Yes!"

"Yes, we did!"

"We did! We did!" The mermaids all began to chime in, agreeing and acknowledging his accounts. He turned back to Katrianna, who stared at him with a face of hope and longing as she waited for him to continue.

"They…brought me to you. You were up there, on that rock. You were crying." Katrianna smiled a bit as a tear flowed down her cheek.

"Yes, I was, but then I saw you." She swam closer to him and caressed his face again as she peered into his eyes.

"That's… right. The mermaids called out to you, and you jumped… no, that's not right. You… flew down to meet me in the water with giant, glorious wings that sprouted from your back." Leland could see a change in Katrianna's eyes, she almost looked scared as she began to shy away, but he wrapped an arm around her and held her close. “The Angel Princess; that’s what the fairies called you the other night, and now I remember why. You were the last thing I saw before I blacked out. The most glorious and gorgeous sight I could have ever hoped to witness.”

****

Katrianna stared back him, searching his eyes for sincerity. She felt herself shaking, but once he held her close, she didn’t pull away. This is what she had hoped for, that he would eventually remember it all, and yet she had feared how he would react to the remembrance of her other features. She forgot to breathe for a moment as she studied him, desperately scanning for any hint of fear or deception, but she couldn’t find anything but wonder and love in his eyes and the tone of his voice.

“You do remember!” She sighed in relief and kissed him. She could feel his heart racing, almost keeping time with hers. The mermaids splashed around them in celebration, as Katrianna beamed with joy. “Come, we must tell Mrs. Doodles!”

The two of them swam to the shore to get dressed

before racing back to the cottage, hand in hand, to call for Mrs. Doodles. When she arrived, Katrianna and Leland had just about dried themselves with towels and were now sitting across from each other at the kitchen table, sharing a bottle of wine. Flying in through the window, Mrs. Doodles landed on of the fruit basket in the middle of the table, excited as can be.

"What's this? Did I hear correctly? Have you recovered your memories, Leland?" Mrs. Doodles could barely contain herself as she jumped up and down and clapped her hands. Leland nodded in confirmation as he reached across the table to hold Katrianna's hand.

"The Princess helped me remember my first night in the lagoon, and it all came rushing back to me, all of it! I can remember how I first met Katrianna, as well as everything about my life before this place."

"Well? Spit it out!" Katrianna laughed at how excited Mrs. Doodles was, and smiled in agreement.

"Yes! Let's hear it. Where are you from? How did you get here? Tell us everything!"

****

Leland proceeded to fill them in on all the details of his life. He told them how he was raised in a prison camp, forced to work in the mines during the day and fight his fellow men during the night. He told them how he had exacted his revenge upon the warden and escaped the camp. Mrs. Doodles was happy to hear of the fellow healer in Crestside, and how he and Melony had taken care of Leland in a time of need.

Leland recounted his journey up and over the mountains, across the endless frozen planes, searching for what could be on the other side. As he recited the significant events of his life to Katrianna and Mrs. Doodles, Leland felt as if he were recalling stories of a life so distant in the past that he could barely recognize that version of himself. It really wasn't that long ago, but Leland's life had changed so much since then, he felt himself to be a different person altogether.

"Well, I'm glad to hear you didn't willingly launch yourself over that waterfall," said Mrs. Doodles as she chuckled. Katrianna laughed as well as she listened attentively to Leland's every word.

“Yes, well, I still can not thank you and the other fairies enough for saving me. I wouldn’t be here to tell you all this had you not acted as you did.” Leland smiled at Mrs. Doodles sincerely. She beamed with joy and nodded.

“Fate, it seems, had put us in the right spot at the right time, and I’m very thankful that it did.” Mrs. Doodles sighed and stood up. “Well Mr. Toller, I’m sorry you suffered through the life that you did, but I’m glad you found your way to us. I feel like I’m finally meeting you for the first time, but I look forward to getting to know you better.”

“You as well, Mrs. Doodles. Oh, I can now remember that my surname isn’t Toller. That was a name the warden wanted to give me. My actual name is Leland Clayton, after my father, Thomas Clayton.” Leland noticed Katrianna suddenly release his hand. He turned to her and saw a look of shock with a bit a pain overtake her. “What? Are you alright?”

Katrianna abruptly stood up from the table and rushed out of the cabin before Leland could stop her. He called for her to wait, and went to chase after her, but Mrs. Doodles flew in his way to stop him. He saw the change of expression on Mrs. Doodles face and knew that she was aware of precisely what had happened.

"Oh, dear."

"I don't understand. What just happened here?" Mrs. Doodles dipped her head and sighed.

"I know. I know you don't. How could you have known? Sit down, please. Give her some space." Leland reluctantly did as he was told and waited anxiously for Mrs. Doodles to explain. "You poor thing. There isn't an easy way to say this, but you have a right to know."

"Please, just tell me." Mrs. Doodles nodded and plopped back down on the fruit basket.

"It would seem your journey to this place was not in vain or by chance. Katrianna's father, the man who found his way to this place all those years ago and fell in love with the fairy Seira, his name was Thomas Clayton."

CHAPTER 15

Leland didn't see the Princess again that day, nor the next day, nor the next. He considered walking himself into the castle in search of her, but having never been invited, he thought it best not to intrude. At night he looked to the castle windows, searching for a light, or a shadow, or any sign of her, but he saw none. No one visited him at the cottage. He feared that the moment he would leave in search of someone, Katrianna would visit the cabin and he'd miss her.

Alone, with no one to talk to, no one to explain to him the details he needed to process everything, Leland was left to speculate and come to his own conclusions. While the story that Daphi and Demmy had told him, about the man who fell in love with a fairy, was pleasant and heartwarming, it now had a second meaning for Leland. His father, the honorable Head Knight of the King's Royal Guard, had left his only son to rot in a prison camp for twenty years. The man, whose wife had been slaughtered by order of King Jerad, had chosen to run away, to fall in love with someone else, and… hide for the rest of his life.

Is that truly the legacy of Thomas Clayton? Could that indeed be the true measure of the man that Leland had dreamt of meeting ever since he was a young child? Every bone that Leland had broken, every crack of the whip, every dreary day in the mine, every horrendous evening fistfight, he had survived in hopes that one day he'd find the man that was his father or at least learn of how his father died. Now, he knew. His father was a coward that chose a new life over saving his son, and eventually became sick and passed.

Everything seemed to set Leland off. Even the cottage itself, knowing that it had been his father's, wondering how many lovely nights his father had rested here while Leland slept in chains. Just the thought of it made Leland want to trash the cottage, break everything, and burn it to the ground. He started with the first part. He busted furniture, toppled over the bookshelf, and tossed about everything that wasn't nailed down, but it didn't help Leland resolve an ounce of what he was feeling.

Leland wanted nothing more than to hate his father and the choices his father had made over raising hell to save his son. The only problem was that Katrianna, the woman who Leland had spent the last few months falling in love with, was the result of those decisions. Had Thomas Clayton not abandoned his son, Katrianna would not have been born. How could such a horrible man raise such a wonderful woman?

"Why does this have to be so damn complicated," shouted Leland as he kicked around the cottage, standing in the middle of his own destruction.

"Because life is complicated, Mr. Clayton." Leland spun around to see Mrs. Doodle's hovering in the open doorway. "Life is never as clear-cut or as simple as we'd wish it to be. Life tends to challenge us, to test our wits and our wills, and when it's all said and done, life is rarely fair."

"Have you come to witness me wallowing in my

misery, Mrs. Doodles?" Leland turned his back to her, now slightly embarrassed at the mess he had made. He picked up the chair from the floor and sat it upright in its proper place. "Take a seat."

"Funny. You've been hiding out here for too long, Leland."

"I've been hiding?"

"You both have. When faced with a solemn truth, both of you locked yourselves away. I sympathize for the predicament you two have found yourselves in, but there's not productive with your current course of action." Leland continued to pick up things here and there around the cottage.

"And what would you have me do?"

"My boy, only a few days ago you regained your memory. You spent the better part of an afternoon telling the Princess and me how lonely and horrible a life you lived; without freedom, without friends, without family. Look at you now?" Mrs. Doodles flew closer to Leland, trying to get him to look at her. "You are a free man. There are those, like myself, that would count themselves as your friends. Most importantly, you have learned that you are not alone in the world.

"I wasn't able to cure your father of his illness, and I'm sorry for that. He was the first human to visit in a century, and I wasn't prepared. You were robbed of a father, and you were robbed of a mother, but now you have a family member, a sister, that still walks the earth. Three months ago, you had no one, and now you have someone, and yet you've chosen to lock yourself away! How does that make sense?"

"That's easy for you to say. You didn't spend the last quarter of a year falling in love with her." Leland sighed and looked down at the floor with his hands on his hips.

"Your tragedy is not lost on me, dear boy. You two may not be able to continue down the path you were on, but at least you have the opportunity to convert that love, that admiration into a new kind of relationship. She's not dead! You're not dead! It might not be easy, at first, but would you truly prefer to cut yourself off completely rather than learn to love her a different way?" Leland stood in silence for a moment. He anger, his misery was only compounded by his knowledge that everything Mrs. Doodles said was right, but he wasn't sure if he was ready to admit that just yet. He turned back to Mrs. Doodles and crossed his arms across his chest.

"I do consider you a friend, and I'm comforted that you thought to visit me, but we both know your loyalty is to the Princess first. That leads me to believe that you've already had this conversation, with her. Since you're here, trying to convince me to be the bigger person and make the first move, I'm guessing the Princess didn't take to your speech either. Am I right?" Mrs. Doodles sighed and nodded.

"You're both equally stubborn as you are cocky." Mrs. Doodles turned to leave. "I'll let you be, for now, but I'm not finished with you, Mr. Clayton. Perhaps in another day or two, when you've cleaned up this mess, you'll be more willing to talk."

Leland took a moment to breathe and scratch his head. He looked around at the cabin, at the devastation he had brought to the place the Princess had granted him to stay. Leland needed fresh air and time away. He set out to find a forest path to walk, to clear his head. He would fix up the place when he returned and then figure out where to go from there.

****

Katrianna had walked the castle halls for days, ashamed and afraid to stick her head outside. She had stormed out of Leland's cottage in a fit of agony and fear. The revelation wasn't something she could have processed in front of him, but she regretted leaving him to find out from Mrs. Doodles. Still, it was a pain that both of them were forced to deal with. They had become so close lately. Perhaps, in this case, the separation was the best way to handle the reality of their situation. It didn't make things easy, though.

She wondered how he was doing. She longed to be close to him. Something had come over her at the lagoon, and for the first time in her life, she had abandoned all of her concerns and allowed herself a moment's release. Everything had been perfect. Everything had been magical.

She felt grimy and stale as she had locked herself away in the castle for far too long. She needed fresh air and a change of scenery. She promised herself to stay near the castle, and not wander too far past the gardens, but before she knew it, she had wound her way around to the west side of the castle walls. She found herself staring at Leland's cottage from afar. There were lights in his windows, but she saw no movement. As she crept closer, Katrianna saw that the door was open, but no one appeared to be around.

Katrianna stepped inside the cottage to find that it had been destroyed. At first, she feared that something horrible had happened and frantically began searching for signs of any harm that had come to Leland. Soon enough it was more apparent to her that the state of the place had been Leland's doing, and she sighed and understood. She couldn't imagine how this place and the memory of her father, his father, made him feel.

She decided she should leave before Leland returned, as she didn't want to interrupt his grief. Mrs. Doodles's words had rung true, but clearly neither of them were ready to deal with it; Katrianna certainly wasn't. On her way out, Katrianna kicked up a stack of papers, sending them flying everywhere. Despite the general mess of the place, she felt a need to gather them up quickly and put them back.

She didn't mean to read them, but after glancing at the contents, she realized these were the writings Mrs. Doodles had advised Leland to partake in, in an effort to regain his memory. Apparently, Leland had chosen not to journal his daily activities as he had been instructed. Instead, Leland had taken to writing poetry, and Katrianna soon realized that she had been his muse. She picks one up at random and reads it aloud.

"The heart, the soul the mind, three different things entwined. When it comes to love, they never seem to agree. The heart knows how it feels, the soul itself is sealed, and the mind thinks many different thoughts. Trust me. Perhaps once, somewhere along the way, on some uncertain day, you might find someone that fits. The confusing three agree, your spirit is set free, and you'll take all the hits for this. This person that you find puts everything in line. A mate, sent from above, full of sheer love." It was simple and purse, and she exhaled as a tear ran down face. She grabbed the rest of the papers and took them with her as she ran out of the cottage. She kept running, without looking back, until she was safe, once again, inside the castle walls.

****

When Leland had worn himself out, and couldn't walk any further, he returned to the cottage and decided to call it a night. The cold night air had been soothing. The swaying of the trees in the dark had been comforting. The lack of walls and furniture confining him to small spaces had allowed him to unwind. He had almost forgotten the state of the cottage he had left it in. Upon his return, he sighed and nodded. Before he could bury himself in sleep, he would need to clean things up a bit.

He started with the larger items, picking up the furniture and moving them back in the place where they should be. He made up the table and chairs, the desk, the rocking chair by the window, and finally the bookshelves. He picked up each book, one by one, and placed them back in their spot. In his first weeks in the valley, when his movements were limited, and he had grown tired of trying to write something, he had turned to these books for distraction. He had read each one of them at least once. The cottage had a nice, small collection of works, and he had taken the time to appreciate each one of them.

As he picked up each book, he was reminded of the state that he had been in when he read them. Each book had a different memory attached to it, a different set of feelings, a different stage of his relationship with the Princess. The memories made him smile as he placed the last book on the shelf and stepped away. Turning around, Leland noticed a leather-bound book that still remained on the floor.

He had no memory of reading that book, and couldn't remember ever seeing it on the shelf. Perhaps it had fallen behind something, or maybe it had been resting on top when Leland had toppled the bookcase. Intrigued, he picked it up off the floor and unwound the string that had been wrapped around it. He opened it and glanced at the first page, before shutting it abruptly and throwing it on the bed.

He walked out a few steps away and put his hands at his sides. His heart was pounding, and his breathing staggered. It made sense that he would find it here, in this cottage, but Leland wasn't sure if he was ready to read it. After taking a moment to calm himself, he took a deep breath and decided he needed to take this step. Returning to the bed, Leland picked up the book and took it to the rocking chair. He opened it once more and began to read the handwritten words of his father's journal.

****

An hour or two later, Leland found himself sighing and throwing the journal back across the room to the floor. If he had not already been confused before about what light he should remember his father in, he was just as torn now. Out of context, the journal read like a redemption tale of a man who had fallen on hard times but finally found a place to call home. The journal started a couple years after Katrianna's birth.

With time to himself, Thomas had recounted meeting and spending time with Seira. He longed for her and missed her greatly. He wrote about all the marvelous things he had witnessed. He wrote about his beautiful daughter, and how anxious he was to witness the woman she would grow up to be. He wrote about developing his illness, theorizing that his younger years of drinking and fighting were overpowering his later life of casual living and eating foreign foods. He was worried how Katrianna would fair in his absence, but he knew the Garden and its residents would look after her.

The words painted Thomas to be a kind man whose life was cut shorter than it should have been. He appeared to be a loving father to Katrianna, and a friend to any that knew him. Again, out of context, Leland enjoyed the insight. Whenever he took a moment to reflect, however, Leland's mind would always return to the same thing. Nowhere in the journal was mention of Leland or his mother. There were no words of remorse or regret or even passing thoughts as to how Leland might be fairing.

Angered by this, as well as ashamed that he had wasted the past few hours desperately searching the text for any mention of a father's love for his son, Leland resided to returning the book to the floor. He rocked back and forth in the chair, staring up at the moon through the window. It was well into the night, and he knew that the only way to calm his raging mind would be to blow out the candles and attempt to find some rest. He looked around the cottage, now tidy and restored to a suitable state, and was glad it no longer looked like a dump. He needed only to pick up his father's journal from the floor, return it to the bookcase, and all would be clean and right.

Leland exhaled as he stood and walked over to grab the journal. Picking the book up off the floor, Leland's thumb slid through a tear on the inside of the back cover. While he may not have liked what he read, Leland didn't necessarily want to destroy the book that Katrianna would likely cherish. He quickly examined the inside back cover to assess the damage.

The fine pasted paper on the inside of the leather had been torn, likely due to age and normal wear, but as Leland rubbed it back and forth, he realized that something had been tucked in behind the paper, sealed in the cover of the journal. Grabbing a butter knife from the kitchen, Leland slowly sliced down the edge of the paper until he could open it enough to retrieve whatever was inside. What Leland found was an additional page, written in the same hand as the rest of the journal, but folded up and hidden. Sitting down and bringing a candle close, Leland unfolded the page, smoothed it out over the table, and read the words written upon it.

****

Katrianna tossed and turned in her bed. She tried entombing herself beneath the sheets and blankets. She tried tossing all the bed linen aside. She was neither too hot or too cold; she was restless. Leland's poems were strewn about on her floor. She had read every one of them ten times over by now. Worse yet, she had heard his voice in her head when she did. How could she remove herself from this? If Mrs. Doodles' advice was to be followed, she would have to let it all go. She'd have to kill the image of Leland she had built up in her mind and replace it with a new version of him; the version in which Leland was her brother, not her lover.

Fate was cruel to deliver unto her a man close to her age, kind, attractive, and accepting of her differences, only to strip him away in such a fashion. The hours crept onward, and her body ultimately rejected her bed. She wanted nothing to do with it as she paced around the suite in her robe, exhausted but unable to sleep. It was still plenty dark outside but was now closer to dawn that it was to yesterday's dusk. Perhaps she'd eventually collapse in enervation and find her rest that way. Until then, she was doomed to stroll about in her sorrow and disarray.

Katrianna brusquely stopped her pacing, however, when she thought she heard a sound in the castle. Standing still, listening to the silence of the night, she waited to hear the sound again. Sure enough, Katrianna could hear the footsteps of someone walking down a nearby hall. She ran to her desk and pulled a dagger from the top drawer before turning to face the door. She always slept with her suite locked, but it didn't comfort her at this moment.

Only a few people were allowed within the castle walls, and most of them tended to fly, not walk, down the halls. Katrianna held her breath as the footsteps neared the door to her quarters. When she saw a shadow cover the small space at the bottom of her door, Katrianna gripped the dagger and prepared herself. Instead of a knock, or any attempt to open the door, there was no movement other than a peace of parchment paper that was slid under the door. Katrianna waited for the shadow to back away from the door before she stepped forward to pick up the paper.

It was old and folded and looked as if it had been ripped from a bound book. Flipping it over, Katrianna immediately recognized the handwriting. Whatever this was, it had been written by her father. She almost toppled over as she clenched it tight. She had read her father's journal and everything else he ever wrote, but she had never seen this page before. She quickly crossed the room to light a candle and sat down near its glow to read the words her father wrote.

"I don't know how many days I have left on this earth. In my youth, I thought my poor decisions would never catch up to me, but it seems fate had something else in mind. I am thankful, at least, to have a handful of things I could be proud of. I refused to bend the knee to a tyrant. Crestside is a resilient place, and I'm sure, over time, the people will work out their troubles. While a part of me always wished I had returned to give that pissant a beating, I'm glad I didn't waste the last ten years of my life plotting how to do it.

"Instead, I met a wonderful, magical woman, and somehow, the stars aligned to give us a chance as a couple. When I think of how kind life has been to me in my final years, I can't help but wish my friend had been allowed to find his own happiness. We had been inseparable since youth, and I had always known him to be the most loyal of friends. He saved my life more times than I could count. The last time, however, resulted in a wound that even he couldn't overcome.

"We tried to make it across that frozen mountain plane together. We braved the cold, the wind, the storms. We trudged through it, side by side, slipping, sliding, falling, and climbing back to our feet together. Eventually, he could no longer make the climb with me. I buried my friend in the snow, in the middle of that blindly desolate place, but I owed him so much more than that.

"Thomas Clayton died after a lifetime of saving Leif Mayvoy's life. How could I leave him like that, and continue on, knowing it should have been me in the snow. I promised him I'd find that hidden place that King Aldiss had told him about. I promised him I'd live a life worthy of his sacrifice. As a personal penance and some near-death need to forever honor my fallen friend, I took his name. I would no longer be Leif Mayvoy. Thomas Clayton, in some way or another, would live on just a little bit longer.

"I may not have wholly believed that I would have survived or lived long enough to find this magical place, but fate found a way to get me here. Seira nursed me back to health, and this Garden took me in. Sometimes it felt like I was keeping a part of myself secret from the people I loved, but I was not about to abandon my promise to Thomas. I have kept his name for the past decade, and I'm not going to dishonor him now.

"Katrianna, my beautiful girl, I'm not sure if you'll ever read this. It's just as well that you never find this page, but if you do come across this one day, know that I never meant to lie to you. Every joy I have experienced in this place, with you and your mother, I owe to Thomas Clayton. I am grateful, and I am happy, and I hope you can understand that. With love, your father, Leif Mayvoy."

Katrianna felt herself shaking as she read and reread the letter, over and over again. She recognized the handwriting, the tone, the words of her father. She heard his raspy voice in her head, saying it all to her. The true name of the man who loved and cared for her, the man she loved and missed and called father, didn't matter in the slightest. He had always been true to her. He had always taken care of her. Obviously, he felt the need to speak this truth before he passed on, but even in doing so, he kept his daughter's heart in mind.

She wiped the tears from her face as she closed her eyes and kissed the last letter her father ever wrote. Remembering to breathe, Katrianna exhaled and beamed down at the letter until she soon remembered how she came upon it. Rising to her feet, she ran to the door and swung it open to find Leland sitting against the wall down the hallway. When he saw her, he jumped up to his feet, but cautiously stayed where he was.

"Where… where did you get this?" Katrianna slowly walked towards him, shaking her head through the tears that continued to flow.

"It was hidden in the back of your father's journal. I found it in the cottage." Leland was visibly nervous, as Katrianna could see him wringing his hands and shaking almost as much as she was.

"Do you know what this means, Leland?" She looked at him with hopeful, watery eyes, hoping he would still return to her what she was so willing to give to him.

"Katrianna, I've been dying inside since the moment you left. After everything I've been forced to endure, I've never experienced more pain than that of the thought of losing you. You... you are the one that haunts my sleep. You interrupt my thoughts, my dreams, my very sense of self. You are the angel that found me in the lagoon, and you're the Princess that owns my heart. I love you, with everything I am, and everything I hope to be. I'd like nothing more than to be yours if you'll have me." Katrianna's tears were flowing freely now as she cupped her face. Her enormous grey wings appeared and emerged from her back, reaching up toward the vaulted ceiling. She rushed toward him and swung her arms around him in a tight embrace.

"I love you, too. You are mine if I am yours." She peered into his eyes, smiled through her tears and then closed her eyes to kiss him deeply.

Nothing else mattered in that moment; not the pain Katrianna had fought through in the past three days, not the loneliness she had endured over the past ten years since her father's death, not the need to breathe. She lips clashed with Leland's, his passion matched with hers, and it was all she needed. Katrianna inhaled sharply as her robe fell to the floor and the cold air of the night attacked her skin. She tore at Leland's clothes until he mirrored her raw and naked state.

Unlike before, Katrianna now longed for her bed, and so she pulled Leland along until they were wrapped up into each other upon it. His hands, his lips, his tongue, roamed her freely. She rose and fell within herself as his touch brought pleasure she had never known before. The morning sun dared to break the far horizon, and Katrianna gazed at Leland. As their bodies fit together perfectly to become one, she felt her heart, mind and soul surrender to him completely. Trembling, she pulled him into her as she kissed his lips once more, longing only for the air that they could share.

CHAPTER 16

Aldiss Castle
3 Months Later

King Jerad casually waltzed down the hallway, wearing his typical morning attire (an open, flowing robe and his favorite pair of rabbit fur slippers) with a bottle of cider in hand that he had already downed about half of so far. He passed the kitchen on the way to the main dining hall, wafting in the pleasant smells of bacon and eggs. The morning was off to an entertaining start so far, so it wasn't much of a surprise to him when he found someone waiting in his dining hall, likely about to ruin his day. Jerad sighed as the Cainate stood and bowed. Jerad waved him off and headed to the opposite side of the table to take his seat.

"This had better be good. I typically don't take visitors prior to noon." Jerad took a swig from the bottle and eyed the Cainate who had remained standing. "Well? Spit it out!"

"Yes, your highness. I have just returned from my inspection of the mines, as you instructed me to do. The work continues, as it has for the past several years, but there has been a… shift in management." Jerad cocked an eyebrow at the statement and looked up at the Cainate sternly.

The Cainate slowly raised his arm and pointed toward the sack that sat in the corner behind Jerad. Jerad groaned in annoyance and snapped his fingers. One of the servants quickly entered the room and, upon direction, retrieved the sack and brought it over to Jerad. Jerad leaned over to inspect the contents and was simultaneously hit with the sight and smell of Captain Fellcer's decayed, decapitated head staring back up at him.

"Oh, what the hell is this?" Jerad stood up and showed the servant aside as he gagged and covered his mouth. The Cainates were ugly already, let alone in a state of deathly decay. He only recognized Fellcer by the long scar that Jerad himself had given him long ago. Jerad threw his now empty cider bottle at the Cainate, who barely dodged it in time. "What is the meaning of this? Speak now, before I have you killed for disturbing my breakfast in such a fashion."

"Please, my lord, I am only the messenger. I discovered the warden's body buried behind his cabin. His men said he was killed about six months ago, just after the winter season."

"He was what? Killed? Which one of the guards killed him? I'm guessing to take over his position? Not my first choice of how to handle it, but it's not the worst choice either." The Cainate shook his head.

"No, your highness. A prisoner killed the warden, one that was set to be released." Jerad groaned and racked the table with his fist. He was becoming increasingly aware of how little he knew about the procedures of the prison camp.

"Released? Since when do we release people? You know what, never mind. Who was the prisoner? What was his name?" Jerad walked to the window to calm himself.

"Leland Clayton?"

"WHAT!? ARE YOU SHITTING ME!?" The livid King spun around and stormed across the room. He grabbed the Cainate and threw him against the nearest wall. "You let Thomas Clayton's son go?"

"NO! No, my lord. Not me! I had nothing to do with it." As the messenger trembled in fear, Jerad yelled out in frustration and punched the wall beside the Cainate's head. He threw the messenger to the ground and stepped over him.

"So, let me get this straight. The son of my enemy was set to be released from his LIFE LONG SENTENCE, and then he somehow slaughtered the best one of your whole savage lot. Then he escaped, and I'm only hearing about this SIX MONTHS LATER?!" Jerad paced back and forth, up and down the dining room.

"The other guards knew who he was. They knew you wouldn't be happy. So, they hid the body and carried on as usual, in the hopes that no one would notice. They were afraid to give you the bad news, my lord." Jerad walked over to the mantle of the dining room fireplace and pulled the sword from its display rack. He pointed it at the Cainate and gritted his teeth.

"Well, they were right to be afraid. I would slaughter every last one of them by hand had they had the balls the come here in person. So, it looks like you're the unlucky one, mister messenger." Jerad slowly walks toward the Cainate, clenching the sword in his hand. "Pray tell, messenger, what good news do you have for your King?"

"Uh…my lord, I…" Jerad shoved the messenger against the wall again, this time bringing the edge of his sword just under the Cainate's neck.

"You better have some good news for your King." He leaned in close as the blade began to draw blood.

"I do! I do, my lord. Please!" Jerad grunted and backed off enough to let the Cainate speak. The Cainate wiped the blood from his neck, but then cleared his throat and spoke. "The guards stated that Fellcer had hired a woman for entertainment that night; a regular.

I tracked her down and forced her to tell me the whereabouts of Mr. Clayton."

"And? Don't tell me he's been walking around the Kingdom, unchecked for the past half-year." Jerad walked back to the end of the table to drink from his chalice.

"No, sir. The woman told me he stole a horse and took it up into the mountains in search of his father." The King spit out a bit of his cider and looked back at the Cainate

"He did what? His father has been dead for two decades."

"May I remind you, my lord, that the bodies of Thomas Clayton and Leif Mayvoy were never found." Jerad nodded and put down his drink. He quickly stepped across the room and rammed his sword into the messenger's gut.

"I do not need some low-level errand boy reminding me of anything, Cainate." The messenger winced in pain as Jerad removed the blade and kicked him to the floor. Jerad drove the sword down, into the Cainate's chest, and left it there as he stormed out of the room. He grabbed the first servant he saw and pinned him against the wall. “I want twelve of our best trackers geared up and ready to meet me in the courtyard in one hour!”

CHAPTER 17

Leland woke to the morning sun and let out a long yawn. He rolled over on the bed to see his love, the beautiful, elegant, Princess Katrianna lying next to him, half covered by the sheet. Though he moved into the castle about three months back, Leland still felt like everything about their relationship was new and thriving. He kissed her bare shoulder and slowly slid out of bed.

The nice thing about the castle was that there was hardly anyone ever around. Without a large royal family, knights, and other staff to fill the castle, there was little to no need for servants, assistants, cooks, barn hands, or much anything else. The fairies used a magic spell or two to keep the place clean and the kitchen stores stocked, and that was about it. Leland strolled into said kitchen and grabbed a large, wide, silver platter from the pantry. He gathered a mix of berries, bananas, and other fruits, a variety of cheese slices, and some other breakfast bits to take back to his love.

"Mr. Leland! Mr. Leland!" Leland froze at the sound as Daphi, the fairy, flew in through the window. Leland lowered the tray to try to cover himself, but it was too late. Daphi came to an immediate halt when she realized Leland was naked and quickly closed her eyes. "Oh my! I'm sorry! I'm sorry! I'll come back! I'll come back later!"

As Daphi tried to blindly fly her way out of the kitchen window, crashing into the wall once or twice before she was successful, Leland sighed and shook his head. Perhaps he should have dawned a robe, or at least a single piece of clothing before making his trek to the kitchen.

Glorious rays of sun peeked in through the stained-glass windows, warming Leland as he walked back down a corridor toward the Princess's suite. He held firm to the handles of the silver platter which, now stacked with all the items he had selected, was now quite heavier than he had planned. As he turned the corner into the hallway leading to their quarters, however, his euphoria was abruptly interrupted by a troubling sight.

On the far end of the corridor, a man and a woman were creeping up the hallway, weapons in hand, with their eyes pinned on the bedroom door. The woman had a bow and arrow trained on the door, and the man gripped long jagged daggers in each hand. Both were covered in tattoos, scars, and clothing that looked to be a hybrid design of armor and furs. The woman's hair was braided tight across her head as she gritted her teeth and covered the door. Her face was painted black and red as she kept her bowstring pulled and ready. The man had little hair upon his head, save for a black, thin strip that ran along the very middle of the top. He too had some paint across his face as he licked his lips and approached the door with his fists firmly gripping his daggers.

Leland came to a stop, just hastily enough to squeak across the floor with his bare feet. As the two would-be assassins halted their assault and noticed him, Leland suddenly regretted not dressing in full battle gear before taking such a leisurely walk to the kitchen that morning. Standing absolutely still for a moment, Leland contemplated a split-second plan before shouting to warn his love.

"Katrianna! Intruders" Leland dumped the contents of the platter and raced down the hall toward the master suite. Seeing the female assassin turn towards him with her bow and arrow, Leland extended his strides as far as he could before diving to the floor and using the large silver platter as a shield to crouch behind. The first arrow was deflected, but a flying dagger managed to pierce the platter just inches from Leland's face. Leland lept to his feet, gripping the platter by a side handle. As he to resumed his sprint, Leland pulled the dagger free from the platter while belting a battle cry toward the assailants.

Closing the gap between himself and the intruders, Leland dodged quickly to the right as the female sent another arrow flying past him with ferocious speed. Leland heard the arrow zip by his ear as he ran up the side of the corridor wall and launched himself toward the daggerman. Leland deflected the first stab from the man with the silver platter as he fell down upon him. Leland attempted to stab the assassin with the dagger, but the man rolled out of the way just in time. Leland pivoted and slammed the platter into the face of the woman before she could string her third arrow. As the woman fell back, Leland positioned himself between the assailants and the master suite door.

As Leland eyed both his opponents, trying to gauge which would make the next move, he attempted to listen for movement within the suite behind him. To his dread, Leland could hear a struggle behind the large doors. Before he could turn and assist, however, a third assailant exploded through the top of the tall doors, flying over Leland and hitting the wall across the hall. Katrianna opened the partially shattered door as Leland rose back to his feet.

"Impressive fighting attire, hun." Katrianna stood beside Leland, wings on full display with a sword in hand.

"I had other plans."

"You've intruded into my lands and my home.

State your business or die." Leland watched the eyes of their attackers as Katrianna spoke. The daggerman was clearly mystified by the wings that stretched out overhead. The woman, with an arrow cocked back and ready, kept her fierce expression as she stared Katrianna dead in the eyes. The third man, now rising from his fall to the floor, smiled in Leland's direction as he unsheathed a sword from his back. After a moment or two, the third man broke his stare and glanced up at Katrianna to address her.

"I would think our intentions would be obvious. King Aldiss has sent us to snuff out those who wish to oppose him."

Leland almost stepped back in shock as his mind started to race. *No! Mercenaries from King Jerad?*

"King Jerad knows of this place?" Leland gripped the dagger tight in his hand.

"He knows of you, scum. Once we return with the heads of you and the lovely lady in a bag, we'll be more than happy to share with him the finer details of this unconquered land. He'll be overjoyed to learn of all the magical creatures...," but before the man could finish his sentence, Katrianna's hand lunged forward to pierce the man's chest with a long sword.

The strike was so quick and forceful, the tip of the sword dug deep into the wall behind the dying man. The other two parties stood in shock for a few seconds, processing what had just transpired. Katrianna took the time to quickly retract her sword out of the wall and the swordman's body, before bringing down her wings to shield her from the simultaneous attacks of the daggerman and the archer.

Once again, the archer's arrow failed to meet its mark, and the daggerman could only slice off a single feather before Leland dove forward to tackle him into the wall next to his fallen comrade. Katrianna lifted her wings to thrust her sword upon the archer, but the woman had abandoned her bow and taken up two long knives from her sides to block Katrianna's attack. The daggerman kicked Leland off of him and lunged at him, swinging his daggers in an attempt to bury one or both of them into Leland's stomach. Leland swiped one blade away by deflecting it with his own but caught the tip of the man's second dagger as it cut across Leland's side.

Leland cried out in pain and anger as he shoved

his leg forward to kick the man in the chest, sending the attacker back against the wall with such force that his body bounced back forward to allow Leland to bury his dagger into the man's gut. The man twisted back in pain, releasing himself from the dagger's grip and fell to one knee as he dropped one of his blades to clench his bleeding wound. The man sprung forward again toward Leland, swiping his dagger to the left and right, up and down, with such speed that Leland tripped over his own feet while backing up. Leland fell back but was caught by the wall enough to spring forward and roll under the man's next swipe.

As he rolled, Leland plunged his dagger down, through the boot of his attacker, to secure the man's foot into the floor. Jumping to his feet, Leland grabbed the man's abandoned dagger from the floor. Quickly, Leland spun around and sliced the man's throat from one side to the other. Leland was bathed in a red mist as he stepped aside, allowing his opponent to fall to the floor in defeat.

Wiping his eyes, Leland turned back down the hall to see Katrianna duck under the swiped blades of her adversary. Katrianna jumped forward to dig her knee into the woman's gut. As the woman was forced backward from the blow, Katrianna quickly raised her blade to slice the girl's face from chin to forehead. As the challenger went limp and collapsed to the floor, Katrianna looked toward Leland.

"Are you alright?" Katrianna stared down at the bodies on the floor.

"I'm fine. You?"

"Of course." Katrianna put away her wings as she walked back into the bedroom. "Get dressed, darling. If there's more in the Garden, we need to find them."

Once he was dressed, Leland followed Katrianna down the castle corridor toward the main library. The room was filled with thousands of books, records, art, and other items collected over the years by the late Queen. Leland imagined how many of these works Katrianna had read in all that time alone. The shelves were endless as they lined the walls and stretched up to the ceiling. In the center of the library sat a small table with a large candle, surrounded by a wreath, serving as the centerpiece. Katrianna produced a key from her pocket and slid it into the side of the candle. With a twist of the key, the candle lit itself aflame and swallowed the key within its wax.

Nearby, several of the beautiful wooden floorboards began to sink and slant into the floor until they formed a staircase leading down to a lower level. The stairs led to a dark room beneath the library. Candles around the room lit themselves once Katrianna entered. Adjusting his eyes, Leland found a sizeable armory filling the space. Knives, swords, crossbows, spears and more lined the walls of the room, as Leland stood in awe.

"This is quite the room to be hiding under a library," said Leland as he looked around.

"Three assassins made it to my chambers. Who knows how many could be out there or where they could be? I'd rather not come across more on the way to the main armory. This room is a nice backup in emergencies like this." Leland nodded as he watched Katrianna grab a sword, a bow, and a pouch full of arrows to sling it over her shoulder. Leland grabbed a belt with a few daggers attached, as well as sword and sheath.

"Where to first, Princess?" Katrianna climbed back up the stairs, and the room darkened behind her.

"We'll start at the riverside and look for tracks where they might have come ashore. If they venture south of the river, death will claim them there. We'll take whoever is left on the northside."

****

Three men, armed to the teeth, waded down the river in the makeshift raft they had strung together from some fallen wood. Then kept their eyes peeled on the trees to the north and south. Every once in a while, something would brush through the foliage on either side, but the men never had a clear shot. Most civilizations tend to set up camp near sources of water, so the men planned to ride the waves until they happened upon something or someone.

"Tearson, you see that? There's someone watching us from the south bank?"

"Open your eyes, Kelo. There are several someones tracking us from that side. They're smart enough not to step out from the brush. Just keep your arrows trained until you see something worth taking a shot at." Tearson nudged Betton once in the side. "You still awake, Betton?"

"Just keeping it quiet, unlike you two, I don't feel the need to chat up a storm at the moment." Betton kept eyeing the trees on the northside, but he hadn't seen much movement in a while. Looking ahead, he noticed a smaller stream separating off to the left of the river. "Heads up, we got a split coming our way. I suggest we go left, see if the stream leads us to anyone not set up along the main river shore."

"Grab your stick, Kelo. Let's paddle that way." Still eyeing the southern shores, Tearson grabbed his stick and helped Kelo steer the raft toward the left. When the raft successfully made the smaller stream, the group found themselves riding deep into the northern forest, leaving the trouble of the south behind. Tearson kept up his guard, out of habit, but wasn't seeing much to get excited about.

The three men had been doing this kind of track and kill work for years. Over time, each one of them had been contacted by the Dark One. The Dark One paid them well and sent them to serve King Jerad in Crestside. The Kingdom was so far separated from the rest of the world that the only troubles it dealt with were internal. Most of the villagers fell in line, but every once in awhile, someone would step out. The Cainates were loyal to a point, and even they needed to be taught a lesson every now and again. For the most part, though, Tearson and the rest of the bandits had learned to live the life of luxury. Their quarters had been set up near the stables of the castle, but the food and wine were plentiful, and that's pretty much all they needed.

Two days ago, King Jerad, appearing more flustered than usual, assigned thirteen of them to band together and find a passage through the mountains. Apparently one too many villagers had run off into the hills and Jerad believed that some rebel camp might have been built in the mountains or on the other side. While they didn't find much of anything in the mountains themselves, the group did find tracks leading to valley on the other side of the ridge. They found an ancient stone staircase that took them to the forest floor and then spread out into small groups in search of anything they could report back. Tearson's group had been assigned to the river, and so far they hadn't turned up much.

"Rapids ahead, should we get ashore?"

"We've been through worse, Betton. Hold onto something." Tearson grabbed onto the rope they had used to tie the raft together and braced for impact. All three held tight as the raft broke through the first waves of rocks, but eventually, their craftsmanship was no match for the rapids' rage. All three men went under and were carried by the rushing waters over a small waterfall which spilled out into a tree-covered lagoon.

Each of the men struggled to get back to the surface, dealing with the weight of their armor and weapons, as they drifted apart in the dark water. Tearson began shedding his dead weight when something suddenly swam past him. He blinked his eyes in the water and twisted back and forth, trying to get an idea of what was around him. Save for the rays of sun that broke through the trees enough to send beams of light into the water; the lagoon was too dark and dense for Tearson to see much around him. He felt something swim behind him, again too swift for him to focus on.

Twisting around again, Tearson then saw a figure floating just ten feet from him. It was too slender to be Kelo or Betton. As it glided across the water in his direction, Tearson saw long flowing blonde hair, shiny, smooth shoulders and arms, luscious bare breasts, a thin torso, and a long, scaled fishtail. Tearson shook his head underwater, unable to believe that a mermaid was floating before him. Still, he couldn't deny the beauty of the creature that now circled around him. He reached out for her, but she only smiled and swam past him, her hand sliding over his shoulder.

He shed another piece of armor and turned around in the water to search for the mermaid again. There were two figures now, floating out of the darkness nearby. Squinting through the murky water, Tearson waited for the figures to reach the light. As the sunbeams began to shift, Tearson recoiled in horror as he saw the figures to be none other than the decapitated bodies of Kelo and Betton! Several mermaids quickly swam into view and feasted on the bodies, like piranhas, tearing chunks of flesh away until there was nothing but blood and guts floating about.

Tearson shrieked in dread and swam as hard as he could upward to the surface. Something collided with him, and he grimaced as a sharp pain took over him.

Tearson glanced down to see that he was missing a leg. He screamed in pain and fear as the last of his air left his lungs. He flayed his arms about, trying to make the surface, but it was no use. He saw the first mermaid swim up to him again, still smiling as she caressed his trembling face. His eyes pleaded for mercy from her, and she pouted her lips in response. She leaned in for a kiss and then proceeded to fill his aching lungs with fresh air. Her lips were so soft, they momentarily made Tearson forget about his pain. He looked up at the lovely mermaid, begging for her help.

Tearson's eyes followed a trail of his own blood, leaking out from the missing leg, float up near the mermaid until it was sucked in through her nose. As she inhaled the blood, the mermaid's eyes rolled back as she licked her lips in ecstasy. Veins began to rip across her now darkened face.

The whites of her eyes were soon riddled with bloodshot until they turned entirely to a shadowy red. Fangs dug their way out of her smile as she grinned at Tearson. Before he could scream again, the mermaid charged forward and sunk her teeth into his shoulder. Several more mermaids rushed in to rip Tearson limb from limb. In his last moments, he reached out for the surface in vein as the mermaids dragged him deeper into the depths of the lagoon.

****

The remaining seven mercenaries trudged their way through the northern forest. Tagen, commander of the group, lead the way through the woods. Tagen had sent Lily Kar and Needum to spy on the main structure in the middle of the forest, the castle. He put three men on a raft up the river. The rest of them, to include Rale, Pawler, York, Wagut, Vaber, and Oscut , he took with him. Though Tagen had seen the steeples of the castle from the waterfall, the valley seemed too desolate to support a hierarchy. He turned around to check on his crew. To his dismay, two were missing.

"Son of a… dammit! Rale! York! Where the hell are you?" The group turned around and scanned the forest, but there was no sign of them. Tagen frowned, knowing full well what the two were up to. "I swear the two of you better be dead before I find you."

****

"You're going to get us in trouble, Rale." Deep in

the forest, Rale smirked as he pulled off York's shirt to expose her chest. "I should beat you and turn you over to Tagen."

"Don't be that way, baby. You might be big and bad to everyone else, but I know what you want." Rale drops his pants and points below his waist. "You've been avoiding me this whole trip, but I know you want a piece of this."

"You're mighty confident." York rolled her eyes and kissed Rale as she quickly unbuckled her belt. Her hands dug into his back as he shoved her against the tree. Jumping onto him, she wrapped her legs against him and held on. Like a rabid dog, his motions were quick and rough. He grunted into her as she bit his neck and growled back. A stick cracked in the distance, and York looked up to see the commander watching them from afar. Rale continued, oblivious to their company until York shoved him away, and grabbed her clothes.

"What? What?" Rale raised his arms in confusion before he was pushed to the ground by the commander.

"You two are pathetic. We are on a mission here, not some holiday vacation. Get your pants on, boy, and then high tail it to the front. You do the same, York." The commander watched her dress for a moment before turning around in disgust and joining the group.

"I can't believe you talked me into that. Take a good look, Rale. You're stupid ass won't be seeing this again," said York as she shoved Rale over.

"Whatever, babe. I know you liked it." Rale turned around to look for one of his knives.

"I wouldn't go that far. I'm pretty sure just about any other man or Cainate could do better than that."

"Yeah well, you'll be lucky if any other man or Cainate actually asks. You're not necessarily the cream of the crop, lady." Rale waited for York's comeback, but it never came. He turned around to bask in his victory, but York wasn't there. She couldn't have scurried off that fast. Rale strolled through the trees a bit, trying to find her. "Come on, York. We've got to get back."

To his annoyance, something fell from above to hit Rale in the head. Turning around and scanning the ground for whatever it was, Rale saw one of York's long boots. He looked up to see where it could have fallen from. Raising his hand to shield his eyes from the blazing sun, Rale squinted upward until his eyes landed York's figure. He fell backward to the ground at the sight. York had been strung up into the tree by a large vine wrapped tight around her broken neck.

York's eyes stared down at Rale; dead and glossed over. The vine then began to move as it loosened its grip and dropped York's body to land at Rale's feet in a heap. Rale backed away from York's crumpled frame in disgust and then looked back up at the tree. His eyes followed the vine up around the branches to see a dark figure with shiny eyes and pointed ears staring down at him. Before Rale could reach for his dagger, the figure pounced from its perch for the kill.

****

"That's it, you two. You've really pissed me off now," said Tagen, returning to the area. He looked around until he found the bodies of York and Rale. York had been strangled, and Rale looked to have been stabbed repeatedly. Tagen immediately unsheathed his sword and crouched low as he surveyed the space around him for enemies.

"Commander, Tagen! Over here!" Tagen quickly

ran through the trees toward Pawler's voice.

"What is it," asked Tagen, as he pushed through the men to step into an open clearing. He didn't see anything at first. "Who's attacking us? How many are there? Where are they?"

"We haven't been attacked by anyone, sir, but take a look over there. Right under those trees across the way. Is that… is that a herd of unicorns?"

****

As the mermaids briefed Katrianna, Leland watched the head of one of the mercenaries bob up and down in the lagoon. He scowled in revulsion, wondering how he'd be able to swim in that water again. The head floated toward him, but before it could reach the shore, it was snatched up by one of the mermaids who dug her teeth into the skull. She looked up at Leland and smiled with her bloody face.

Leland turned away from the sight and kept his eyes on the woods. Two assassins at the castle, three more in the lagoon. He wondered how many more there would be. He gripped the top of his sword and stayed alert until Katrianna was finished. He heard her thank the mermaids for their service, and soon she was by his side.

"I guess the mermaids sensed something wrong with the lagoon's latest visitors, huh?" Leland frowned and looked over at Katrianna.

"They tend to be thorough." Katrianna sighed. "The mermaids have no idea how many more are out there. I say we continue heading east and look for any sign of them."

"Sounds good," but before Leland could take a step, the quiet air is pierced by the frantic neighs of a unicorn. Though the unicorn clearing was a couple miles away, the sound was loud and clear. "Oh, no."

"Hurry, Leland. They need our help!"

****

"I haven't seen any trace of the Clayton's, but at least this is something we can take back to the King. Now there may only be five of us, but all we have to do is surround them, and then maybe we can cut off a few of those alicorns. Spread out!" Tagen crept closer to the unicorns as his men spread off to either side. The few unicorns already in the clearing circled together, protecting one or two foals between them. He signaled Vaber and Pawler to try to shoot one down. Pawler takes aim first and fires, but the unicorns dispersed quick enough to avoid the arrows. One of the foals jumped out from behind the group's protection. "There, nab the young one!"

Oscut grinned as he sprinted toward the foal. Likely only a month or two old, the foal stumbles about, unable to get his footing right enough to run away from Oscut in time. The larger unicorns neigh and shriek, but only one of them runs after the foal. Tagen grunts deeply and rushes the unicorn. As Oscut grabs hold of the foal, Tagen leaps into the air and wraps his thick arms around the unicorn's neck to pull it to the ground. Wagut pounced on top the unicorn to help the commander hold it down. Tagen, being as big as he was, knew that he and Wagut had only caught the beast off guard and therefore only had a moment to do what they needed to do. The young foal screams as Oscut throws a sack around its head and ropes it tight.

As the unicorn in Tagen's grip lets out a bloodcurdling cry, the rest of the unicorns rush off back toward the forest. Tagen had to stab the beast enough times to keep it down, but now the job was down. Climbing to his feet, covered in the unicorn's blood, Tagen winces at the pain of what was surely a broken rib. Still, he had acquired what he came for. Leaving the carcass of the unicorn to rot in the sun, Tagen walked back to his men, flipping the shiny, severed alicorn in his hand.

"Good work, Oscut. You've bagged us a prize for the King. And wasn't Pawler good for nothing? Who taught you how to shoot, Pawler?" Pawler hung his head in shame. "Come on, let's find the river and meet up with the others."

"You're not going anywhere." Tagen looked up to see a man and a woman only a few yards away in the clearing. The man had his sword drawn, and the woman pulled back on an arrow. The two stood just at the right spot to catch the glare of the sun, making it hard for Tagen to see who they were.

"Lily? Needum? Is that you two," called out Tagen as he held his hand in front of his face to block the sun.

"Nope," was all Katrianna said as she released the arrow, sending it speeding straight through Tagen's hand and into his left eye. He hollered in pain as his men drew their weapons. "Release the unicorn."

Tagen continued to moan as he snapped the arrow in half, allowing him to slide his hand off one side while keeping the rest of it stuck in his eye. He stumbled back and forth for a moment but caught his balance. Had his hand not been in front of his face, the arrow would have cut through to his brain. He grunted through the pain and pointed his bleeding hand at the woman.

"This unicorn… is property of King Jerad, first of his name, ruler of Crestside and soon to be the conqueror of this shithole you call home. Now step aside before I come over there and wring your neck." Leland raised an eyebrow at the commander's boldness; even the remaining four mercenaries looked at him as if he were crazy.

It was only then that Katrianna noticed the alicorn sticking out of the commander's pocket. She scanned the clearing around and saw one of the unicorns lying dead in the grass. Katrianna found herself shaking in shock to see one of her lovely friends lying so lifeless and still. She channeled her emotions into a rage as she looked back the Tagen.

"Did you… did you kill that unicorn?" The commander turned around and looked at the dead unicorn.

"What, that one? Yes, yes, I did. Then I took my dagger, and I cut myself a nice little trophy. Would you like to see it, I have it right…" but before the commander could turn back to the woman and finish his sentence, he felt another two arrows pierce through his back. He turned around to see Katrianna tossing her bow to the side as she walked up to him.

She grabbed the daggers from his belt and, with a roar at the top of her lungs, she plunged them both deep into his chest. As he fell to the ground, the commander shrieked in agony as Katarine reached down and yanked out the arrow stuck in Tagen's left eye, only to slam it back down into his right eye. Tagen's cries of agony continued until Katrianna drove her sword through the man's head and deep into the ground beneath. Turning to the remaining four men, Katrianna pulled out her sword and raised it high.

"Who's next?" All four men dropped their weapons. Oscut removed the sack from the foal's head, allowing it to run off and find its mother. Oscut dropped to his knees before Katrianna and began to beg.

"Please, miss, just let us go. We'll leave these lands, and never come back. We won't tell a soul about anything we saw here; I promise you that." Katrianna poked her sword in the ground and leaned on it a bit.

"I'm actually a little disappointed. I had hoped you all would put up more of a fight. Leland hasn't even had the chance to raise his sword yet." Leland shrugged in agreement. Katrianna kicked the man onto his back and stood over him. "None of you will be leaving this valley, but that doesn't mean you have to die here and now."

"Wait. What?" Leland stepped forward, confused, but Katrianna put out a hand to stop him.

"Tell us what to do. We'll do whatever you say," begged Oscut.

"The river. Cross it and head south. Remain on that side of the river and never cross north again. So long as you don't enter the northside of this valley again, I will not kill you." Oscut nodded quickly and scurried to his feet. He looked to his fellow mercenaries, and they all nodded in return. All four men took off south as Leland raised his arms in confusion.

"What are you doing? Why grant them mercy?" Katrianna waited until the men were out of earshot before responding.

"Oh, I've granted each of them nothing but horrible ends. Have you forgotten one of the first rules I gave you when you came to this land? Once they cross that river, they will enter the Forest of Death, and they'll soon wish they were never born." Katrianna sheathed her sword and started walking back to the castle. "Let's go. If these men came from your King, we must prepare for the worst. The rest of the Garden must be warned."

CHAPTER 18

Aldiss Castle

Awakened by a loud crackle of thunder, King Jerad sighed as he stared up at the ceiling. It had been at least a week since he sent his twelve best Mercenaries over the mountain pass to find out just what the hell was going on up there. Thomas Clayton and Leif Mayvoy had both disappeared into the mountains twenty years ago. Now Leland Clayton looks to have followed suit. Jared wanted nothing more than to believe that the men had died, somewhere in the snow, alone and unwell. Though that was the most likely reality, it wasn't enough to satisfy him. He wanted to see the bodies. He wanted to mount the head of Thomas Clayton on his wall. Unfortunately for the King, the hired help provided by the Dark One continued to disappoint. The assassin couldn't kill Thomas Clayton all those years ago, and now it seems that a full dozen mercs couldn't come back with a single trophy. Jared was infuriated by their lack of results.

Having been King now for over two decades, Jared was tired and bored. He honestly did not understand how his father had kept from killing himself out of sheer boredom. The Kingdom of Crestside had fallen in line, and there was no one left to protest or challenge Jared's claim to the throne. Anyone that had dared to speak out against King Jared had either been killed or thrown into the mines years ago. Now Jared's days were full of food, wine, and finding someone to keep his bed warm.

Hoping to share his bed with someone new, instead of the same old hags he had been rotating in and out for the past 20 years, Jared had wrenched a young girl from the arms of her mother the previous night. When he was finished with her, Jared did not allow her to go home but forced her to remain in the King's chambers with him, citing a need for company in order to sleep. Jared turned his head on the pillow to look at the girl but was both surprised and frustrated to find that she was not there. His bedroom door still appeared to be locked from the inside, which meant the girl had not left the master suite.

Jared sat up in bed and peered around the room, trying to spot the girl in the dark. He swung his legs over the side of the bed and put his feet on the floor, only to recoil them quickly when he stepped in a warm puddle. Jared looked down in shock to see a dark pool of something flowing out from under the bed. While this had not been the first time a woman had committed suicide over his antics, Jared had not expected the young girl to be capable of such measures. Jared crawled across to the other side of the bed, figuring he would find the body of the young girl sprawled out on the floor with something sharp in her hands. Instead, he saw a naked, beautiful woman crouching over the dead young girl.

"What the hell is this," yelled Jared as he backed away. The woman quickly looked up at Jared, her eyes full of shock. Half of her face, her chin, and her neck were covered in blood. She wiped her cheeks clean, licking her fingertips as she stood next to the bed and smiled down at Jared.

Despite his disgust, Jared could not help but notice two things. First, was the fact that he had never seen this woman before. She was not a citizen of Crestside, and he did not remember her arriving with any of the mercenaries sent from the Dark One. The second, arguably more critical thing that Jared noticed was the fact that this woman was absolutely stunning. Her long dark hair flowed over her shoulders and down to her large, perfectly shaped breasts. Her body had all the right curves in all the right places; a perfect combination that Jared had never imagined he would see.

"Apologies for startling you, my King, but from the looks of it, you are more aroused than disgusted. Am I right?" Before Jared could answer, the woman crawled up on the bed, bent down and ran her lips and her tongue up the inside of his thigh. Her fingers, tipped with sharp black nails, scratched their way across Jared's body. To the King's surprise, the pleasure far outweighed the pain.

Perhaps this was all a dream; some sick, demented fantasy that Jared had cooked up in his head to spice things up in the bedroom. He had struggled, lately to find things to satisfy his cravings. The only problem with being King, Jerad had nothing to long for. Too much of a good thing, meant Jerad would grow tired of it quicker. He had indulged himself in every delicacy he could get his hands on. He had bedded pretty much any woman he wanted to bed; young, old, married. He had cuckolded several men, he had forced parents to watch him defile their young ones, he had abused and used whoever he could, but even that had become tiresome.

The strange woman left blood smears all over his body as she kissed and licked her way up to his face. She pushed him down as she spread her legs to straddle him. Jared moaned in pleasure when she slid down into place.

"Oh! Oh, my King! The stories of your manhood have certainly not been exaggerated! I've heard you prefer to mount your women from behind. While I admire a confident man, I prefer to ride my men on top. So, let's see how you perform." The woman ran her hand down Jerad's chest, digging her claw-like nails into his skin. For the first time in his life, Jerad cried out in both pain and ecstasy. The woman arched her back and rode the kill like a bucking bull. She reached down and slapped Jerad across the face as she sped up her rocking. "Keep up with me, your majesty."

Jerad looked up at the woman in shock. No one had ever touched him like that before, let alone struck him during sex. He wasn't entirely convinced that he liked being dominated in the bedroom, but he wasn't currently in a position to protest. Having never been in this position before, Jared found himself grabbing whatever he could and holding on for dear life.

"That's it, my King, surrender to my will." The woman controlled the pace, speeding up when she wanted, slowing down when Jerad was on the verge. She was there to ensure her own pleasure, not his. She bent down to embrace him, leaning in to share a blood-soaked kiss as she neared her finish. Her hand slid around his. Jerad grabbed her wrist and tried to pry free her hand, but the woman only tightened her grip in response. When the time came, the woman cried out in pure pleasure before sliding off to the side to collapse on the bed. “Well done, my liege, well done.”

Jerad stared at the ceiling, catching his breath as he contemplated everything that just transpired. As the euphoric high wore off, Jerad remembered how everything started. There was a dead girl sprawled out on the floor at the foot of his bed. A stranger, whom he had never seen before, somehow snuck into the castle, broken into his locked master suite, killed the girl and then assaulted the King. When he considered it all at once, Jerad knew the sex, while pleasurable, wasn’t enough to forget the rest. Jerad quickly rolled off the side of the bed and crossed the room to grab his sword.

“Guards! Get in here!” Jerad swung back around and pointed his sword at the beautiful woman now stretching across his bed.

“Oh, sweetheart, they can’t hear you.” Jerad sidestepped over to the door and pushed it open. Spread across the hallway, Jerad’s two guards laid still and pale. “Sorry, love. I didn’t want them to spoil my entrance but don’t worry. I only killed the two.”

“Just who the hell are you, and what is it you want?” The gasped and pouted her lips.

"What? Don't you recognize me? Here, perhaps this will help jog your memory." She slid off the bed like a snake and tip-toed over to him in the darkness. She slowly leaned close to him, locking eyes as she flashed a grin. "Wait for it."

Jerad stared back at her, not quite sure what was about to happen. Another bolt of lightning ripped across the night sky. In that split second flash, as the room was lit, the woman's face changed to a hideous old woman with a face full of scars, moles, missing teeth and graying thin hair. Jerad fell backward to the floor, stretching his sword between them. The heinous woman's face reverted back to the young and beautiful version when the lightning ceased, but the image had been seared into Jerad's mind.

"Get away from me, witch." Jerad crawled away, keeping his sword trained pointed at her. Suddenly, before Jerad could react, the witch swiped the sword away, lunged at Jerad, grabbed him by the neck, and lifted him at least a foot up in the air. The witch turned and pinned Jerad against the wall, still holding him high off the floor.

"I've warned you before not to forget your place.

I do not appreciate your tone, considering everything I've given you; the throne, the crown, this castle, the very bed in which you sleep." Seeing Jerad being to gasp for air, the witch dropped him to the floor and walked away. She pulled up a chair and sat down. She leaned back and crossed her legs, relaxing while Jerad caught his breath. "I gave you everything you hold so dear. So, I don't think it's too much to demand a pinch of respect."

"The Dark One," croaked Jerad, sheepishly as he pulled himself up along the wall.

"Bravo, you've finally caught up with the class." The woman gave a half-hearted round of applause. Jerad choked a bit as he righted himself. "Did you think I wouldn't be around to check up on you."

"It's been twenty years since I saw you last."

"Yea, well twenty years pass a hell of a lot faster in the world out there than they do in this corner of the world. You're not my only investment, Jerad. I have other things that tend to be more worthy of my time than the state of things in Crestside." The Dark One basked in the moonlight as she stared at Jared. "Still, I'm flattered that you've counted the days since our last meeting."

"Considering your decrepit state at the time, I figured..." The woman raised an eyebrow and cocked her head to the side.

"What? You thought I died?" The Dark One nodded over toward the dead girl on the floor. "I have certain habits that prevent that. I'm the oldest woman to walk this earth, and I'll be damned if I leave it on anyone else's terms, let alone time's."

"The habits you speak of, they aren't magic." Jerad limped over to his wardrobe and began to dress himself. "They're Vampiric, aren't they?"

"Jerad! I'm impressed you know the term. How did you come across it?" The Dark One leaned back and swiped a bottle of wine from the desk.

"I read about it." Jared sat down at his table, pouring himself a glass of wine.

"Oh? Give me all the details, my little bookworm." The Dark One, still naked and without a care, leaned forward and smiled, like a schoolgirl aching for a good story.

"In The Alphabet of Ben Sira, the author referenced to a conversation with the ancient Nebuchadnezzar. The King's son had grown ill, and Nebuchadnezzar did not know what to do. Ben Sira wrote an amulet, and on it, he inscribed the names of three angels: Snvi, Snsvi, and Smnglof. When Nebuchadnezzar asked who they were, Ben Sira told him a story. As mentioned in Jewish demonology, there was once a demon called Lilith who, among other female demons, roamed the night for infants. Blood hungry creatures, these demons would either kill or infect the young infants. Now, the myth behind Lilith is that she was, in fact, the first wife of Adam."

"The first wife? Everyone knows the story of Adam and Eve. I don't remember anything about another one." Jared heard the sarcasm in the Dark One's voice but continued to play along.

"Yes, well in the first chapter of the book of Genesis, it states that the creator made a male and female in his own image. The creation of Eve, however, is not actually mentioned by name until well into the second chapter. So, there are those that believe there was another woman, named Lilith, who had been created first. The myth suggested that Lilith and Adam weren't a happy couple. Lilith saw herself as superior to Adam and refused to lie beneath him during sex. Instead she wanted to be on top, to remind Adam that she was in control. She ended up leaving the Garden of Eden and fled to the shores of the Red Sea. It was there that she gave birth to thousands of demons. After hearing Adam's plea to bring Lilith back to him, God sent out three angels to retrieve her. Snvi, Snsvi, and Smnglof were given orders to kill off one hundred of Lilith's demons every day until she agreed to come back.

"Lilith refused, and in turn, she swore to bring sickness to the descendants of Adam. The only way to stop her, and heal the young, would be to mention the names of the three angels or one of the secret names of Lilith. According to Hebrew texts, Lilith made a resting place in the destruction of Edom. The name of Lilith was later associated with demons that lurked the night in search of blood. While stories of corpses coming back to life were spread around, it was widely believed that this addiction to blood was simply a sexual fetish of the sick-minded. Combing the horror tales and the sexual activity, the process of sucking blood from another living being was thus given the name of Vampirism."

"My, my! As I said, I am impressed. I knew you had a spark of ambition within you, but I honestly did not take you for such a historian. You continue to surprise me, Jerad."

"I'll take that as a compliment, and ignore the insult you wrapped it in. So, Dark One, to what do I owe this pleasure of your visit?"

"I was horny." The Dark One laughed and took another long pull from the wine bottle. "In all seriousness, though, I came to cash in on my investment. I have a score to settle, and you are going to help me settle it."

"And why would I do that, oh Dark One?"

"Since I'm going to be here awhile, we're going to need to drop the formalities. I can only be called 'the Dark One' so many times before it starts annoying the shit out of me." The woman stood and waltzed over to Jerad, pinning him against the wall once again. "You can call me Satrina."

"Is that a joke?"

"Excuse me?"

"Oh, don't play coy. You expect me to believe that?" Satrina just smiled and stared at him, acting as if she was clueless to his inquiry. "Amongst the passages of Jewish demonology, it is written that Lilith had an encounter with Elijah. While it is not known precisely if this was Elijah the Prophet or an Angel of God, but Lilith was forced to tell him her secret names. Lilith confessed to Elijah seventeen names; Satrina was one of those seventeen.

"Are you trying to tell me that you're her? You're Lilith?" Satrina winked at Jerad and then walked out of the suite and down the hall. Jerad chased after her. "Hey! Where do you think you're going?"

"I'm famished, my King. While the blood of your guards and that fine little girl was great for my skin, I still need actual food for sustenance. You wouldn't let your guest starve now, would you?" Jerad rolled his eyes as she tried to keep up with her pace. As the two of them headed for the dining hall, Jared found himself almost embarrassed at the gawking looks his servants gave the naked woman walking past him.

"Perhaps you'd like to put something on while my chefs prepare breakfast." Satrina looked at him and laughed.

"You are adorable. How refreshing to see this side of you! And all it took was a woman to use a little force." Jared growled, growing tired of her pokes. "I walk the earth as I please. If it would make you more comfortable, however, feel free to send for your tailor. Ah, here's the kitchen. Should we just eat in here?"

"My cooks prefer their privacy," said Jerad as he tried to pull the woman back to the hallway.

"You speak so highly of them. Why do they deserve such respect and regard from you?"

"They don't, but they are one of the few members of my castle staff that I've kept from my father's regime. The head cook and his wife have cooked here since before I was born. I have grown to appreciate their cooking, and I'd rather not have to break in a new chef to my liking."

"So the Chef and his wife are essentially holding you hostage with their cooking. Their jobs are ensured by the mere fact that no one else knows your tastebuds?" Satrina laughed at the thought. Jerad sneered at her.

"Quite the opposite. They loved my father and would like nothing more than to leave my service. I've enslaved them to their duty. Their family, in fact, are the hostages that stand the risk of death should my cooks not continue to serve."

"Clever, but tell me, King, where are they now? This kitchen is bare!" A loud ***bang*** abruptly resonated through the kitchen as Jared turned to see the chef and his wife staring at Satrina. The wife had dropped a large crate of food along with a couple of bottles of goat's milk.

"What is the meaning of this!? How dare you make such a mess in front of your King!" Jared slammed his fist down on the baking table as the chef and his wife fell to their knees. "What do you have to say for yourselves?"

"Forgive us, my King! We were… unprepared is all." The chef lowered his head, but his wife couldn't take her eyes off of Satrina.

"Unprepared? For what? This is my castle, is it

not? Am I not allowed to step into my own kitchen?" The chef was trembling. Jared looked at the wife, who had barely blinked. "And you, just what the hell are you staring at?"

"The Queen, my lord. As my husband said, we weren't aware of your mother's return. We would have prepared something." The woman continued to stare at Satrina with a confused look on her face. "You haven't aged a day, my lady. How… is that?"

"My mother?" Jerad looked back and forth between Satrina and the chef's wife. "What the hell are you talking about?"

"Welp, guess she spilled the beans along with the rest of that food on the floor." Satrina shrugged her shoulders and then leaned down and grabbed an apple. Taking a giant bite, Satrina leaned back against the stove and smiled at Jared. "Surprise."

CHAPTER 19

Aldiss Castle

"What the hell kind of sick game are you playing? My mother died giving birth to me." Jerad paced around the study as his tailor took Satrina's measurements.

"I don't play games, sweetheart. I conquer things; that's all I do. I have survived on my own for ages, and I've only grown stronger over time. Nothing can kill me, let alone giving birth to you. That's a lie some sad old man told you." Satrina looked down at the tailor, winking at him as he measured her inseam. "David and I disagreed on several things; raising you was one of them. He wanted another cookie-cutter copy of the kings that came before him. What number would you have been? Thirteen?

"You have no idea how excited I was to hear that you had changed your name. I would have picked something better than Jared, but it still made me giggle. I had plans for you and for this Kingdom, but your father wouldn't have it. He tried, bless his heart, to deal with me, but our marriage was doomed to fail. When he found out my true purpose in these lands and realized our entire marriage was based on a lie, he banished me from Crestside. On the eve of your first birthday, I was escorted out of the kingdom. I guess David hoped that he could convince you that I was never a part of your life. Apparently, it worked."

"I don't believe you. My mother's name was Natrisa."

"If you haven't figured out similarities between the names Natrisa and Satrina, then you're dumber than I thought. Your father was well-read. I couldn't waltz into his life with one of my known names." Satrina ran his fingers through the tailor's hair. "Why do you think you never got along with your father? Out of all the books in your father's master library, why do you think you read the ones on demons and vampires. I may have only nursed you for a year, but I whispered into your ear every night before bed and every morning when you woke. Clearly, my influence stuck along long after I was forced to leave."

"But… this morning…in my chambers."

"Oh, get over it. I needed to get a quick read on you, and a lot can be read from sex. If you believe any of the old stories about the birth of man, you'll understand that certain families shared…relationships for some time. How else do you think the population got to where it currently is? Do the math, babe." Satrina took a seat on the couch and motioned for Jerad to join her. "Don't overthink it, Jerad. It was a one-time thing. I told you, I like to conquer things. You're just another man, hun, no different from the rest."

"Oh, I'm plenty different," said Jared, as he eyed the tailor out of the room, "and you'll address me properly when others are present. That is unless you've come to claim my throne. Is that why you're here, Satrina? Is that the revenge you seek; the score you have to settle?"

"That, baby boy, is another story altogether."

Jared took a seat across from Satrina.

"Fine. You've had your fun this morning. You've certainly made an entrance. You want my attention? You've got it. So, let's cut the shit and get straight to it." Jerad leaned forward and pointed. "What do you want with my Kingdom?"

"Huh." Satrina leaned back in the couch, a look of disappointment on her face.

"What?"

"Well, if you truly don't know the answer to that question, it means you failed to do what I asked you to do." Jerad shook his head.

"You told me to reopen the mines and dig east. I've had prisoners digging for years."

"That's not the only thing I told you to do." Satrina looked around and raised her hands. "I mean, this is a nice place, but it's certainly not the largest castle I've seen. Are you telling me that in twenty years you failed to find your father's archives?"

"My father's archives?" Jerad mimicked Satrina's

movements, swing his arms open wide. “We’re literally sitting in the library, Satrina. I mean, what’s so special about a bunch of books.”

“Come with me.” Satrina walked out of the library, swaying her hips as she headed toward the study. Walking behind the desk, Satrina started grabbing books off the bookcase in the wall. She cleared an entire shelf, throwing the books to the floor, revealing a small slot in the wall. Jared watched as Satrina reached into the slot and pulled on something. The bookcase responded with a loud creek before swinging inward to give way to a small hidden passage.

“Well if you knew where it was this whole time, why the hell didn’t you have that Assassin, Fitch, tell me?” Satrina stopped in the dark and turned around to Jerad.

“Because I shouldn’t have to do every single damn thing for you! For shit’s sake, Jared! Are you incapable of taking any kind of initiative?” Satrina stared Jared down for a moment before turning back around in the passage. “Only a handful of people know of this room’s existence, Jerad. You really think I was going to tell some hired hand where it was, in hopes he'd do the honorable thing and only tell you? Again, I thought you were smarter than this."

"Well if you already know about this place, and how to get into it, why did you need me to find it?" Jerad looked around the room, noticing the age of the binding on some of the books and the stacks of scrolls that lined the walls.

"I had hoped to deal you in. There are secrets in this room, secrets that date back to the first men to hold your father's name. What your father didn't know was that I was there when the deals were made to keep those secrets." Satrina found the scroll she was looking for and gave it to Jerad. "Read that, then come find me. I'll fill you in on the dirtier details that weren't put down in writing."

"Oh, fun. Reading." Jerad took the scroll and brought it over to the desk. Satrina rolled her eyes and headed out of the room.

"Shut up and do as you're told." Satrina slid her hand along the walls as she headed back through the passage to the study. "Your tailor better work fast. I'm tired of you looking at my tits."

CHAPTER 20

The Garden

Leland followed Katrianna through the forest. She hadn't said a word since they left the castle that morning. She hadn't spoken much that day at all. Leland had risen that morning to find Katrianna pacing back and forth in the bedroom. She had apparently already made breakfast, and she had stuffed two sacks of supplies for them to take on a journey. Leland had tried to get her to talk, to find out what was going through her head, but Katrianna's mind was made, and she told him she wasn't in the mood to talk about it. So, loyal to her, Leland put on his clothes and followed in silence.

To Leland's surprise, Katrianna led him straight to the river and then began to cross it. Again, Leland had questions, but Katrianna didn't appear to have time to stop and answer them. Leland was very aware of where they were heading. Among his earliest memories of the Garden was the moment when Katrianna told him never to cross the river south. Katrianna and everyone else on the northside of the river referred to the south as the Forest of Death. For as peaceful and cohesive as this place was sold to be, such a name for a forest seemed a bit contradictory. As they crossed the river, Leland looked up to see four bodies hanging on pikes stuck in the water. Their bodies were riddled with holes, their throats had been cut, and their eyes were missing. Despite this, Leland was able to recognize them as the four mercenaries from the unicorn clearing.

"Katrianna, wait. This goes against everything you've told me since I've been here. Can you clue me in on what we're walking into?" As they stepped on the southern shore, Katrianna turned to Leland.

"This is the Forest of Death. Those that live within it know who I am, and they know who you are. They've accepted me, but they don't trust you. They will kill you at the first opportunity. So, keep close to me and keep quiet." Leland nodded and followed her as she stepped off the beach and in through the first row of trees.

They walk for a mile or two in silence. Leland recognized the forest to be thicker than the north. The trees stood fatter and taller. The brush at their feet was thicker. There was no sound but the steps Katrianna and Leland were making. From what Leland could tell, the land used to be riddled with canyons. At some point, a flood of green had taken over the place and turned it into the lush Garden that it was. Katrianna led Leland up toward the edge of a cliff. She ducked down and crawled toward the edge, telling Leland to follow suit. Looking over the edge, Leland couldn't believe his eyes.

"They are called the Childlike Elves, but they are not to be underestimated by any means." In the forest beneath them, Leland witnessed a large population of little elven children, laughing and playing about with each other. Their ears were slanted back to a tip. The skin was smooth and pale. The area was full of huts and tree-houses. Leland looked around the community, but couldn't find any adults around to care for the little ones. In fact, all of the young ones seemed to be the same age. He looked down in awe at the elves, but he was ultimately confused by it all. He couldn't imagine how these adorable little creatures could warrant such fear within the Garden.

"I don't get it, Katrianna. What are we hiding from?"

"You're speaking too loud, Leland! They're more dangerous than they look." Katrianna grabbed him and looked into his eyes. He could hear the fear in her voice. Looking back over the cliff, Leland was shocked to find that all the elves were gone. The community was empty with no sign of the hundreds of elves that had been running around just moments before. Leland felt a shift in the air and spun around to see five adult elves standing over them. They stood six to seven feet tall. Their eyes were dark, their fangs were long, and their sharp swords were drawn and placed in a pentagon around his neck. A sixth elf, larger than the rest, stepped forward and grabbed Katrianna by the throat. He lifted her up and slammed her against a tree trunk as he growled and bared his teeth.

"I told you once before, Princess. You're not

welcome in this forest." Leland tried to get up, but then quickly turned to hiss at him as the pentagon tightened around his neck. Any further movement and he'd be dead for sure. The leader turned back to Katrianna and growled again. "What are you doing here?"

"You know what I'm doing here. You've got four men hanging in the river, and one of your scouts killed two more in my forest near the castle, so don't act like you don't know." The leader roared and gnashed his teeth as he pointed down to Leland.

"Four of his kind. Not only that, but they were sent here for him, which means the garden has been compromised."

"I apologize for invading your sanctuary, but you clearly know what's at stake here. Leland is not your enemy. The agreement Asielle made all those years ago has been broken, and we need to prepare for what comes next." The leader growled again.

"Anyone who does not reside in our forest is my enemy. That includes you, Princess."

"Please. He can provide you with details on the other side. He had information that could benefit us all.

He's no threat to you." The leader stared at her for a moment before releasing her. As Katrianna fell to the ground, the leader turned to wave off the swords around Leland's neck.

"Of course, he's no threat to me. I don't need a sword to take this man's life." The leader walked over to Leland, standing above him with his hands on his hips. "My name is Ip Toma Yetto. As you can see, we do not take kindly to strangers in our forest. I'm the leader of my people. Until you give us a reason, you shall not be harmed. If a reason does arise, however, know that your death will be by my hands."

"What my husband is trying to say is, welcome to the realm of the elves. My name is Atsvi Hyaka, and I'm definitely the more diplomatic between the two of us. Let's go somewhere where we can talk." Katrianna nods and takes Leland by the hand. The two follow Atsvi down and through the village to a large hut with a long table and chairs around it. Atsvi, accompanied by several guards, sits at the opposite end of the table. Ip Toma Yetto stands behind her, arms crossed. "Speak your piece, Leland Clayton."

"Thank you. Those men you killed were part of

an expedition team sent out by King Jared of Crestside. Crestside, as a Kingdom, knows nothing of this place. From what I read in the journal belonging to Katrianna's father, the former King was a distant descendant of the King Aldiss that forged a bond with your late Queen Asielle. His son now rules with a bloody fist, and he either got lucky by sending that kill team to find me, or he has an idea of what this Garden is. There is a chance he will abandon the search when his men fail to return, but there's also a chance he might send more forces. Without eyes on Crestside, I can't tell you more than that.

"All I know is that he has an army of Cainates who, despite their appearance, could present a problem to this place if they were to find a way to get here. I only know of the waterfall and its staircase as an entrance. If that's the only way to get in, we could easily bottleneck their troops." Atsvi raised a hand, and Leland stopped.

"I can sense goodness within you, Leland, but we elves live only as a private community. We have cut ourselves off from civilization for centuries, and we prefer it that way. We may recognize this Garden as our home, but we do not recognize Katrianna's royal designation as anything but honorary. She has no authority over us and therefore has no power to snap her fingers and call us to arms. We live here, but we don't interfere or entertain the lives of anyone outside of our own.

"However, we are aware of the threat, as well as it's potential to grow large enough to affect our lands. In fact, nothing you have come here to tell us is news to the elven people. The elves have always had a watchful eye on Crestside and the people that lived there. We likely know more about the Kingdom's history than you do." Atsvi stood up to leave. "If a threat presents itself, we will handle it. You can return to your home."

"Wait. The Princess and I came here to help you, not to stand on the sidelines." Ip Toma Yetto shook his head.

"We don't want it."

"Why not?"

"Is it truly that hard for you to understand? From the beginning, the very beginning of everything, your race has brought nothing but suffering and pain to our race. Stand your most capable, you're most formidable man next to me, and tell me who between the two is superior. We are stronger, we are smarter, and yet your race, the human race, was the creator's favorite. Then your race bit the hand that fed you, and everyone suffered. We lost our home. We had to drastically change our way of life. We became nomadic and estranged, and it is not a stretch to place the blame solely on your shoulders."

"If not for a human, Asielle, your kind would have drowned like everybody else," said Leland.

"Yes, one woman tried to make a difference. She found us and convinced us to move to this land. She may have found this place, and saved us from the flood, but then she turned right around and burned us. She told a human king of our existence. She entrusted his family to guard us against the outside; as if we needed humans to guard us at all. This valley, this Garden has been held hostage for hundreds of years since that poor decision. Now, that poor decision could cost us our home again.

"We do not care that your Princess is a hybrid.

She has enough of the blood of your race within her. We don't care if she or any of the other creatures in this valley vouches for you and your earnestness. You ran away from your troubles to come here, and now your troubles could cost us everything." Ip Toma Yetto growled and pointed at Leland. "So, do you see now? Do you understand now why we despise you? Is it clear enough why we do not wish to speak to you, to coexist with you, to have anything to do with you? If I had it my way, I'd kill you right where you stand."

"You can try." Leland dropped his sack to the ground. As Ip Toma Yetto roared, Leland tore off his shirt and threw it at the elf. Leland stepped forward and spun around, giving the elves a full view of his history of scars. "I feel for you and your people, but I'll be damned if I let you put the blame on me. I've paid for the sins of my father, ten times over. If you think you can take on Jerad and his army, good for you. I hope you slaughter every last one of them. I'm only here to lend a hand."

"We don't need your help." Ip Toma Yetto stepped forward. "We don't want your help."

"Well, I don't give a shit." Leland closed the gap

between them and stared up into the eyes of the beast. "After twenty years of torment, I wanted a different life. So yeah, I ran. But now that new life is being threatened, and I refuse to let you or anyone else tell me that I don't have a stake in the fight."

"This isn't your home, boy. This isn't your land to defend." Katrianna stepped forward beside Leland.

"No, but it's mine, and it's the home of everyone north of the river, whether you choose to interact with them or not. The fairies and the mermaids might not be able to the toe the line with you, but Leland and I can. We don't need your permission," Katrianna pulled Leland back away from Ip Toma Yetto, "but we'd like your blessing."

Just then, the door to the hut slammed open as two elves ran inside and straight to Atsvi. They whispered something into her ear, and even Leland could see her pale skin flash whiter. She looked up at Ip Toma Yetto and then over at Katrianna. She cleared her throat and stepped forward.

"It would appear that this threat is much larger than what we had initially anticipated." Ip Toma Yetto turned back to his wife with a questioning look.

"What is it? What news from our spies causes such fear in your eyes?"

"King Jerad's benefactor has arrived in Crestside. It's Satrina."

CHAPTER 21

Crestside
The Road to the Mines

"So, let me get this straight. The Garden of Eden was home to more than just humans, and the rest of the magical creatures that lived there, now reside in a hidden valley on the other side of these mountains." King Jerad leaned back in the royal carriage as he spoke to Satrina. "And you used to live over there until the Queen Asielle kicked you out."

"Yes. In her travels to gather the former inhabitants of Eden, we crossed paths. I displayed a little dark magic which she mistook to mean that I was one of the magical creatures she was looking for. Not knowing who I was, Asielle took me back to the valley and saved me from the flood. Over time, Asielle and I began to disagree on things and eventually I was banished from the land." Satrina sat on the darker side of the carriage, admiring the craftsmanship of the dress the tailor had made for her.

"So what? Now you want your revenge?"

"I've told you time and time again. I conquer things. It is what I do. It is what I have always done. I will not let some flock of fairies and elves tell me what I can and cannot do." Satrina almost hissed as she spoke about them. "If I can't have what I want, I'll burn their whole valley to the ground."

"Well then what do you need me for? Why haven't you taken your dragon, and your armies and stormed the place? What's taken you so long to come back here?" Jerad played with the dagger in his hand.

"Oh, I wouldn't risk my dragon in an attack. She is too rare a creature. Such an incursion takes time to plan, and numbers to support it. The army I delivered you would be slaughtered in a heartbeat when pitted against the elven army of the Garden. That's why I've brought you more sons of Cain to supplement your forces." Satrina peeked out the window of the carriage as they rode through the town. "As far as the time I've been away, I've already told you all you need to hear. I have other investments across the world. I'm a busy woman with things to do. I may have needed to wait and bide my time a bit, but I never forgot about the Garden."

"Everything I've been told suggests that the Claytons found a passage in the forest to the north. Why are we heading south?"

"The northern passage isn't fit for an army. Its terrain is too treacherous, and it leads to a very narrow entry point. I didn't tell you to reopen the mines for nothing. The tunnels that your prisoners have been digging for the past two decades should lead deep enough into the mountain for my dark magic to do the rest. Your supplemental troops should arrive at Crestside in the next two or three days. I'll open the passage, and your army will march through."

"I guess I'm just all questions today," Jared said as

he ate some cheese and groaned at how slow the carriage was going. “Say you win. Say the army burns down the valley on the other side. I’m still waiting to hear WHAT IS IN THIS FOR ME?”

“Did you lose all sense of drive and ambition since the last time I saw you? That's the problem with getting everything you wanted at such a young age without earning it. By the time your father inherited the crown, he had plans in place to make his reign truly his own and not a continuation of his father's. You just wanted to own everything for the sake of owning it. Are you satisfied and genuinely ready to die or don't you now need something new to yearn for?

“There is a reason I’m out here with you instead of sitting on a throne somewhere with a crown on my head. I like to conquer things. I like to break people and bend them to my will. I don't care to stick around and sit on a throne above them. That lifestyle is meant for someone like you. You are the king of this land, and the valley is just next door. Ideally, you would reign supreme over both. You would have an influx of new servants, new subjects, new people to torment and do your bidding. Does that not interest you?

“You are my son. Though you aren't my only son, that does not mean that I do not wish to grant you things. I would like nothing more than to gift you the survivors of the valley, but again, that is something you must learn. I made you take your father's life for your current crown. In order to rule over the valley, you’ll have to ride with your army into battle and earn it.” Jared rolled his eyes before sitting up straight to look across at his mother.

“And what if I don't want it? What if this idea you have in your head about who I truly am and what I truly strive for is nothing more than a fantasy? Perhaps I am satisfied with what I have. What if your words have fallen on deaf ears, and I truly want nothing to do with your initiative? What then?” Satrina raised an eyebrow but then stretched out her lips into a ling, wide grin.

“Then, I would end you. I would take over your armies, your crown, your throne, and your kingdom until I have replaced you with someone else. As cliché as it sounds, I brought you into this world, and I am more than happy to take you out of it.” Satrina sat up and peered across the carriage at her son, locking eyes with him. "So far, you've only proven to me that you're commendable in the sack. Convince me that you're still worthy of the crown on your head, or I will take it away from you."

****

Forest of Death

As if things had not been on edge before, Leland was overwhelmed by the stark tension that filled the forest. From the moment that Satrina's name was mentioned, Ip Toma Yetto cared about nothing but preparation of the attack. He seemed no longer concerned about barring Leland or Katrianna from joining the fight. The elves were not allowed to revert back to their child-like states until the threat was over.

Katrianna confessed to Leland that she had no idea who Satrina was or what history she had with this valley. From the look in their eyes to the quickness in their steps, it was beyond apparent that the elves were both afraid and angry. Whatever had happened in the past, Ip Toma Yetto and his people were certainly driven to prevent it from happening again.

Katrianna called upon the unicorns to join the

cavalry along with the horses owned by the elves. She called upon the fairies to serve on standby, ready to give medical attention when needed. The mermaids were obviously confined to the water, but that didn't mean they were stuck in the lagoon. Katrianna tasked them with keeping an eye on all parts of the river and the waterfall.

Ip Toma Yetto, however, did not believe the attack would come from the waterfall. His spies had observed Satrina and the King touring the mines in the southern part of Crestside. While Leland had always figured that the tunnel work was just an ongoing, endless form of punishment, with no true objective, Ip Toma Yetto believed that Satrina would use the mines to forge a new entrance into the Garden. So, in anticipation of such an attack, Yetto assigned elves to build barricades, dig trenches, and erect boardwalks within the trees in the general area where Satrina's forces could emerge. When Leland wasn't assisting the builders, he joined battle training sessions. One evening, Yetto took notice of this and watched Leland practicing his sword work on a tree.

"You've got a lot to learn, but I can see you're

making progress with some of your techniques." Leland put his sword away, wiped his brow, and turned to face Ip Toma Yetto.

"For obvious reasons, I didn't receive weapons training when I lived in the prisoner camp. I'm better with my hands, but I figured those wouldn't get me very far in a battle." Leland leaned against the tree and peered up at Ip Toma Yetto. "Why the change of heart? Three days ago, you wanted to run me out of this forest. In fact, I'm sure you were considering whether or not to add me in with the mercenaries hanging along the river."

"I was. While my feelings on the matter haven't changed, priorities have changed." Yetto watched his people working all through the night. The forest was lit was hundreds of torches as his people rotated in shifts to rest. "It was one thing to deal with a tyrant king who stumbled upon something he shouldn't have. It is now a completely different matter when considering that one of the darkest souls on this earth is involved."

"You're talking about Satrina." Yetto clenched his teeth when Leland spoke the name. "Who is she? What history does she have with this place that causes such a reaction from you and the rest of the Garden?"

"Think of every evil thing your race has done. Calculate every crime, every travesty, every single horrible act committed by a human being. Satrina is the summation of all those things. She is one of the oldest creatures on this earth with so much blood on her hands; nothing could ever clean her skin again." Yetto sighed and leaned against the tree near him. "Like everyone else, she was banished from Eden, but she was the first. She would have you believe that it was all over some petty thing like wanting more control over her lover, but that wasn't it at all.

"Satrina was attracted to chaos. Tell her not to do something, and she would do it ten times over. She was allergic to any state of peace and calm. Addicted to turmoil, Satrina loved to infect the lives of those around her, break them down, and destroy them. Asielle had no knowledge of Satrina or what she was capable of. She did not know that Satrina used to collect magical creatures and sell them in dark magic markets. Asielle had no idea the horrible, torturous things Satrina use to do to our kind and other magical creatures for money, for pleasure, or simply for lack of better things to do."

"She would torture your kind? For no reason?"

"For plenty of reasons. Magical creatures are magical in many ways that could benefit humans. The wings of a fairy, the scales of a mermaid, the teeth of elves, the blood of any magical creature, all these things have magical properties that could be valuable to people who know dark enough magic to use it. If more of your kind knew the things that could be done with a single vile of my blood, they'd hunt every one of us down." Yetto stared out at the night, the fire from the torches reflected his eyes. "When Asielle became aware of Satrina's history, and what she planned to do with the residents of this new valley, Asielle banished Satrina. Asielle wasn't a killer, but I wish I could have served as an executioner. Letting Satrina go only meant that we would one day have to deal with her evil heart sometime again. That's what Satrina represents, Leland; the worst of humankind."

"How can I prove myself to you, Ip Toma Yetto? I'm just as invested in the survival of your people and this place as you are. What can I do to prove to you that I'd do anything to protect the Garden?" Yetto pushed off the tree and began to walk away. Leland didn't figure he would get an answer, but he called out to Yetto anyway. Yetto then stopped in the dark but didn't turn around.

"You want to prove your intentions? Your word isn't enough. Your pledge isn't enough. There's only one thing you can do to prove your allegiance to the Garden." Yetto looked down at the ground and then continued to walk away. "You could die for it."

CHAPTER 22

Crestside Prisoner Camp

King Jerad squinted his eyes as he walked out of the warden's cabin into the blazing morning sun. He and Satrina had slept at the prisoner's camp for the past few days as they inspected the mine tunnels and waited for the additional troops to arrive. As Jerad acclimated his eyes to the light, he turned to see hundreds of rows of Cainates, armed to the teeth, ready for war. Most of the Cainates looked the same; diseased, dismembered, and worn. At first glance, the Cainates could be mistaken for crippled weaklings.

Jerad saw the rage in their eyes, the anger and madness pumping through their brains. Satrina had found these poor souls from all over the world, and she had used her dark magic to numb their inner chaos. No longer would they run rabid. They would hear, understand, and obey an order given to them. Once they were set loose, however, they would be a force to be reckoned with.

"Join us, King," called Satrina from a nearby table. Satrina was joined by twenty or so men and women, all rugged, battle-tested, and mean. Jared grabbed a plate of food and sat down at the table. "Your Majesty, I would like to introduce you to your generals. These men and women have known their fair share of combat. They are war-ready and prepared to lead your armies into victory."

"No offense, but the last batch of professionals you sent my way were quite easily disposed of." Jared took a bite of sausage as he looked over the generals. "What makes these people any different?"

"Let's just say I saved the best for last, my lord." Jerad gritted his teeth at the level of sarcasm in Satrina's voice. Still, he nodded and continued to eat his food.

"Now then, you have a combined count of twelve hundred Cainates at your disposal. I've adjusted the tunnels to fit ranks of ten across. I have just enough dark magic within me to punch through the mountain to the other side. When your army is in place, I will do so, and you and I can ride the waves of Cainates into victory."

Jerad wasn't concerned with battle strategies, with the resumes of his of new generals, or with the dimensions of the tunnels. What Jared couldn't help but focus on, however, was the fact that Satrina's magic had limits. Would today's acts deplete her power to a degree where she would be vulnerable? Is it rechargeable, and how does she accomplish that? Is it all in the blood of her victims, or must she source her dark magic from somewhere else? The wheels in Jerad's mind were turning and he found himself overwhelmed with intrigue.

"Twelve hundred Cainates sounds like a sizeable force. What size of opposition could they be facing?" Jerad drank down a cup of cider and poured himself some more. "And what are the chances that they know we're coming?"

"When I left the Garden, the Elven people were

maybe three or four hundred strong. Even with the time that has passed, I wouldn't expect their population has increased more than double that. I imagine we would easily outnumber them two to one." Satrina not so discreetly pulled the cider bottle out of arm's reach of the King. "They are a resourceful people. I imagine they have some idea of our activities, but we haven't given them much time to prepare. If we proceed as planned, we should reach the Garden by nightfall."

****

Forest of Death

Katrianna rode Aubade through the forest until she came to a stop next to Atsvi Hyaka and joined the ranks of the Elven Cavalry. While Ip Toma Yetto had initially decreed that the female elves would not be joining the fight, his decision was reversed once Satrina became a factor. Those female elves capable of engaging in battle were assigned to the Cavalry and placed away from the front lines.

"This is such bullshit. I still can not believe my own husband would not allow me to fight with the males. We are just as strong, just as vicious, and all-around just as suited to fight as any of them are, and yet he persists with his stubbornness." Katrianna smirked in understanding.

"He's likely just hoping to keep you safe." Atsvi hissed at the comment.

"I never needed a male to fend for me before, I certainly don't need one now. He wanted to cart us off to some secluded cave somewhere. That's not safe, that's solitude. You can engage an opponent from a strategically safe advantage." She sighed and tightened her grip on her reigns. "Now is not the time for my husband's misguided attempts at chivalry. The Garden is at risk, and every able body needs to be here to defend it."

"Well, then I'm glad you convinced him to accept the Cavalry idea. Trust me; I don't plan on trotting around back here in the dark. When things kick-off, we'll be just as much in the fight as the rest of them. I don't know about you, but I definitely plan to bloody my sword." Atsvi grinned at Katrianna.

"We'll see how your unicorns match with our elven steads." Atsvi took out her sword and inspected it as the last rays of the evening sun ran along its edge. "It's been a long, long time since blood touched this blade. I look forward to joining you in the hunt."

CHAPTER 23

Forest of Death

Leland stood on the catwalk within the trees, drenched in the pouring rain that had started falling just after dusk. Now, a few hours after midnight, the forest was silent and still as all eyes were pinned on the mountainside. According to Yetto's spies, Satrina and King Jerad had marched their troops into the mountain earlier that day. If he closed his eyes and blocked out the sound of his own beating heart, Leland could hear the groans of the mountain. Somehow, King Jerad's army was pushing its way through. By the sound of it, they would arrive at any moment.

Ip Toma Yetto could be seen down below, pacing behind the front ranks of his troops. Each member of the elven army was fitted with slick, thin, silver armor, a diamond-encrusted sword, and shield. When the clouds allowed it, the moonlight danced off the elven armor and briefly illuminated the scope of Yetto's forces. When the clouds covered the moon once again, the forest went dark.

At the sounds of falling rock, the army tensed up and prepared for war. Leland watched as a crack began to form along the large mountain barrier. The mountain shook and rumbled as the crack began to widen. It tore across the mountainside, ripping open the rock. Several elves along the catwalk, as well as on the ground, drew back the strings of their bows, training their first volley of arrows on the opening. Ip Toma Yetto raised his hand, waiting to give the command to fire. The hole in the rock wall continued to grow until it stopped at about the size of a standard doorway.

Leland stared in disbelief as the opening appeared before his eyes. What kind of magic could do such a thing? Still, Leland found himself more dumbfounded by the size of the opening. While the feat in itself was impressive, the doorway provided a very small and simple target that Yetto's forces could easily cover. Leland would have thought a more significant exit point would have been made for Jerad's forces. To Leland's dread, the mountainside suddenly erupted as massive chunks of rock the size of elephants were sent flying into the forest. The explosion shook the area as several of Yetto's forces took cover from the gigantic flying blocks of debris. When the dust settled, and the ear-shattering rumble of the mountain ceased, Leland could see the advancing army; a crescendo of war cries emitted out of the throat of the rock wall.

As Ip Toma Yetto signaled for the first volley of arrows to be released, several different elves began dipping their arrows into buckets of tar. Lighting the tar tips on fire, the elves shot the flaming arrows out into the night sky to shower down on the waves of Cainates that came spewing out of the giant opening. Some arrows dug deep into Cainate flesh, while others found their targets within the trenches dug between the mountainside and the forest. Large blankets of fire shot up from the tar filled trenches, engulfing the area in flame, lighting the pitch-black night, and limiting the direction King Jerad's army could flow.

"Kill them all!" Leland jumped down from his perch and joined the infantry ranks as Yetto's cry filled the night air. Leland lent his battle cry to surging roar of the elven army as they advanced as one upon King Jerad's forces. More arrows, some enflamed and some hiding within the darkness, overhead to pierce through the hearts of Cainates still emerging from the mountain. If not for the adrenaline pumping through his veins, causing all his senses to be hyper-focused and amped up to an incredible degree, Leland likely wouldn't have been able to make out half of what was happening in the battle.

Elven armor clashed with Cainate steel as the two opposing forces met on the battlefield like crashing waves. The elves moved with such swiftness, digging their blades into Cainate flesh, severing limbs, decapitating heads, and tossing bodies aside left and right. The Cainates, while not as large as their elven opponents, were just as quick and malicious as they descended upon the elves like rabid beasts craving for blood. Some used their weapons while others seemed to abandon all sense of civility as they gnashed their claws and teeth into anything that moved.

Leland watched as a Cainate pounced upon one of the elves, digging its fangs deep into the elf's neck and ripping out the throat. The Cainate's eyes shined in the dark, reflecting the flames, as it launched itself into the air toward its next target. Leland scaled a fallen body on the ground and hurled himself into the air to dig his sword through the Cainate's heart. As they both crashed to the ground, Leland pulled his sword free to swing around and block an attack.

Swiping the Cainate's sword away, Leland shoved the beast back and ran his sword into the Cainate's side. Dropping down to grab a dagger from the Cainate's belt, Leland spun around to throw it into the face of an approaching aggressor. The Cainate falls backward into the swarm of battle as Leland finds another target to pursue. A high-pitched whistle can be heard over the shouts of war, signaling the Cavalry to advance.

As Leland and the infantry continued to strike down anything in their path, horses and unicorns stormed through the chaos to trample over Jerad's forces in bulk. Leland could see Katrianna tearing into Cainates left and right as she swung her sword along either side of her unicorn, digging her blade deep before finding another body to strike. More Cainates began shooting up into the air to tackle the Cavalry riders. Some met their targets while others were shot down by arrows from the catwalks. Some of the larger Cainates focused their attacks on the horses themselves, attempting to dig their fangs and talons deep enough to rip out enough muscle and bring the steads down. Screams erupted from some of the steads as they were pulled down to the mud and torn to shreds, while others buried their hoofs into their assailants and carried forward.

Leland could see several men and women riding horseback within Jared's army. He assumed these were some kind of commanding officers. As they made their way out of the mountain and into the fight, Leland saw Yetto and some of his top lieutenants take notice. Leland watched as Yetto fought his way through the horde of Cainates to attack the nearest man on horseback. Yetto pierced his sword through a Cainate and threw the beast's body aside. He then ran up the side of another falling Cainate and jumped into the air toward one of King Jerad's generals. Before the man could react, Yetto's broad sword slices down through the man as well as through the horse's neck. Covered in the blood of his victims, Yetto roared in the faces of his enemies and continued to attack.

The battle raged on for hours as the Cainates kept flowing out of the mountain like roaches from a hole in the wall. The elven army was clearly growing tired, but a mix of momentum, adrenaline, fear, and rage kept them engaged in the fight. The Cainates began to abandon personal attacks as most of them posed little to no threat when matched one on one with an elf. Leland witnessed groups of Cainates group together to swarm and overpower their prey. One would dive for the knees, another would target the torso, several more would attack the upper body, and together they would pull down and rip apart the unfortunate elf.

Katrianna continued to ride Aubade through the pandemonium. Aubade's crisp white coat was drenched and matted in the blood and guts of any Cainate dumb enough to get in the way. As the Cainates banded together to attack their foes, it was only a matter of time before several became fixated on taking Katrianna down. Aubade was less of a target. Though large in frame, the unicorn was fast, strong, and quick to dig its alicorn through anyone that attempted harm.

Katrianna, on the other hand, could only fend off so many beasts flying in her direction. Slicing her sword through one Cainate reaching out to her on the left, Katrianna twisted to her right to run her sword through another Cainate gnashing its teeth at her throat. As the Cainate fell, Katrianna found her sword to be stuck and struggled to pull it free. Prying it loose, Katrianna swung her sword back to her left but was too slow to stop the growling beast from tackling her off the unicorn.

As she crashed down into the mud, Katrianna held her sword across her body, desperately trying to keep the Cainate's teeth out of range of her face. Katrianna elbowed the beast in the side of the head and rolled on top of it while she pulled out a dagger to slam down through the Cainate's head. She climbed to her feet in a puddle of blood and rainwater. The clouds above had cleared, but the ground was soaked and covered in mud and wet patches. Katrianna found her footing and swung her sword to block a blade to her left. Wearing armored gloves that covered her forearms to her fingertips, Katrianna reached out to claw across the Cainate's face before dropping down to twirl on her knee and dig her sword up through the beast's stomach.

Out of the corner of her eye, Katrianna could see several Cainates sprinting toward her, eager to dogpile on top of her. She grabbed the closest fallen Cainate's sword with both hands and threw it end over end into the chest of the first beast. Katrianna whipped around her own sword in hand, cutting everything nearby in half before sprouting her wings and lifting off the ground.

From the air, Katrianna could see her unicorn falling back to the safety of the forest. She could also see a few rows of Cainate archers firing streams of arrows back toward the elven catwalks. As the morning sun began to peek out over the mountains, Katrianna's wings caught the light, and she immediately realized how large of a target she was for several of the nearby archers. She twirled around in the air, as she tightly wrapped her wings around her to deflect several incoming arrows. After the first volley was unsuccessful in bringing her down, Katrianna shot upward out of any archer's range.

Leland heard the cries of Atsvi Hyaka from across

the battlefield. As he pulled his sword from the torso of a fallen Cainate, Leland followed Atsvi's eyesight to see a mob of Cainates tackle Ip Toma Yetto to the ground. Leland sprinted in Yetto's direction, striking down any enemy in his path. Having lost her horse, Atsvi started running toward the same destination from the opposite direction. Leland watched as Atsvi tore off her cloak to reveal mini crossbows attached to her arms. Sheathing her sword, Atsvi raced across the war zone toward her husband. A Cainate dove threw the air to tackle her, but Atsvi was too quick for it.

Dropping to the ground, Atsvi slid underneath her attacker and fired several mini arrows into its face. Back to her feet, Atsvi reached Yetto before Leland could and sprayed the top of the dog pile with all the arrows she had preloaded in her crossbows. Some of the Cainates rolled off the pile to their deaths, while a couple took notice and launched themselves toward Atsvi. Leland tackled one in the air and stabbed it repeatedly with his blade before the two hit the ground. With fewer Cainates on top of him, Yetto could be seen fighting off those closest to him. Leland and Atsvi worked together to kill as many of the mob as possible until Yetto was able to get to his feet and the slaughter the rest of them.

Yetto was covered, from head to toe, in gashes, bite marks, and stab wounds. Bleeding profusely, Yetto let out a sigh before momentarily dropping to his knees. Leland covered them as Atsvi dropped beside her husband and helped him back to his feet. In the distance, Leland could see a man and a woman sitting on horseback, watching the battle from the safety of the tunnel.

"There! I can see Satrina and the King!" Yetto growled and turned around to see the same thing. Before Yetto could call for his men to follow him, however, a horn sounded overhead. Leland looked around, trying to determine where it was coming from. "What is that? What does it mean?"

"It's not ours," said Atsvi. The horn sounded again as the Cainates began to fall back to the mountain. "They're retreating!"

Leland finally found the source of the sound, one of the King's generals blew into his horn as he turned his horse around and fled back into the tunnels. The elves began picking off what Cainates they could without following them into the mountain. The Cainate archers released their last arrows, showering the area and allowing their troops to withdraw. Leland could no longer see the King or Satrina, but he did see several Cainates launching spears out of the tunnel to ward off Yetto's troops from following. Giant beasts hurled the spears through the air.

Most dug deep into the ground as if drawing a line in the dirt that the elves shouldn't cross. Other spears found their mark, falling from the sky with enough momentum to impale several elves and pin them to the earth. Leland took cover, but not before noticing that several of the Cainates began looking to the skies and chucking their lances higher and harder toward the clouds. Leland's eyes followed the flight path of the spears into the sun until he saw Katrianna flying in and out of the sunlight, dodging what flying spikes she could. To Leland's horror, one of the spears struck through, breaking through the veil of Katrianna's wings and piercing her through the chest.

"Katrianna!" Leland ran out across the battlefield as the final arrows and spears dug into the earth around him. Overhead, Katrianna was clearly struggling to stay airborne. As she began to drop, Leland jumped over bodies, pushed aside Cainates struggling to get to their feet, and sprinted across the mud to get under her. Katrianna's wings finally gave out, causing her to plummet to the earth. Unable to cover the distance in time, Leland was forced to watch his love hit the ground with a hard ***thud!*** Several Cainates crawled towards the fallen princess, ripping through her feathery wings with their claws. "Get away from her you sons of bitches!"

Leland dug his sword through the spine of one Cainate and threw his dagger into the right eye of another. He grabbed the back of another Cainate and tossed it aside, retrieving his sword and sending it back down into another beast. When he had cleared the area, Leland slid down to the side of Katrianna and pulled her up into his arms.

Her wings dripped with blood as the spear had punctured out her back. Katrianna spat up a glob of blood as she looked up at Leland and smiled through dark red teeth. She tried to speak but struggled as more blood flowed out of the corners of her mouth. Leland broke down in tears as she touched her face and tried to comfort her.

"It's ok; it's alright. You'll be fine." Leland didn't know what to say and didn't know what to do. The strong hoofs of Aubade dug into the earth next to Leland as the unicorn neighed and grunted to get Leland's attention. Understanding, Leland broke off the long end of the spear and then picked Katrianna up off the ground to place her on the unicorn's back. The unicorn turned and sprinted off toward the tree line, towards the medic camp where the fairies had been working on the wounded throughout the night. Leland turns back to see the mountain crumbling apart, sealing the giant hole and covering the retreat of King Jerad's troops. Unable to avenge his love's attacker, unable to chase after King Jared, unable to do anything but hope the fairies can save Katrianna, Leland dropped to his knees and screamed at the top of his lungs.

****

She tried to hang on, she decided to keep her eyes open and her mind away, but everything felt like it was closing in on her. The world around was hazy, as Katrianna struggled to process the sounds around her. As the unicorn galloped across the blood-soaked battlefield, Katrianna could focus on nothing by the stream of blood flowing out of her body and down Aubade's coat. The ground was covered with bodies, many of them staring up in death, they all bared witness as Katrianna was carried over them and into the forest.

She could barely hear the fairies and the elven healers as they removed her armor and ripped open her shirt to address the wound. Katrianna felt as if her soul was being yanked out from within her when they removed the spear from her ribs. She fought to breathe through her tears, through her pain, through the blood in her lungs. Multiple people stood over her, their hands upon her, their sweat and tears dripping to her, as they tried to save her. Her head was turned to the side as they tried to clear the blood from her airway. She longed to see Leland's face one more time, but she knew she wouldn't last that long. As her body began to shake, Katrianna lost all ability to process her own thoughts and emotions as she drowned in her own blood.

CHAPTER 24

Crestside
Prisoner Camp

King Jerad walked through the prisoner camp, looking at the remnants of his army as they ate, drank, and conversed about the battle. It had taken them half a day to march back out of the mines. His twelve-hundred Cainate army had been reduced to a mere three hundred. He looked at each of them in disgust, still not sure why they had surrendered when so many of them still stood. Satrina was nowhere to be found, but Jerad quickly found the table with the remaining generals. He had started with twenty, and now ten sat at the table drinking their cares away. He walked up in the middle of the group laughing at a joke.

"Do you think this is funny?" Jerad leaned in and swatted away a goblet of beer from one of the generals. "You lost the battle today! Then you turned tail and ran! I saw their numbers. We might have had closer to three times the army they had, and yet each of you failed to secure a victory for your King. So, tell me what is so funny?"

"Our apologies, my liege." The closest general bent down his head as he addressed the King. "We are definitely disappointed in the loss today, and we know that we failed you. We were only trying to burn off a bit of steam."

"Oh, I understand. Really I do." Jerad's sarcastic tone did not go unnoticed as he plopped down at the table. "You all deserve some relaxation after a hard day's work. I look out across this camp and see at least three hundred Cainates taking a load off. Now, if we still had three hundred well-bodied Cainates, then why the hell did we retreat? I sure as hell don't remember giving the order."

“We fought for you, King Jerad, and for Crestside, but we had other orders to consider,” said another one of the generals. Jerad jumped up at the comment and stepped closer to the general that spoke.

“Excuse me? What the hell did you just say? You had OTHER ORDERS?” The generals all kept their heads down, several of them shaking their heads at the one that had spoken. Jerad grabbed the general and shoved his head down upon the table as he took out a dagger and stabbed it into the wood by the man’s face. “Pray tell, what other orders were you given?”

“We were told to pull back if the battle wasn’t going in our favor. Satrina didn’t want to leave you or Crestside defenseless. Had we stayed, all of your armies would have been killed and you wouldn’t have anyone left to defend your throne back home.” Jerad shook his head and walked around the table, flipping his knife back and forth in his hand.

“No, no, there’s more to it than that. I refuse to believe that your secret set of orders were purely for my benefit.” Jerad grabbed one of the female generals by the hair and slammed her face down on the table. Stabbing the knife next to her face, he sneered at the rest of her comrades. “What else? What other orders were you given? Tell me, or I swear I’ll put each and every one of you in the ground.”

“Your majesty, please!” One of the generals stood up from his seat, arms out in the air, to reason with the King. Jerad raised an eyebrow as he hovered his dagger over the female general’s head. “We did not conspire against you in any way. We thought you were aware of Satrina’s agenda. She rode by your side.”

“Speak up. What agenda?” The general sighed as he quickly glanced at his fellow generals, many of whom seemed to glare at him for speaking. Jerad snapped his fingers to regain the general’s attention. “Tell me!”

“We only lost the battle today because Satrina commanded many of our forces to refrain from killing the enemy. They were only to wound the enemy” Jerad frowned in confusion as he stared at the general and then around the table.

“What? That.. that doesn’t make sense. I saw your soldiers unleash hell upon those elves. I saw the true rabid behavior of the Cainates on the battlefield.” The general shook his head at Jerad's words.

"Not all of our troops were given these commands, but enough of them were. We didn't want to look weak in battle, so a small amount of our army was, as you said, unleashed. The rest had orders to disable the enemy, but not kill them. I believe the victory would have been yours had our forces not been held back by such an order." Jerad reached across the table and grabbed the general by the throat.

"Even if this is true, why would Satrina give you such an order? The elves aren't the only inhabitants in the Garden. If Satrina was hoping to gift me with more servants, there are apparently plenty of other creatures on that side of the mountain. Why would she risk losing the battle just to ensure that I'd have elf slaves at the end?" The general struggled to breathe until Jerad released him. The general choked on the air as he gasped for air. "Answer me before I grab you again."

"She didn't plan to gift the elves to you. Any magical creatures that we apprehended, wounded or not, were to be shackled and shipped west. Satrina planned to sell them. She never intended any of the Garden residents to become new citizens of your

Kingdom. The journey west is a long one. Dead bodies, magical or not, would rot by the time they reached their destination, rendering them useless to any market." Jared stepped back.

"So, all this time, Satrina wasn't at all interested in expanding my Kingdom? She wasn't planning on burning the Garden to the ground? Instead, she was planning on enslaving the inhabitants and taking them away to make a profit? And she was merely using my armies to acquire what she couldn't claim herself." Jared clenched his fists in rage. "And all of you actually followed these orders, allowing three-quarters of my army to perish in the process?"

Jerad pulled out his sword and cut down the general who had been so willing to fill him in on Satrina's plans. He pointed his sword to the rest of the generals. He stared into the eyes of each of them.

"From now on, you will obey my commands, and my commands only. Rest assured this war is not over. We must be prepared for the Garden to strike back. Gather the army and move camp to the fields in front of the castle. I want them close should an attack occur." Jerad sheathed his sword and turned to leave.

He stopped and turned back to the group, pointing at each of them. "I expect your complete allegiance. Should you choose to flea Crestside, I will have you hunted down, castrated, and dragged back here to feed to my pigs."

CHAPTER 25

The Garden

The morning sun shined down upon the Garden, lighting the treetops, breaking through the fog, and illuminating each and every drop of dew. The valley was quiet, save for the chirping of birds, the murmurs of trees swaying in the gentle breeze, and the soft crashing of waves along the river stream.

Leland waded out into the waters, solemnly, slowly, with a large group of individuals standing on the shore behind him. Every fairy, every mermaid, every unicorn stood and watched him. On the other side of the water, between the trees, several elves stood in silence. Ip Toma Yetto, wrapped in numerous bandages and wearing a sling, stood next to his wife as they peered out across the water at Leland.

Leland took his time as he walked out into the depths of the stream, coming to a stop when the water rose up to his waist. Rose petals and other flowers floated all around him, covering the water top with beautiful colors and shapes. His hands shaking, Leland held onto the corners of the coffin as it floated in front of him. His tears flowed down his cheeks and dripped into the water below as Leland held on tight to the wooden box that held his love.

Katrianna had died on a table hundreds of yards away from him on the day of the battle. He had not been able to hold her hand, to comfort her in her final moments. He had not been able to tell her how much he loved her, how much she meant to him. He had not been there to wipe away her tears, to clean her face, to help her breathe. She had died alone, and now he too was alone without her.

With all the magical creatures, all the wonder, and awe that existed in this Garden, Leland wondered where Katrianna was now. In the prisoner camps, the elderly prayed to God. They believed in an afterlife, in a place called Heaven. Leland didn't know enough about it to believe it himself, but he desperately wanted to. He wondered if that's where Katrianna was now. If so, perhaps he would one day be there as well. Would he find her there, walking the last corridors of the great beyond?

Would she even recognize him, or does one not take the memories of this life with them? He could not imagine an afterlife without her, and that only made his current reality that much harder to process. Having spent almost every day with her since he escaped his personal hell at the prisoner camp, Leland had grown accustomed to her face, to her voice, to her presence. Where would he go now? What purpose would he have on the earth? His head was full of questions, his heart was full of pain, and his soul was trapped somewhere in between.

The current surged around Leland, the water washing over his hands, slipping between his fingers, loosening his grip. Suddenly the coffin pulled away from him in the water. Leland reached out for it, trying to grab it once more. He attempted to swim after it, but the current pushed it farther away from him. He cried aloud, sobbing into the water around him as he stood and watched Katrianna float away from him. The flowers chased after the coffin as they flowed farther and farther away, eventually disappearing out of view. He hung his head and stood in the river, alone with his thoughts.

When he finally walked ashore, the crowd had dispersed to allow him to mourn. He sat down and stared out at the water. The elves had disappeared back into their forest, but Ip Toma Yetto and Atsvi Hayaka remained. Eventually, they walked across the river and joined him on the northern shore. Atsvi gave her condolences and then stepped away to visit with the fairies. Ip Toma Yetto sat down next to Leland and looked out at the flowing stream.

"The Princess fought valiantly yesterday; you both did. I am sorry the healers couldn't save her life." Leland nodded but didn't respond. "We elves have lived alone for centuries. We abandoned our fellow creatures of magic. We blame humanity on all of our hardships. We acted as if we were alone in suffering. I am grateful, every day that Asielle found us and brought us here, but on this morning I can only think of how many magical creatures that weren't so lucky.

"Satrina comes from a dark side of the world where creatures like me are brutalized. She, and others like her, have profited off the torment and torture of magical creatures for hundreds of years. They are the enemy, the true evil of the world." Yetto sighed and looked over at Leland. "Anyone who is willing to pick up a sword and put their life on the line to oppose that evil, should be welcome in my home and recognized as a friend to my people.

"I am sorry, Leland Clayton. I am sorry for how I treated you, how I treated the Princess for years, and how my people have behaved in this new Garden. We should be allied with every other creature that lives here instead of standing apart. I'm sorry that you lost your love, but know that my people will not forget the example she set, and the sacrifice she made so that this Garden could remain." Ip Toma Yetto reached out and put his hand on Leland's shoulder. He then stood up and joined his wife as they headed back across the river.

"This isn't over." Leland stood up. Yetto turned

around to listen to him. “We won the battle, but the fight isn’t over. Satrina remains, King Jerad remains, and many of their Cainate forces remain. That’s too many ill-intentioned people with knowledge of this place. That can’t stand, and you know it.”

“I do.” Ip Toma Yetto looked at his wife and nodded. “Mourn for your loss today. Come find me tomorrow, and we will discuss it further. The elves won’t abandon you in this fight. The Garden must be protected, even if that means stepping outside of it to destroy those that would harm it.”

CHAPTER 26

Aldiss Castle

It had been three days since Jerad had seen Satrina. The Cainate army had set up camp in front of the castle, the generals had scouts in the hills looking for signs of an attack, and the King found himself constantly on edge. He was enraged to know this his mother had used him, but he needed every ounce of help he could get. He knew an attack was pending, and he hated the wait.

During the battle, Jared had seen the totality of the elven army's bloodlust. While the rapidness of the

Cainate knew no rival, Jared saw the elves to be nothing but the most effective killers he'd ever laid eyes on. They could shoot an arrow, throw a dagger, or wield a sword so fluidly that most of the Cainates didn't stand a chance. If by some stroke of luck, a Cainate had managed to disarm an elf, the elf still had its fangs and claws to wage war with. The Cainates, while vicious and cruel, felt tame when pitted against an enraged elf.

Jared had also seen the Clayton boy on the battlefield. Though Leland didn't quite match up to the size or veracity of his elven comrades, Jared noticed how well Leland held his own in the battle. Leland was the only human Jared witnessed in the battle, so he figured Thomas Clayton had died some time ago. Jared wanted nothing more than to end the Clayton line by engaging Leland in battle, and part of him wished Leland would attempt an attack on the castle. If there was even the slightest chance that some of those elves followed Leland over the mountains and into Crestside, Jared knew he needed Satrina's help to survive.

More than several of the castle's staff had been reported missing over the past day or so. Jared didn't pay it much mind at first, but now he was beginning to believe Satrina had something to do with it. He searched everywhere in the castle, checking every room, every hideaway, every dark corner, but came up with nothing. Finally, he made his way down into the catacombs beneath the castle grounds and knew that this is where Satrina had been hiding.

From the moment Jared entered the tunnels leading to the catacombs, he could smell the stench of death. He lit a torch and walked down the long, dark, dirty tunnel until it opened to the large room where his ancestors had been buried. The walls were lined with the bones of his relatives, and in the middle of the room, surrounded by the bones, blood, and organs of at least ten bodies, Satrina sat on her knees.

"Satrina?" The woman was bent over, bowing, as she had strung up four bodies on makeshift crosses hung in front of her. One body had been castrated, one had been decapitated, one had no arms or legs, and the last body had been stripped of its flesh entirely. On the ground near Satrina were several bowls, some containing body parts, and organs, some containing the ground-up dust of bones, and others were filled to the brim with blood. As Jared stepped closer he could hear the faintest of sounds coming from his mother. She was praying, chanting, speaking tongues of some dark language into the earth.

Jared circled around to see Satrina from the front. Her head faced toward him, but her eyes were pure black, and she didn't seem to react at all to his presence. Her face was pasty and covered in white powder that Jared guessed was from the bowl of ground-up bones. Jared sat down on the ground and watched for hours as Satrina chanted over and over again. The chants would only cease for a moment here and there when Satrina would feast on an organ, or inhale the bone powder, or drink from the blood bowls.

Sometimes Satrina's chants were barely louder than a whisper, while other times Jared had to cover his ears at the volumes of her screams. Jared watched Satrina's body morph back and forth between an old woman, a middle-aged woman, and a young girl. Her skin decayed and rejuvenated, her bones cracked, her veins rippled across her body. Jerad noticed a breeze enter the catacombs from some unknown source.

His torch snuffed out, Jared found himself sitting in the dark. Satrina had stopped her chanting, and the space was eerily quiet. A spark lit up the middle of the room, as the four crosses began to ignite themselves. The heat became intense as the four were lit aflame. The fire grew until it licked the vaulted ceiling. Jerad shielded his eyes from the heat but peered through the flames to see Satrina's eyes glowing white as she stared at him and smiled. Just as abruptly as they started, the crosses quickly doused themselves, and the room was once again dark.

The room was engulfed in a cloud of smoke that scorched Jerad's insides. He tried to peer through the darkness, but the smoke only burned his eyes. Jerad coughed and choked on the smoke until suddenly his torch became lit once again and the room was clear of any fire or smoke for that matter. Jared repeatedly coughed as he massaged his throat and stared down at the torch in his hand, not sure how the fire had returned. He then looked up to see Satrina standing over him.

"Aagh!" Jared screamed and hollered as he tried to back away from her, but Satrina was quick to reach out and grab him. She leaned in close, her eyes back to normal, her fangs retracted, and smiled at Jared.

"Come, my son. Let's get you out of here." Satrina took Jerad by the hand and guided him out of the catacombs. When they reached the surface, the sun bearing down on them, Jerad dropped to his knees in the dirt and gasped. As the clean air filled his lungs, Jerad wiped the soot that had caked around his eyes. He looked up at Satrina who seemed to be enjoying herself in the sunlight.

"What was that?" Satrina didn't answer, but looked down at Jerad and smiled. She pulled him up to his feet and proceeded to dust him off.

"Hush now, my child. You don't want your people to see their King distraught." Jerad looked around to see several of his servants staring in his direction.

"What are you all staring at? Get back to work," Jerad yelled out at them. The servants quickly jumped back into their work and dispersed from the area. Jerad righted himself and looked back at Satrina. "Tell me."

"My apologies if I scared you, my King. I was performing a ritual and was unaware of your presence." Satrina looked down at herself to see that she was naked and covered in dirt, blood, and bone dust. "Look at me. I must have ripped apart that fancy dress your tailor-made for me. Allow me to clean up, and then meet me in front of the castle. If there is a chance of an attack from the Garden, I need to prepare what remains of your army."

Jerad stumbled over to a trough of water and splashed his face with it. He wasn't sure how long he had been down in those catacombs, watching Satrina perform her ritual, but his body was aching all over. He watched as Satrina walked off down a corridor, only to stop abruptly and return to him.

"Inform the generals that they need to procure some livestock for me. Take one bull and one male horse from every farm in the Kingdom. They need to arrive no later than this evening." Jared nodded as Satrina turned back around and walked away. While he had no idea what the livestock was for, Jared knew this wasn't the time for him to argue.

****

Later That Evening

As the sun began to set on Crestside, King Jerad

stood next to Satrina outside the castle walls. Some three hundred Cainates had formed a single line. At least twenty large bulls and thoroughbred horses had been gathered and were corralled in a small fenced-in area nearby. Satrina called for the first bull to be brought out. One of the generals brought the bull over, pulling it by a rock, and secured it to a post that had been stuck in the ground.

"Your army may now be small in numbers, but I can build them up to be stronger than they've ever been." Satrina stepped forward and motioned for the first Cainate to approach and kneel before her. Jared stayed back and watched. "All they need is some borrowed muscle."

Satrina stepped between the Cainate and the bull. She placed her hand on the bull's hide and dug her fingernails into it. The bull bellowed out in pain but was frozen in place. Its legs buckled as the bull crashed down to the ground. As blood ran down the side of the bull, Satrina dug her fingers deeper. Finally, Satrina pulled her hand out of the bull, a large chunk of meat within her grasp.

She then turned to the Cainate and smothered

and spread the meat across the Cainate's back. She chanted into the air, hissed and moaned as she massaged the meat against the Cainate. Jared watched in amazement as the meat penetrated the Cainate's skin. The Cainate groaned as its muscles began to expand. When Satrina was finished, the Cainate had doubled in size. Satrina called for the next in line as she pulled another chunk of meat from the bull to repeat the process.

Several hours later, Jerad had watched Satrina brutalize all of the bulls and switch to the large horses until she had transformed his entire Cainate army. As the last Cainate stumbled back to the camp, Jerad watched as Satrina struggled to get back to her feet. Just as he had witnessed in the mines before the attack on the Garden, Jeradd saw that Satrina was weak. Her dark ritual must have restored just enough magic for her to perform this task.

Jerad dismissed his generals and helped his mother to her feet. Satrina held onto him as they walked back to the castle. Jerad noticed his mother to a bit dazed, but the longer they walked, the more she regained her wits. Thankfully for Jerad, Satrina didn't seem to notice that he had been guiding her down to the dungeons instead of back to her quarters. When they reached the cell, Jerad tossed her in and closed the gate behind her. Satrina hit the ground hard and then looked around her. When she realized where she was, she frowned up at Jerad.

"What is this?"

"Now that you've secured my victory, should Leland and the Garden attack, I can address your betrayal." Jerad leaned against the bars. Satrina snickered as she crawled towards him.

"Excuse me?"

"Your generals told me everything. I know all about your plans, you conniving bitch." Satrina lunged at Jerad, clawing for him through the bars, but Jerad quickly stepped back out of range.

"What did you call me?" Satrina pulled herself up by the bars.

"I didn't stutter." Jerad leaned back against the dungeon walls across from the cell. "You used me, you used my army, you conspired against this Kingdom, and to top it all off, you lost! Had the battle been won, a deal could have been made to split the spoils, but you had no interest in that. You spent all that time spinning lies about getting your revenge and escalating my reign. You were going to cart off as many magical creatures as you could find and make a fortune, while I would be left with nothing for my trouble. You lied and conspired to steal from me. Deny it!"

"Steal? From you?" Satrina gripped the bars and pressed her head against them as she glared at Jared. "What do you own that I didn't give to you? Did I not gather a Cainate force for you to command? Did I not acquire generals to serve under your reign? They were my armies, my Cainates, and mine to let die if their deaths served my cause. I conspired nothing. I took what was mine, and you should count yourself lucky I didn't decide to claim your life as well." Jerad sprang forward and pushed Satrina back hard enough to send her crashing to the floor of her cell.

"I know what's happening here. I can tell that you're weak. You depleted your dark magic in the tunnels, and you depleted it again just now in the fields. You may still appear youthful for now, but I can tell you're not near as powerful as you've been before. Tell me I'm wrong."

"How dare you touch me. How dare you accuse me of anything other than giving you your life and everything in it! I'm just as powerful as the day you met me, and you best watch how you speak to me, boy." Satrina rose to her feet and pointed at Jerad as she warned him. Jerad reached through the bars, grabbed her by her hand, and pulled her to him. He clenched her by the throat and pulled her firmly to the bars of the cell.

"Prove it, mother! Strike me down, right here, right now. Use that magical strength and speed of yours that I witnessed when you killed my father's men all those years ago. Cast a spell on me. Obliterate me to pieces. DO IT!" Satrina hissed and flashed her fangs at Jerad but quickly retracted them when Jerad tightened his grip on her throat. "I thought so. What purpose do I have for a powerless witch?"

"You stupid, selfish, insolent brat! I have destroyed tens of thousands of men greater than you. No man has ever crossed me and lived to tell of it. No King has ever disrespected me as you just have." Satrina struggled against Jerad's grip, but couldn't pull away "No son of mine would dare treat me this way!"

"No?" Jerad slid his hand up her neck to grip Satrina by her face. He wrenched her jaw open and, with a quick slice of his blade, Jerad cut Satrina's tongue from her mouth and threw it to the floor. "Well, no mother of mine will speak."

CHAPTER 27

Crestside
A Day Later

Leland peered down at the village in the center of Crestside from his perch in the trees. He watched the men and women going about their days, and wondered what his life would have been like had he accepted his fate and did as the warden had saidd. He would have learned a worthy craft, he would have been a hardworking servant of the community, and he would have had to learn how to exist under King Jerad's rule. Though he was happy that these men and women had found a way to make their lives work in a horrible situation, he was thankful that he had chosen another path.

"That's the main village. It looks like more of the Cainates have joined the army ranks and left the townspeople to themselves for now. To the south is the mining camp, where King Jerad had marched his army through to your forest. There's a bunch of farmland to the west. Then there's a large field to the north before you reach the King's castle." Leland turned to Ip Toma Yetto, who crouched down on the massive tree branch next to him. Yetto had taken Leland over the mountains via the path that the elven spies frequented when relaying information about Crestside. The path let out about midway between the mines and the northern passage Leland had used.

"That's where my spies said the army is currently camping. That is where we will meet them in combat. They still have a few hundred Cainates, but that shouldn't be an issue for my brethren. I've brought eighty elves with me. The rest have remained in the Garden. The bulk of my people need to remain on our side of the mountains, but this small group should do the trick." Yetto sharpened his dagger as he sat in the tree. "Do you have a preference on when we attack? I would rather get this done sooner than later."

"I agree, but there's something we must do first. Your fight is with Satrina, King Jared, and their army. It is not with the Kingdom of Crestside. Those people in the village, the farmers, and the prisoners at the mining camp have suffered under Jerad's rule for decades. They need to know that you are not an invading force, but an avenging one. While your eighty elves could likely slaughter the Cainates with ease, you should not deny the citizens of Crestside. They have a stake in this as well and should be allowed to fight alongside us." Yetto didn't seem very convinced, but he allowed Leland to continue. "Allow me to take ten elves to the mines. We will free the prisoners and kill any Cainate stationed there. You can then join us on the road as we escort the prisoners into town. We will slaughter any Cainates still in the village, and make a call to arms for any human willing to grab a weapon and fight for their Kingdom. We will them assemble overnight and attack at daybreak."

"Did you not run away from this land, from these humans, when you came to the Garden? You appeared to be fine, at the time, to abandon them to their enslavement. What changed?" Yetto leaned against the tree trunk and waited for an answer.

"I was a wanted man, and I ran because my life was in danger. You're right, though, I had no plans of returning or finding a way to free my fellow man. I might have been a prisoner, a slave, like everyone else, but I didn't feel like this place was my home. I didn't feel any loyalty or sense of duty to the people of Crestside." Leland looked out at the town and the people within it. "Seeing the community your people have built in the Garden, the sanctity of that place, made me wish that I could help these people who have been forced to live under a tyrant's reign for far too long. My father fought for these people, and I should honor him by doing the same. I'm not just here to kill Jerad for taking Katrianna from me. I will gain nothing from that act but provisional satisfaction. This fight has to be about more than that, and so I choose to fight for the freedom of these people, and the continued safety of yours. You agreed to come this far, Ip Toma Yetto. Let me do this."

"You have much passion within you, Leland. I

will not stand in the way of your redemption." Yetto smiled and nodded. "I'll grant you five elves to take to the mines. They will then accompany you into town afterward. The rest of my elves will remain hidden until the early morning, where we will join you on the battlefield. I'll be interested to see how sizable a force you are able to recruit."

****

The road to the prisoner camp was barren. From their earlier reconnaissance, Leland knew that there were still several guards who remained to watch over the prisoners. Through the mines had collapsed, most of the prisoners had still been forced to move rock and dig into the mountain like they had every previous day before. Why King Jerad continued to punish these people were beyond Leland's understanding. While many of the prisoners were middle-aged when they were first sentenced, and now were likely too old to join Yetto's forces, Leland knew there were some that could fight. More importantly, he knew that it wouldn't be right to attack the castle without liberating the people first.

Once satisfied that the area was clear, no Cainate

attack parties hiding in the trees, Leland gave the signal for the elves to take the road. As the five elves rode their horses out from the tree line, Leland heard Aubade neigh beside him as the unicorn stomped its hoofs into the ground. Leland pulled himself up onto the saddle as the two headed onto the road to catch up with the elves. The six of them started with a light trot as they headed toward the camp gates, which stood at least twenty feet high.

"You there. Stop where you are!" A Cainate could see Leland and the elves as he looked through a small peephole in the gate. "In the name of the King, that's far enough."

The elves and their horses advanced on the gate, now galloping at top speed as they raced down the road toward the gate. Leland and Aubade chased after them as Leland pulled out his sword. Two of the elves charged ahead of the group as they threw several long daggers into the wood of the gates. At the last moments of their approach, the horses each came to an immediate stop, launching the elves into the air. The two elves scaled the gates with ease, using the daggers as stepping stones to assist with the climb. The two elves dropped down behind the barrier with daggers in hand, and moments later, the gates swung open.

Leland led the charge as he and Aubade stormed into the camp. At the sight of invaders, several Cainate guards jumped up to attack with whatever they had in hand. Leland slashed his sword down across the neck of one guard and then turned to his other side to dig his sword into the chest of another. Leland could see a large group of Cainates huddled around the fighting pit, seemingly unaware of the attack. As he and the elves had not made much noise in the charge, Leland wasn't necessarily surprised. Leland rode toward the group and shouted at the top of his lungs.

"Your champion has returned!" Leland jumped off his horse and tackled as many of the Cainates as he could. Swinging his sword around, Leland got to his feet and stabbed the closest guard to him. He kicked one guard in the stomach and turned to punch another one with the hilt of his sword. Two elves joined the mix and growled as they began to tear into the Cainate group. Leland kicked another guard down and moved to slash his sword down upon the Cainate, when a whip suddenly wrapped around Leland's arm and wrist, preventing him from doing so.

Leland gritted his teeth at the sting of the whip, remembering every time he had felt its licks before. He spun around and stepped toward the guard. The Cainate cracked the whip and then swung it toward Leland again. Leland caught the whip with his sword, allowing it to wind and tangle all around it. Leland spun around, pulling the whip away from the guard while taking out a dagger to dig deep into the Cainate by the time Leland faced him again. Leland bent down and grabbed the keys from the guard's belt and walked back to the fighting pit. Stepping over all of the dead Cainate bodies, Leland grabbed the small ladder and dropped it down into the pit.

"You there. Stop fighting amongst yourself and help me." The two prisoners climbed out of the pit and looked around to see their fallen jailors. Leland handed each of them a sword and gave one of them the keys. "Go to the tent and unlock everyone's chains. We'll take care of the rest of the guards. I want all the prisoners gathered by the front gate as quickly as possible."

Leland and the elves dispensed of the rest of the Cainates in the camp, killing anything they came across. Leland rode up to the warden's cabin and broke down the door. He walked through the seemingly empty home, remembering his first moments inside the warden's quarters. He slowly inched down the back hallway, checking every room. When he finally made it to the backroom, Leland found a large Cainate, apparently the current warden, asleep in a tub of filth. The sound of Leland's boots on the wooden floor woke the warden, but the Cainate could not reach for his weapon before Leland's sword was buried into his chest. Leland pulled free his blade and let the warden bleed out in the tub as he exited the cabin and headed for the crowd of prisoners that had formed by the front gates.

"Good evening, fellow prisoners of Crestside. My name is Leland Clayton, though some of you might remember me as Prisoner 452. I hereby release you from your enslavement. You have suffered for too long at the hands of a false king. I have found friends from beyond the mountains to aide us in taking back this Kingdom, but we need all the help we can get. My friends and I will escort you back to the village tonight where you can reconnect with your friends and loved ones and find shelter. In the morning, we will attack the castle, and I am hoping some of you more able-bodied men and women will be willing to join us."

Leland looked out at the former prisoners, recognizing many of them as the people he had fought in the pits, scavenged for food with, or served beside in the mines. They were tired and broken, so much so that they stood in silence before Leland and the elves without the strength to even celebrate their liberation from the camp. Leland wondered if it was too much to ask any of these people to fight, knowing precisely the hell they've all been through.

"Hey!" A man pushed forward through the crowd. He stopped and stared at the unicorn for a moment before addressing Leland. "I've been digging tunnels and slinging rock in those mines for the past twenty damn years!"

"I know you have." Leland nodded down at the man. The former prisoner looked at the crowd and turned back to Leland. He pointed up at Leland.

"Well, I didn't do all that work for nothing! So, you better believe I'm able-bodied enough to kill some of those filthy Cainates. To hell with them!" The crowd cheered behind the man and Leland raised an eyebrow and smiled. He looked over to the elves who nodded and laughed. The man reached down and grabbed a dagger from the hand of a fallen Cainate. "Well what the hell are we waiting for?"

CHAPTER 28

Crestside
The Next Morning

Leland stood on the edge of the great field, a good mile or so from the castle. A morning fog blanketed the space just enough to separate Leland's group from the Cainate troops. He knew they were there, armed and already standing in formation, waiting for Leland to make the first move. The elves stood ready to attack, while the people of Crestside were knelt down to the ground, praying for strength and endurance. Leland watched them for a moment as he stood off to the side. He was thankful to have them there, to have the elves there, but wished Katrianna was there with him. Believing he had nothing to lose, and knowing they needed all the help they could get, Leland stepped away, walking off to his own spot in the fog, and knelt down to the ground.

"I don't know what to call you. Lord, your holiness, father… those names all sound disingenuous since I've never spoken to you before. For years, I hated the idea that you existed. If true, it meant to me that you had allowed all my misfortunes to occur. You allowed my mother to die, and my father to be banished. You allowed me to be beaten and broken, time and time again, for years. You offered me a sliver of grace when I found the Garden and fell in love with Katrianna. Then you took her from me as well.

"Perhaps you're nothing more than a puppeteer, pulling our strings for your own selfish entertainment. Perhaps you are the opposite, so much so that you feel it would be wrong to intervene in our lives, even when times are hard. You clearly have followers here in Crestside; men and women who have truly suffered, but continue to believe in you, to pray to you, to beg for your help. If you do exist, I ask that you consider their pleas and show favor upon us as we advance on those that seek to spread evil across the world you created. I hope you exist because that would mean that Katrianna might now be in a better place than this. Perhaps, on the day that I die, I'll find out for myself."

Leland rose to his feet and returned to the battle line. He called for Aubade and pulled himself up on top the unicorn. He rode up and down the line, looking at every elf, man and woman that had chosen to appear. In the night, Leland and the former prisoners had convinced several families to take up arms and join in the fight. At least one hundred people now stood willing and ready to fight. Blacksmiths, bakers, farmers, and more gripped their pitchforks, knives, hammers in hand as well as any other weapon that could be found. They looked up to Leland as he came to a stop to address them.

"Citizens of Crestside. Thank you for standing beside us. Do not think ill of those that chose to stay behind. None of you should be made to fight. Each and every one of you deserves justice and freedom from the tyrannical rule of Jerad Aldiss and his Cainate horde. You've all been through hardship. You've all suffered at the hands of the king that shows no love or care for any of you. You don't deserve the sentences you've lived out over the past twenty years.

"On the other side of that field is King Jerad's last stand. A week ago, the elves that stand next to you wiped out over 900 hundred of Jared's forces. Jared was a fool to try to invade their lands, and now they've come to help you win back yours." Leland raised his sword in the air. "Citizens of Crestside, I have seen many magical things, but nothing stirs my heart more than seeing each and every one of you here, now, ready to take back what King Jerad stole from you. I commend you, and I'm proud to fight beside you!"

The crowd raised their weapons in the air and cheered. Leland rode his unicorn across their line, tapping his sword against each of their weapons, cheering with them. He then stopped his unicorn at the center point in front of their lines. He nodded to Ip Toma Yetto who signaled for his troops to form ranks in front of the villagers. The elves would strike first, but the people would be hot on their heels to join the fight. Twenty of the elves sat on horseback on either side of Leland. Yetto rode up next to Leland and nodded.

"Good speech." Leland smiled and looked forward as the morning sun began to dissipate the fog bit by bit.

The elves began to chant, starting at a whisper and rising slowly. Across the field, Leland began to see the outline of Jerad's Cainate force. He saw several men and women, Jerad's generals, riding their horses up and down the Cainate lines. The sky was cloudy above, but enough of the sun's rays peeked through to clear up the fog. As the foggy blanket lifted, Leland's eyes widened at the sight of the Cainates. These were not the same beasts they had fought in the forest or at the prisoner camp. Their deformed bodies had doubled in mass, and they now stood taller and wider, almost as large as the elves. Even from his distance, Leland could see the size of their claws and the length of their gnashing fangs. They wore no armor and held no weapons. The roared and dug at the earth, like caged beasts aching to be set free upon Leland and his army. Leland looked over at Yetto.

"This must be the work of Satrina." Yetto just smiled as he bared his teeth and continued to stare across the field at his enemies.

"She's desperate, Leland. She knew we'd cut through her remaining ranks like butter. She's scared, and she's hiding somewhere in the castle behind that horde. I mean to kill every one of those creatures and then storm the gates to find that witch." He looked over at Leland with bloodlust in his eyes. "We shall claim our victory this day."

"Leland Clayton!" Leland faced forward at the sound of his name. Sitting on a large stead in front of the Cainates, King Jerad stretched his arms out beside him. "Your pitiful gathering of peasants and lost creatures does not frighten me. I am thankful to you for bringing them here to die. I'm not here to offer you mercy. I'm not going to give you one last chance to surrender. I just wanted to see your face before my army rips your body to pieces. I hope you'enjoyed your freedom for the short time that you enjoyed it. Your family name dies with you today. I hope you die slow."

Jerad turned around and rode his horse through his Cainate army until he was safe behind their ranks. The elves began chanting again, but the Cainates now were growling and roaring every much as loud.

"Cainates! Serve your master well, and you will

be rewarded." Jared unsheathed his sword pointed it toward Leland, the elves and the people of Crestside. "Feast on their hearts, rip them limb from limb, and kill every last one of them!"

Leland watched as the Cainate army took to the ground and sprinted toward him. He pointed his sword forward and hollered alongside the elves and the men and women of Crestside as they charged forward. Aubade galloped forward with strength and rage alongside the elven horses. Leland could feel the adrenaline pumping through his veins. He let out a battle cry and swung down his sword as he and the first rank of elves plunged into the Cainate horde.

CHAPTER 29

Somewhere Beyond

A bright light radiated over everything, making it hard to focus, let alone see exactly where she was. Katrianna squinted her eyes as she covered her face from the glare. She was unaware of where she was or how she had come to be there. The last memories she had were of the battle, of the apparent Cainate retreat, and of the spear striking through her. She remembered the pain and clutched her chest. Looking down, she found that she was wearing a silky white dress. She felt no pain, saw no scars or stitches, and couldn't see any sign that she had been injured at all.

She tried to examine her surroundings, but she

could see nothing. The spaces appeared so hazy, like a fog that surrounded her. Everything was brightly lit, but she could not find a source for the light. Even the floor beneath her bare feet was bright white. Had she not felt the floor against her soles, she wouldn't think she was standing on anything at all. The more she attempted to understand, the more anxious she became. If this white nothingness was supposed to be peaceful, she was not reacting to it well.

"Hello Katrianna, it's nice to finally meet you." Katrianna spun around to see a beautiful woman standing before her. The woman wore a long gold and silver dress, with open shoulders and a bare back. Her long hair was pulled to one side and flowed over her shoulder and down her right side. She was without flaw, with graceful blue eyes and a sparkling smile.

"My, have you grown. Like your mother, your beauty is beyond measure. I'm so happy to see how you've come into your own."

"Who… who are you? How do you know my mother?" The woman walked around Katrianna, admiring her frame. Katrianna stood still, not sure what was happening.

"I've been watching you, all the days of your life. I've seen your hardships, your highs, and your lows. I was so happy to see you fall for that young man that found his way into the Garden. You two seem like a proper fit for each other. I watched you put your life on the line for the Garden, riding your unicorn into battle with all the courage of a lion and the grace of a swan. It was a majestic sight to see, I assure you." The woman stood still once more, in front of Katrianna. She reached out and caressed the side of Katrianna's face. "I saw you sacrifice everything for the Garden. It broke my heart to see you suffer. It was both an incredibly heart-wrenching and yet tremendously proud moment to witness."

"Are you," Katrianna looked into the woman's eyes for reassurance, "are you Queen Asielle?"

"I am Asielle. It warms my heart to see that my memory is still alive in the Garden, enough that a young woman like yourself would know who I am more than a century after I passed. Your name, Katrianna, the Angel Princess, will be known forever in the Garden as well. You were the child that gave her life in battle, the bridge between the magical creatures, the sacrifice that brought the inhabitants of the Garden together." Asielle stepped forward and embraced Katrianna. Gracefully wrapping her arms around Katrianna, Asielle hugged her tight and kissed her on the cheek. "It was a noble thing you did, and the Garden will never forget it."

"I am honored by your words. While I had not planned to die on the battlefield, I was proud to serve the Garden." Katrianna took a few steps, peering into the haze that surrounded them. "What is this place? Is this where I am to spend eternity?"

"Heavens no." Asielle chuckled. "That next place, the place you will arrive at when your time has come cannot be described by any vocabulary you or I know. You will know no pain, no heartache, no longing, and no need for anything. You will be at peace, and you will be complete."

"How long must I stay here before I am allowed to go to that next place?" Katrianna turned back to Asielle, smiling at the thought of finding such peace, but saddened by the idea that she would be that much further away from the one she had grown to love. Asielle smiled back at Katrianna while shaking her head.

"Sweet child, you misunderstand. This space is but a meeting place for you and me to speak. It is not your time to go to that next place, you still have work to do, and a life to live." Katrianna gasped as a tear ran down her cheek.

"Are you saying I'm… not dead?"

"I would never allow such a thing to happen to you. I was proud of you and allowed events to play out like they did, knowing that you would be brought here, to me. There is so much we have to discuss, so many things I wish to tell you; to teach you. If you are to be the new Queen of the Garden, I would hope to instill in you as much knowledge and power that I can give." Asielle reached out to wipe the tear from Katrianna's cheek. "The world is too young to lose you. The Garden is too vulnerable for you to leave it. You have yet to official seal your union to Leland, and that bond will only make you and the Garden stronger."

"I'm confused. I'm shocked. I'm humbled and willing to learn so that I may serve the Garden to the best of my abilities. I apologize, however, as I'm worried I don't have the time. If I am not dead, then I need to return to the Garden. The people of the Garden need every ounce of help they can get, and I need to be there to fight with them." Asielle held up a hand to stop her.

"Don't worry, my child. Time works much differently here. Focus on me, and these things I need to teach you, and I will then send you along your way." Asielle smiled to assure Katrianna of her words. Katrianna dropped down to her knees and looked up at the Queen.

"Teach me, then, my Queen. Share your wisdom with me, that I may honor you and the Garden with my life."

CHAPTER 30

The Garden

Mrs. Doodles sat in the grass by the side of the river. Overwhelmed by her anxiety and depression, she had little will to do anything else. She knew that Leland and several elves had crossed over the mountains to seek revenge. She wished she could have gone with them, to be of some kind of help. She wondered what help she truly could be, however, as she looked over at the waters. Days ago, she watched the coffin holding the Princess float away down the stream.

She had failed to save the Princess's father, and now she had failed to save the Princess herself. While she had assisted in healing several injured elves after the battle, she let Katrianna's life slip through her fingers. She now sat alone by the water, lost and without purpose. Suddenly something emerged from the water. Mrs. Doodles heard a gasp and looked up to see Katrianna choking and heaving as she broke through the surface of the water.

"Princess!" Mrs. Doodles jumped up into the air in shock and flew out across the water to help pull Katrianna to shore. Katrianna fell limp against the earth for a moment, sucking in as much air into her lungs as she could. She wore the same white dress that Mrs. Doodles had helped dress her in for the funeral. "I… I don't understand. How are you here? How can this be?"

"Asielle sent me back." Katrianna coughed up some water and then pushed herself up to her feet. She stumbled back for a moment, but then caught herself. She looked around and sighed. "I'm actually here."

"You are, Princess. Please, now, sit for a moment and rest." Mrs. Doodles tried to pull her back down to the ground, but Katrianna shook her head.

"No, there's no time. The battle is about to start in Crestside. I need to get there." Katrianna sprouted her wings and shot up into the air and toward her castle. Mrs. Doodles flew after her and followed her through the castle corridors.

"You only just came back, sweetheart. You have returned to us from the dead! You're in no condition to fight." Mrs. Doodles watched as Katrianna shed her dress and put on new clothes.

"I feel amazing, Mrs. Doodles. I have so much energy pulsating through my bones at this moment; no amount of restraints could hold me down." Mrs. Doodles stared in awe at the Princess's skin; perfect and without flaw. There was no sign of her injuries; no holes, no stitching, no scars. Once dressed, Katrianna ran to the armory to don her gear. She grabbed her breastplate ran her hand over the large hole left from the spear that had pierced through her. After a moment had passed, she tossed it aside and grabbed another one from the wall. She equipped herself with a sword and shield, then stormed out of the armory and headed to the library.

"I don't see how you could make it there in time to make a difference, Princess. Even with your wings, it would take hours to fly over the mountains."

Katrianna ran over to the bookcase against the wall and pulled free a bunch of books to reveal a slot hidden behind them. She reached through and pulled on a lever.

“Not to worry. Asielle told me of another way.” The bookcase swung backward and to the side to reveal a passage. Mrs. Doodles followed Katrianna through the passageway which opened to a small study. “After Asielle formed an alliance with the first King David Aldiss, she had two identical secret rooms constructed; this one, and one that exists in Aldiss’s castle.”

Katrianna pulled a desk away from the only wall not lined with a bookcase. She placed her hand on the center of the wall and then slid it down to the floor. With her hand, Katrianna traced the shape of a large doorway along the stone wall. When her hand completed the rectangle, she slid it back up to the center and removed her hand from the stone. A spark ignited where Katrianna’s hand last touched the wall. The spark expanded and glowed a brilliant white light as it encompassed all the space upon the wall within the outline that Katrianna had traced. The glowing increased in brightness until it suddenly faded away to reveal an image of a room very similar to the one Katrianna was standing in; reversed in shape and filled with different looking furniture. Katrianna turned to Mrs. Doodles.

"This portal was meant to be used to maintain the relationship between the Garden and Crestside. When Asielle died, that relationship died with her. Perhaps it can be resurrected someday." Katrianna took in a deep breath and walked through the doorway into the other room. She turned around and waved her hand across the doorway. Before she knew it, Mrs. Doodles found herself alone in the room, staring at a blank wall.

"Good luck, my dear."

****

Katrianna made her way quickly through the passage and pulled the lever to open the bookcase. She found herself in what looked to be the King's study. Not knowing what opposition she would find in the castle, Katrianna picked up a chair and tossed it through the stained-glass window. Leaping out the shattered window, Katrianna sprouted her wings once more and made her way toward the sky.

Soaring over the castle, Katrianna quickly found the battlefield and saw the chaos on the ground below. The number of bodies on the ground seemed to indicate that the battle had only just started. Katrianna watched as the rabid Cainates attacked the elves, striking them off their horses and fighting them on the ground. The Cainates were humongous, now thicker and taller than they had appeared in the first battle.

Katrianna saw Leland riding Aubade into the fray. She watched as Leland swung his sword left and right, cutting down anything in his path while Aubade refused to be brought down. Behind the elves, Katrianna could see a group of villagers, holding pitchforks and other weapons, charging into the fold and attacking the Cainates. She was impressed at the sight but could tell that these new, larger Cainates presented a more formidable force than the elves had encountered before.

She saw the same chaos that she had witnessed in the elven forest. The Cainates moved with unrelenting viciousness and rage. The elves fought with honor and bravery, and they clashed with the violent beasts. As the Cainates tore through the elven ranks to attack the villagers, several of Yetto's troops threw themselves in front of the carnage in attempts to save their weaker comrades. The humans pushed forward, attacking whatever they came across. Many of them began to fall, as well as the elves, and Katrianna knew she needed to act.

Flying high up into the clouds above, Katrianna called out to the sky as she unsheathed her sword. She could feel the power of the Garden within her. Asielle had shown her so many things and had instilled in her the confidence to face any foe that would threaten the tranquility of her home. The clouds came alive around her as bolts of lightning struck out on either side of Katrianna. She flew higher, holding her sword high above her. When she had reached her peak, Katrianna saw the surrounding clouds reach out to her with ropes of bright light. The bolts of lightning struck her from every angle and wrapped around her armor. She dropped from the sky, falling toward the earth with unflinching speed.

Katrianna closed her eyes and endured the pain as she felt the lightning pierce through her, all over her, again and again. At the last moment, Katrianna opened her eyes and crashed down into the ground in the center of the Cainate army. On impact, Katrianna struck the earth with her sword and shield and cried out as several bolts of lightning shot out from within her and rippled through the Cainate forces. The lightning penetrated the bodies of the nearby Cainates, frying them to the core. Katrianna exhaled and stood to her feet. Around her, burned to a crisp, laid the bodies of at least half the Cainate army. The remaining beasts stood around the black singed earth and looked at Katrianna with fear.

Katrianna turned to her right to see Leland cut down a Cainate and then jump off Aubade to stand on the ground at stare at her in awe. She stared back at him and smiled. Finding their courage, several Cainates on her left charged toward Katrianna. She let out a war cry and turned to face them. She slammed her shield into the face of the first Cainate to reach her. She felt every bone in its face shatter upon impact as the Cainate screeched in agony and stumbled to the ground. Katrianna spun around and dug her sword through the gut of the next Cainate. The Cainate stopped in its tracks, bellowing in pain, but then began to claw its way forward, inching closer to Katrianna.

Gripping the sword with both hands, Katrianna pulled it free from the Cainate's belly, ducked and rolled under the beast's attack, and stood up behind it to swing her sword down to severe the Cainate's head from its body. She turned to face the next Cainate, which was already flying through the air down upon her. Before it could tackle her, however, a large spear pierced the Cainate's eye with such force that it fell backward and hit the ground near Katrianna's feet. She turned to see the elves advance on her position, more swords and spears in hand.

"We've got this, Princess." Ip Toma Yetto stood next to Katrianna as his elves attacked the remaining Cainates. "King Jerad has retreated to the castle. Perhaps you and Leland can hunt him down."

Katrianna nodded and ran past him. She ran across the scorched ground, through the elves and citizens of Crestside until she found Leland, still standing there in shock. Katrianna collided with him and wrapped her arms around him. As the two of them fell to the ground, she held him close. She looked down at him, locking her eyes with his, as she leaned in and kissed him with every bit of passion she could muster.

Leland didn't respond for a moment, but then eventually wrapped his arms around her tightly and returned her kiss.

"You're... here! You're alive." Katrianna kissed Leland again and then pulled him to his feet.

"I am. I have so much to tell you but now is not the time. We need to end this." Katrianna grabbed hold of Leland and flapped her giant wings as they ascended into the air above.

CHAPTER 31

Aldiss Castle

Jerad drank the last drops of wine from the bottle and screamed as he threw it hard against the wall. The bottle hit the wall with such force that several of its shattered pieces flew back across the air to dig into the side of Jerad's face. He screeched in pain as he ripped the shards of glass out of his cheek and temple. He slammed his fists down upon the table as he cried out in anger toward the painted picture of his father on the wall.

"I had you! I struck you down and wiped out anyone connected to you. I have walked around this castle for twenty years, reigning supreme over the

Kingdom you once protected. I had everything! I would have kept it all too, had your friends from the other side not intervened!"

Jerad had seen the angel bring down the lightning upon his troops. He witnessed the devastation and knew the end was near. It would only be moments until his castle walls were invaded. He only hoped he had the chance to defend his crown one last time. He saw a shadow fly past his window. He wiped the blood from his face and grabbed his sword as he made his way down the hall to the balcony overlooking the courtyard. The angel, wrapped in golden armor, stood next to Leland Clayton as they stared up at him from the ground.

"It's over, Jared. Your reign has come to an end. Give up the crown." Jerad grabbed a bottle from the table on the balcony. He broke the nect against the stone banister and held the bottle over his head. Showering himself in wine, Jerad emptied the bottle and then threw it into the courtyard.

"It's over, you say? You want me to give up my throne? You want me to take off this crown? Who's going to take it from me?" Jerad screamed at the top of his voice down to Leland. He pulled the crown from his head and held it out in the air. "You want this, you piece of shit? Come and get it."

****

Leland stepped aside as the flying bottle struck the ground by his feet. He stared up at the drunken king and smiled. Jared might still be breathing, but he had been defeated in every other way. His army was being slaughtered in the fields beyond the castle. His witch was nowhere to be seen. He could barely stand as he screamed down at Leland and Katrianna before stumbling back into his chair. Leland nodded and stepped forward. Before he and Katrianna could advance another step, however, something burst through the walls of the courtyard to their right and left.

Two large Cainates, three times the size of anything Leland had seen out front on the battlefield, crawled into the courtyard to stand between them and King Jerad. The beasts were so massive, they couldn't stand up straight on their own two feet. Instead, their hulking mass forced them to lean over on all fours, like giant apes, as they roared at Leland and Katrianna. Between the beasts, a few men and women appeared, slinging swords, daggers, and spears about them.

"Oh, my apologies, Leland. You didn't think I'd just let you waltz in here and take my crown without a fight, did you? Allow me to introduce the last of my generals, as well as my two largest Cainate friends; gifts from my mother." Leland looked up to see King Jerad lean over the balcony banister, a new bottle of liquor in his hand, as he smiled down at Leland. "You're going to have to earn the right to fight me, boy."

The generals advanced first as Leland and Katrianna gripped their swords in anticipation. One of the women and two of the men sprinted toward Leland. The woman tossed her spear directly at Leland's head. He ducked under the spear just in time, feeling it graze his hair as it flew overhead to dig into the wall behind him. Leland rolled to the right as two daggers dug into the ground where he had stood before. He jumped to his feet and swung his sword to block the attack of the third man.

He pushed back on the general as he spun around and kicked the other man in the chest. Leland exchanged a few blows back and forth with the general, clashing their swords together until he was able to lunge forward, swipe away his opponent's sword and punch the general in the face. Leland dove to the ground, retrieving the two daggers in the dirt and spinning around to throw then into the chest of the daggerman and the woman who had thrown her spear. Leland then returned to his feet to clash swords with the third general once more.

Katrianna blocked the sword of a general on her right and used her wings to block a stab from the general on her left. A third general launched himself up in the air and rain down upon Katrianna with his spear. Katrianna launched herself into the air, swiping the spear away with her sword. She grabbed the general by the neck and flew him high into the air before releasing him to fall to the ground. As the body of the general hit the dirt with a nasty ***thud***, Katrianna dropped down and slammed her sword against the sword of the general on her right.

Katrianna hit his sword with enough force that the general's arm gave out. Unable to defend himself, the general's throat was sliced clean by the edge of Katrianna's sword. The general fell to the ground as he watched Katrianna do the same thing to the general on her left. As blood flowed out from his gaping neck, the last thing the general saw was that of Katrianna picking up a fallen spear and throwing it forcefully across the courtyard to run through the last general contending with Leland.

Leland blocked a sword swipe from the last general and then watched as a spear struck the general in the chest and pinned him against the wall. Leland looked across the way and nodded at Katrianna, thanking her, as the two massive Cainates roared at the far end of the courtyard. Leland turned and braced his foot against the dead general's chest as he pried free the spear from the wall and the general. As Katrianna flew up into the air to attack the Cainate closest to her, Jerad started sprinting toward the Cainate roaring in his direction.

Leland gripped the spear in his hand and tossed it as hard as he could. The spear flew across the courtyard and dug deep into the left knee of the Cainate. The Cainate recoiled up and back as it hollered out in pain. Leland slid across the ground, underneath the massive beast, and sliced his sword through the Cainate's right ankle. The Cainate falls forward in pain, crying out in anger and agony, as Leland got to his feet and attempted to run up the Cainate's back. He climbed halfway up the beast's back, hoping to run his sword down through the back of the beast's neck. Before long, Leland's feet began to sink into the lard of the massive beast, and he wasn't able to climb anymore. The beast reached around and grabbed Leland and threw him halfway across the courtyard.

As Leland crashed hard to the ground across the courtyard, Katrianna flew down toward her Cainate giant and dug her sword deep into one of its eyes. The beast shrieked and attempted to swat at her, but Katrianna kicked off its face and flipped backward into the air. Leaving her sword in the Cainate's eye, Katrianna dropped to the ground and grabbed the swords of two of the fallen generals. She launched herself back into the air, flying between the beast's massive arms to dig one of her swords into the Cainate's other eyes. Blinded now, the Cainate stumbled forward in anguish and rage. It dove forward toward Katrianna, but she flew out of the way. As the Cainate crashed down to the ground, Katrianna dropped down on the back of its head and dug her third sword deep into its skull.

While the Cainate twitched in its dying moments, Katrianna looked across the courtyard to see the other Cainate limping toward Leland. Katrianna watched as Leland ran back to retrieve the other spear that his female general had attempted to strike him with. Leland pulled the spear from the wall and turned back to the Cainate. The beast roared and reached out for him. Leland dodged the attack and dove forward. Rolling to his feet, Leland shoved his spear up and into the thick neck of the Cainate.

With all his might, Leland wrenched the spear to the right and then to the left until he ripped open the Cainate's throat and showered himself in the beast's blood. Diving to the side and rolling out of the way of the falling beast, Leland stood up and watched as the Cainate fell hard to the ground and bled out in the dirt. Leland turned to look up toward the balcony, but Jerad was nowhere to be seen. Katrianna quickly flew over and lifted Leland up in the air and over to the balcony. Dropping down, Leland held his sword out in front of him as he walked into the castle.

Following the drops of blood on the floor, Leland made his way down the castle corridor until he arrived at the library. In the center of the room, Jared sat back in a chair with his sword in one hand and a bottle in the other. He grinned and sat up as Leland entered the room.

"Did you know I still refer to this place as Aldiss Castle? I refuse to allow anyone to refer to me by the name, but I like it for the structure. It reminds everyone around here of the man that I killed and the legacy I snuffed out with that kill." Jared drank from the bottle and smiled at Leland as he gulped down the wine. "Perhaps I'll name a wing after you."

"I've defeated your goons, Jared." Leland gripped his sword in both hands as he inched toward the king. "Now it's your time to die.

"Oh, is that so? You think because you killed some hired help, you're now worthy enough to face me? You don't have the skills to contend with me, boy, and I don't have the time to instruct you." Jared took another swig from the bottle and then tossed it down to the floor by Leland's feet. He climbed out of the chair and staggered toward Leland. "I killed my father with this sword. I killed several of his knights with this sword. I disciplined many capable Cainates with this sword. Now, I'm going to run you through with it."

Jared lunged forward, slicing his blade through the air toward Leland. Leland blocked the attack and slid to his left to bring his sword up for another block. King Jared cried out in annoyance as he swung his blade, again and again, striking Leland's sword left and right. Jared wiped clean his face, his temple and cheek still bleeding from the glass. Leland went on the offensive, swinging his sword down upon Jared. Jared dodged to the side, allowing Leland to hit the table with this blade, granting just enough time for Jared to punch the boy square in the face. Leland stumbled backward to the floor, but quickly righted himself. The two clashed swords again and pushed against one another.

"No man has ever beaten me at this game, boy. My skills with the sword are unmatched." Jerad grinned at Leland through the space between their blades. Leland gritted his teeth and headbutted Jerad hard in the face. Jared stumbled back and was chased by Leland who kicked him solidly in the chest. Jared hit the wall hard behind him. He swung his blade forward to block another of Leland's attacks. Leland quickly swung his blade to strike and deflect Jared's sword, then leaned in to punch Jared in the face. Jared stumbled over to his side, clenching his jaw.

"I believe you Jared, but when's the last time your skills were tested?" Jared groaned and lashed out at Leland. Swinging his sword left and right, forcing Leland to back away and give Jared some space, the king stood up and stumbled into the hallway. Leland followed quickly, and the two clashed swords once more. Steel hit steel, again and again as Jared backed his way down the hall. Leland advanced, again and again, forcing Jared backward with every strike. Eventually, Jared found himself back on the balcony overlooking the courtyard. Jared slipped on a large piece of broken glass and fell backward to the floor of the balcony. Leland kicked away the broken bottle and stood over the king. "Perhaps if you weren't just a drunken, useless mess, your skills could have bested me."

"How dare you!" Jared pulled a dagger from his belt and dove forward to drive it down into Leland's boot. Leland winced in pain as Jared climbed to his feet and swung his sword. Pinned to that spot on the floor, Leland swung his sword to block Jared's attack. Jared swiped Leland's sword to the left and leaned in to punch

Leland in the gut. The two clashed swords again until Jared deflected another strike and hit Leland in the face. Leland fell to the floor, his boot still pinned through with the dagger. Jared reached down and hit Leland again, knocking Leland all the way down. “Not so cocky now, are you Clayton?”

Leland spat a glob of blood across the floor as he tried to push himself up. Jared grabbed Leland by the arm, pulled him up, and struck him in the jaw again. Leland crashed back down to the floor as she Jerad dragged his sword along the floor around him. Once again, Leland pushed himself up. Unable to reach his sword, Leland rose up to a kneeling position beneath King Jared.

“There you go, boy. You’ve finally learned to show some respect. It may have taken you all your life to get to this point, but at least you learned your place in the seconds before your death.” Jared raised his sword for the final blow. Leland cried out in pain as he quickly reached for the dagger lodged through his boot and foot. Pulling the dagger free, Leland ducked under the King’s swing and lunged forward to dig the blade deep into Jared’s gut.

Jared stumbled backward, away from Leland, as he looked down at the dagger. He reached out for something to keep him upright but went crashing into the balcony table. Jared fell to the floor of the balcony and then turned to pull himself up to the banister. As he leaned over the edge, Jared saw that the courtyard was filled with people. Elves and humans stood side by side as they stared up at him. Jared smiled his bloodied teeth down upon them as he gripped the handle of the dagger in his gut. He shouted out in pain as he pulled the blade free and then twisted around to look at Leland.

"It appears we have quite the audience," said Jared as he leaned back against the banister and gripped the dagger. Gathering all his strength, Jared pushed himself off and dove toward Leland with the blade. "Why don't we give them a show?"

"Agreed." Leland stepped forward and kicked Jared squared in the chest, sending the King over the banister and down to the courtyard.

****

Jared hit the ground hard from the twenty-foot drop. Gasping for the air that had escaped him on impact, Jared spat out a stream of blood across the dirt. The crowd backed up, giving the fallen King some space as Leland made his way down to the courtyard. Jared finally found some air and breathed in deep as he rolled over to his back. He looked up to see Leland standing over him, as well as the woman with angel wings.

"Where is Satrina? Where's the witch?" Jared could see the woman talking to him, but could barely make out her words. The woman leaned in and spoke again. "The witch, where is she?"

"Who? My mother? Oh… I locked her away… in the dungeon." Jared struggled to speak but somehow forced out the words. He tried to get to his feet, but his body was broken from the fall. He looked up to see all the faces staring down at him. Men, women, and elves all seemed to take their time to walk past his line of sight. Leland remained in this spot, standing over Jared, content to watch him take his last breaths. Jared smiled and spat out some more blood. Jared spat up into the air and felt his blood rain back down upon his face. He smiled in his own disgust and rolled his head to the side. Jared watched as his crown rolled away from his head and fell to the ground a foot or two away from him. He snickered and turned his eyes to Leland. "I guess…I guess that means… you win."

****

"I guess it does." Leland stepped forward and swung his sword down for a final blow, decapitating Jerad in one clean cut. As Jerad's head rolled a few feet away, Leland looked up at Ip Toma Yetto and Katrianna. "He said she's in the dungeon. Let's go."

The three left the courtyard as the villagers gathered around to see the dead King. Leland ran down the hall until they came upon the steps leading down into the dungeon. Ip Toma Yetto went first, followed by Katrianna, with Leland bringing up the rear. The three slowly descended the stairs down into the darkness. With only the light of a few torches along the wall, the area was hard to see. Leland tripped over the bodies of two fallen Cainate guards as he followed Katrianna and Yetto over to the cells. They all stood still as they stared into the one cell that was locked. Crouched in a corner, hiding in the dark, sat a bloody, ragged woman.

"What do you want? Come to bask in your victory over my son?" The woman croaked as she chewed on a liver, she had clawed out of one of her guards.

"No, Satrina. We're here to finally rid you from this earth," said Ip Toma Yetto as he bent down to pick up the set of keys on the floor. Satrina laughed as she leaned out from the dark. Her eyes were sunken in a bit, but she still appeared to be somewhat youthful.

"I may be lacking enough dark magic to free myself from this cage, but as you can see from the bodies on the floor, I'm far from defenseless. I've killed millions in my lifetime. You think you're the one to bring me down?" Satrina took another bite of the liver and then threw it aside. As she chewed and swallowed, she pulled herself up by the bars and stared at them. "I can't die, stupid. I can be hurt, sure. Hell, Jared cut off my tongue a day or so ago, but I've grown it back. You can try all you want, but I've never been killed. I bet you couldn't even come close, elf."

"I'm willing to take that bet," said Yetto as he clenched the sword in his hand. Satrina pressed her face against the bars and smiled at him. Suddenly a roared boomed overhead from somewhere outside the dungeon. Satrina's eyes opened wide as she grinned.

"Too late." Leland and Katrianna both grabbed Yetto and dove to the side as a colossal claw dug through the ceiling above. As the ceiling collapsed, giving way to the sun, Leland looked up to see a giant dragon using its claws to dig out the dungeon. Satrina climbed the bars up through the gaping hole and scaled the dragon's wing until she pulled herself on top the dragon's back. Yetto pushed aside part of the ceiling that had fallen on him and stood up to face Satrina. "Maybe another time, elf. Then again, maybe not."

The dragon hissed and spewed a ball of fire down into the dungeon. Yetto stood to face it, but Katrianna pushed him down and shielded Yetto and Leland with her massive wings. She winced in pain as she took the brunt of the flames. Eventually, the fire ceased as the dragon turned its head away and climbed out of the castle. As Katrianna turned around, shaking away any burnt feathers, the three of them watched as the dragon launched up into the sky and flew away.

EPILOGUE

In the weeks following the fall of Jerad Aldiss, the kingdom of Crestside slowly started to put itself back together. The residents of the prison camp were brought back into society. Citizen housing units were torn down as people moved back into their homes. The Cainates had been completely wiped out, and so nothing stood in the way of the people taking back what was rightfully theirs.

For the first time since Crestside was founded, the people were forced to elect a new King. Jerad was the only descendant of King Aldiss the twelfth, and so the Aldiss name was now retired to the graveyard. For now, it seemed that the best choice was to elect their liberator, Leland Clayton, as the new King of Crestside. Not only did Leland lead the efforts to rid the land of the Cainate horde, as well as kill the tyrant King, he also had established a bond with the people of the land on the other side of the mountains. The people of Crestside didn't quite understand what that land was, but they knew it was filled with magical creatures, like the elves, and that Crestside needed to maintain a relationship with them.

Leland promised to one day officially introduce the people of Crestside to the inhabitants of the Garden. Until then, Leland wanted the Kingdom to focus on healing. After years of slavery, tyranny, and torment, the Kingdom was finally allowed to grieve. Many had died, and the population was dwindling, but the villagers were persistent and felt that enough youth existed to bring Crestside back to all its glory in a generation or two.

The villagers dug a spillway to branch off from the river. It would flow into a man-made lake that was dug to encompass the field where the last battle against the Cainates had been waged. The body of water was named "Lake Aldiss," in honor of the Aldiss family and everything they had done for Crestside. Beside the castle, a memorial was constructed, showcasing paintings and statues of the kings of the past. The names of everyone who had fallen to the Cainates during Jerad's reign were carved into the walls. It became a favorite place for Leland to visit and think of his parents.

A few months after Crestside had begun to reconcile itself, Leland married Katrianna in front of the entire Kingdom. For her efforts in protecting the Garden, combined with the knowledge that Asielle had blessed her, the inhabitants of the Garden named her their Queen. The elves recognized her authority over the Garden and pledged to co-exist with every magical creature in the land. The Forest of Death was no more.

The union of Leland and Katrianna was special and full of love. While Katrianna was recognized as the married Queen of Crestside, Leland was not seen as King of the Garden. The Garden looked to him as a friend and their preferred ambassador to the outside world. The passage between the two castles allowed Leland and Katrianna to tend to their duties while never being far apart.

Leland and Katrianna grew closer and closer to each other with each passing day. Their love fulfilled each other, and their longing to care for one another, as well as the people they served, never ceased. Leland cherished every moment he spent with Katrianna, knowing full well that his life could have led him in so many other directions.

Leland would treasure every second he had with his love. He had been lucky enough to have Katrianna returned to him, and he wouldn't waste a single moment. Together, Leland and Katrianna reigned in fairness and with compassion and were loved by all around. Crestside remained in place, guarding the secret passages over the mountains to the magical valley on the other side. Joy, love, and peace returned to the land, as Leland and Katrianna worked to build Crestside back to it's prime.

Though their lives became blissful and full of enchantment, the royal couple knew that, with Satrina still out there somewhere in the world, the threat to Crestside and the Garden was ever-present. Leland knew that one day, Ip Toma Yetto would call upon him and his bride to ride out and hunt down the witch.

Satrina wasn't the only evil in the world, and the longer she was allowed to live, the more likely she was to form alliances that could bring hell back to Crestside and the Garden. Until Satrina was dead, no one was truly safe. Leland and Katrianna swore that one day, they would rectify that wrong so that the Garden would always remain a safe, vibrant, halcyon shelter to all that called it home.

Fin

APPENDICES

LELAND CLAYTON'S POEMS

Love

Life is so vague, it is so fragile.
It can be given, and taken away so easily,
and yet it is one thing we don't cherish
enough.
Some things in life make us realize
that we're lucky to be alive.
Then again, some things
make us want to run and hide.
One thing stands firm, though.
One thing keeps us going.
One thing survives when all else is dead.
That, my friend, is love.
Love fills us up when we are empty.
Love allows us to drop our pride and cry.
Love heats up our blood, keeps it flowing.
Love opens up our eyes.
We must remember who we are
and who we care about.
For without love, we all will surely die,
in that, there is no doubt.

Happiness, I sing

In return,
for the feelings that you've given me,
I'd like to tell you something
from the bottom of my soul.
When I'm alone
in this darkened room I'm sitting in,
I can only think of one thing:
how you make me whole.
I'm surrounded by your love.
I am drowning in your oceans.
I'm astounded by the happiness you bring.
So, I sing.
You're abounding from above.
You control my every motion.
I scream aloud about your understanding.
So. I sing.
Let the valleys hold my echo.
The people of the crowds, let them know,
that I will go anywhere, I will do anything.
So, I'll sing... forever after now

Skin

Tender as an unsailed sea
who's waves I gently wade within,
no gritty sense of salty tarnish,
no eerie sense of death below,
but isolation of bountiful ambition.
A liquidy landscape of which I caress,
a taste as soothing as the sight,
smoothly lulling my ever need for comfort;
a delight that can persuade my mind.
Like no other surface,
like nothing else created by God's hands,
I long to search its every inch,
every crease and corner, dip and dimple
every bump and curve, rising to drop off;
an adventure I foresee to last lifetimes.
Already I am seduced to never leave.
While an earth is yet to be seen,
my imagination lies only in knowing
every secret and utter beautiful surprise
that lies within you gorgeous skin.

Trust

Tis a funny, yet very dangerous thing, trust.
It can build our relationships
and, when abused, it can tear them down.
It can lift you up to the joys of heaven.
It can drag you down to the pits of sorrow.
It can redeem you, save your soul.
It can forsake you, and burrow in your heart, a hole.
When entwined with love,
it is both lovely and deadly at the same time.
I, myself, have learned this many times.
When you mess with such a sacred thing,
you mess with your life, and all things in it.
You mess with your heart,
and with those who love it with their own.
To all those I have broken my trust
or doubted in any way, shape or form,
a forgiveness of a thousand seas
would never save my soul.
The love of one heart, of one being, however
might give me the chance to live on.

ILLUSTRATIONS BY
ILARIA APOSTOLI

Thomas Clayton finds his wife and the Cainates

King Jerad beats Captain Fellcer.

Prisoner 452 fighting in the pits

Katrianna introduces Leland to the Unicorns

Mrs. Doodles and the fairies find an ill Thomas Clayton

The Angel Princess

The Mermaids find the Mercs

Four Mercs hung on display outside the Forest of Death

Katrianna takes Leland to the Elves

King Jerad wakes to find a stranger near his bed

Katrianna's funeral

Katrianna meets Asielle in some place beyond

Katrianna attacks the Cainate horde

The union of Leland and Katrianna Clayton

Made in the USA
Middletown, DE
01 March 2022